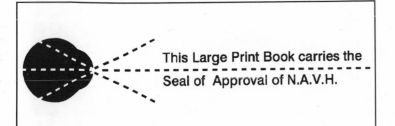

This Large Print Book carries the
Seal of Approval of N.A.V.H.

I Burn for You

I BURN FOR YOU

SUSAN SIZEMORE

WHEELER PUBLISHING
An imprint of Thomson Gale, a part of The Thomson Corporation

THOMSON
━━━★━━━ ™
GALE

Detroit • New York • San Francisco • New Haven, Conn. • Waterville, Maine • London

THOMSON

GALE

LIBRARY OF CONGRESS CATALOGING-IN-PUBLICATION DATA

Sizemore, Susan.
    I burn for you / by Susan Sizemore.
      p. cm. — (Wheeler Publishing large print romance)
    "Crave the night #1" — T.p. verso.
    ISBN 1-59722-310-7 (alk. paper)
    1. Vampires — Fiction. 2. Telepathy — Fiction. 3. Security consultants —
Fiction. 4. Los Angeles (Calif.) — Fiction. 5. Large type books. I. Title. II.
Series: Wheeler large print romance series.
PS3569.I95I14 2006
813'.54—dc22

                                                    2006014996

Published in 2006 by arrangement with Pocket Books,
a division of Simon & Schuster, Inc.

Printed in the United States of America on permanent paper
10 9 8 7 6 5 4 3 2 1

Constance Howard Brockway,
this is all your fault!
Thank you.

Very special thanks to Winifred Halsey
for staying awake all night to provide
me technical help.

CHAPTER ONE

He was growing hungry for the night.

Despite modern advances that made dwelling in daylight both possible and enjoyable, Alexander Reynard felt the longing to return to darkness stalking him. Especially right now, when driving through the heavy morning traffic in bright sunlight gave him a blistering headache, despite his tinted windshield and dark sunglasses. He used to enjoy the gift of being able to greet the dawn and all the bright hours after, but lately, light hurt. And he feared he was reverting.

Alec had forced himself to sleep last night through stubborn tenacity, to prove that he could still do it. He would not let nature conquer will. He *had* slept, and that may have been a mistake. For in his dreams, a woman came into his bed.

She had floated into his senses on a fragrant mist. Her skin had been warm and wet, her flesh firm and slick as satin. He'd woken up hot and hard in a tangle of sweat-soaked sheets. There'd been blood on his lips and molten hunger in his veins.

Head back, he'd howled his need into the dark. Though it had been a dream, the woman was real; he was certain of that. All he had to do was find her. Claim her. It had taken all his will not to run out into the embracing night and start the search then and there.

He didn't want this now. This was not a good time or place for the beginning of a quest.

Head pounding from the sun, Alec found a place to park on Hill Street near the huge Central Market. It was at least a three-block walk through bright sunlight to his destination; if he cut through the market, he could get out of the sun for a while.

Domini Lancer woke from disorienting dreams of angels, peaches, and making love. Once awake, a powerful craving for peaches remained. She even smelled peaches while she took a long, hot shower to try to wipe the dream from her mind. But she couldn't forget it, or the strong urge to buy some peaches on the way to work. She'd tried to ignore the ridiculous urge, yet here she was at the Center Market, right where her premonition had demanded she be. This absolute *need* to follow a dream had never happened to her before, and she was a little scared. Scared that maybe she was going crazy. More scared of whatever was about to happen. And even worse, scared that nothing was going to happen. She'd never had such a powerful premonition before, so if this turned out to be the usual petty crap her visions pulled on her, instead of something momentous, she was really going to be pissed off.

As was her boss, whom she'd called to say she'd be late.

Old Man Lancer didn't make any allowances for Domini being his granddaughter. His deep, whiskey-growly voice had been annoyed when he said, "Fine," and hung up the phone. Though he'd always comforted her when she had dreams that came true as a kid, as an adult he didn't cut her any slack, and she didn't bring up the subject of being psychic anymore. Maybe because both of them wished she wasn't.

Domini heard music, and turned around. Melissa Etheridge's "Angels Would Fall" was coming from a radio at a fruit vendor's stand — where a pyramid of peaches was piled high at the front of the stand, gold as the morning sun, almost shining with their own light in the dim market. She couldn't help but take a step closer. The music swelled around her, bright, lively, and full of aching secret passion.

Swaying to the sound, Domini picked up the peach at the very top of the pile. Its velvet fuzz brushed sensuously across her palm, more tempting than Eve's apple. She felt as if one bite of it might send her into a Sleeping Beauty trance — or make her fall in love.

She raised it to her lips.

"You want to pay for that first?" the vendor asked.

The music faded into the background; reality came rushing back in.

Domini blinked. She smiled apologetically and quickly dropped the fruit into the vendor's outstretched hand. "I'll have a dozen," she said, and handed eleven more peaches to the woman.

After she'd paid and taken the plastic bag of fruit from the vendor, Domini headed toward the nearest exit, boiling with frustration at the universe that had cursed her with such pointless foresight. For God's sake — was that *it?*

Why had it been so desperately important to race to Central Market, when all she'd been *meant* to do was listen to a song on the radio?

10

"I could have stayed home and done that," she grumbled.

"Do you always talk to yourself?" a male voice asked, his voice soft yet self-confident — caressing?

Domini turned to look for the man who'd spoken. When she moved her head, something soft as a breeze, intimate as a kiss, brushed against the back of her neck. It sent a cold shiver of fear down her spine and heat racing through her blood. The combination was as dizzying as peach brandy.

Though the market was crowded, suddenly she felt as alone as if she were standing on the moon.

And someone was watching her.

Domini turned slowly around, alert to any threat, to anything out of the ordinary. The routine of running a visual sweep of her location helped calm her.

The market was a huge open space, full of noise, bustling with people shopping at aisle upon aisle of stands, and breakfasting at the snack bars. Despite the overhead lights, neon signs, and sunlight flooding in from entrances on all four sides, there was a shadowed quality about the warehouselike building.

Nothing seemed out of place. It was a normal morning, with people going about their business and enjoying the sights and sounds of the place. There was no threat within.

Domini turned her attention to the entrance and instantly saw him standing in the doorway, just across the street from the Angels' Flight sign. He wore sunglasses, yet she knew the eyes behind the dark lenses were fixed on her. She stared boldly back.

His tall, broad-shouldered silhouette was haloed by the California sunshine. His features were shadowed by the brim of the sort of hat that reminded her of Indiana Jones. All she could make out was a square jaw and cleft chin, covered by dark beard stubble.

But how could he be the one who had spoken to her, when he was halfway across the market? Unless . . .

Unnerved, Domini turned and hurried for the opposite entrance. She didn't know what to make of all this; all she knew was that she had to get out of here *right now.* It was all she could do not to run, or look back over her shoulder to make sure he wasn't following her.

Alec watched the tall beauty go. He was left with a memory of long dark hair, a wide, full mouth, long legs, and lithe movement. As she fled, he fought down the urge to follow her with all the will he could muster. Her confusion and fear clawed at him. He forced himself to remain still as pain surged through him, wanting her with all his soul, bleeding inside at knowing she rejected anything to do with him. He told himself she had every right to run, and didn't let his primal response to flight rule him. He stayed on the leash, though breathing came hard and every muscle in his body tensed solid as stone.

Let her run. It will be all right.

Even as he told himself this, the shrouded part of him hated her for running — that creature believed in soul-bonding passion at first sight. But Alexander Reynard was more civilized than that. Or so he must believe, for the woman's sake, even more than his own.

What was happening to her was beyond her ken. And very nearly beyond his, at this moment. If they touched now, it would be raw and rough.

He hadn't expected to find her so soon, and losing her instantly dealt a blow to his soul. He wanted to throw back his head and howl, the way he had last night. But he would live with the loss for now, would fight down the arousal their brief touching of minds brought him. Or at least he'd live with it until he could offer her a man, not a monster.

He could have followed her easily. Her scent perfumed the air; her aura cut a bright swath easily discernible even in the tangled mix of life signs within the crowd. But he deliberately turned his back on that path. In a few minutes, he had a meeting at a nearby hole-in-the-wall joint, a meeting that was his purpose in coming into downtown Los Angeles. He would stick to that purpose, and endure what needed to be endured.

Alec made his tightly fisted hands relax, then he made himself walk through the market and out the other side, just as he'd originally planned.

CHAPTER TWO

Many towns and all the big cities had a meeting place for the fringe peoples of the world. In Chicago, it was a boutique hotel. In New York, it was a bookstore. In New Orleans, it was an outdoor café famous for its coffee and doughnuts. Here in Los Angeles, the meeting place was a bar on the seedy side of downtown. It had a sleazy, dilapidated look that intentionally put off unwanted customers, which included most of the population. The bar's clientele paid very well for their privacy, and learned not to complain about the dirt and aromas to the bar's touchy proprietor.

While the establishment never closed, Alec was the only customer at the moment. He sat at a small scarred table in the center of the room and nursed a drink that looked like, but was not, a beer.

He hated to be kept waiting, and every

now and then glanced toward the door with a look that grew more laser sharp with annoyance.

Finally, Alec made himself stop watching the door and reached for his glass again. The brew looked like a dark, rich stout, but was an herbal concoction that tasted something like — no, he didn't want to think about what it tasted like. Later, if he was lucky, he'd be able to enjoy a beer again, but for the immediate future he'd been told to abstain for medical reasons.

If things didn't work out — if the worst happened, and he went feral — it wasn't alcohol he'd be craving.

He rolled back the cuff of his white shirt and looked at the small tattoo of a stylized fox on the inside of his left wrist. It was fading, which wasn't a good sign.

Then the door opened, slammed shut, and Shaggy Harker bounded up to the table and swung into the other chair.

"Hey, buddy!" Shaggy's deep voice boomed through the room, the sound filling all the shadowy spaces. "Long time, man."

Alec was so startled he very nearly snarled at Harker, and that could have turned a meeting of old friends into a bloody mess, with both of them reacting on primitive instinct rather than thought. Alec's mouth and

16

fingers ached as he controlled the reaction.

He managed something like a smile. "Long time," Alec agreed. "You look — hairy."

Shaggy threw back his head and let out a bark of laughter. "You look like shit."

"I feel like it, too," Alec acknowledged.

With a swift move, Shaggy wrapped his big hand around Alec's left arm. His grasp was surprisingly gentle. Alec went very still as Shaggy studied the fox tattoo.

"Ink's fading," Shaggy finally judged. "Bummer."

"Yes."

Shaggy loosed his hold and sat back with his arms crossed over his wide chest. Most werewolves were not bikers, despite the stereotype. Shaggy Harker just happened to be a werewolf biker. He was big and bearded, his long, silver-streaked hair tied back with a red bandanna. He was dressed in leather and denim and an old black T-shirt. A faint musky aroma washed across the table to tickle Alec's sensitive sense of smell.

Shaggy was smart, perceptive, and very much had his nose into everything in his territory. If someone supernatural blew into Los Angeles needing something, Shaggy was the one who could fix them up. If it was legal.

"You in town for the cure, man?" Shaggy asked, after the bartender brought him a beer that was really a beer. "The docs at the clinic do good work," he added after taking a gulp of the cold brew. "You'll be fine."

Alec had little patience for sympathetic reassurance, but he let it go with only a cold look. His nerves were strung tight, which was his only excuse for acting so prickly. Or like a prick, to be more precise.

He signaled the bartender to bring Shaggy another drink, then made himself finish the glass he'd been nursing.

"I have an appointment at the clinic later this morning. There are stipulations about receiving treatment."

"Yeah, yeah," Shaggy said. "I know the drill for your folk. Part of your twelve-step is that you have to have a job, one that serves humanity."

Alec bristled at the casual comment. "I am a Prime of Clan Reynard," he sternly reminded the werewolf, whom he'd met on a mission to rescue embassy hostages several decades before. "The Clans serve. We are guardians, protectors," he said proudly.

"And touchy," Shaggy added. "I've never known anyone who could get bent out of shape faster than a vampire. Thanks," he said as the bartender deposited another beer on the table. He gulped down the brew, then wiped his mouth with the back of his hand. "Good thing you're buying, Alec —"

"You used to call me Colonel."

"Yeah, but that was before you went into Delta and got all casual."

It was true that the members of the army's elite covert fighting force acted like civilians much of the time, and rank was generally a nonissue. Yet . . . "I didn't know you knew about my transfer."

"Guessed when you disappeared so sudden-like." Shaggy shrugged. "We're both civilians now. You *are* out, right?"

"Unfortunately." Alec had reluctantly resigned his commission when the symptoms started. Delta Force was no place for a vampire when the drugs that let him function in the daylight world were losing their potency.

"You need a job?"

Alec rubbed the back of his neck, then rolled his head from side to side. "I need a job," he answered, when he'd worked some of the tension out of his muscles. The memory of seeing his woman in the market rose before him for a moment, but he pushed it away. "I very badly need a job."

"Think I might have something for you," Shaggy told him. "Heard old man Lancer's looking to add to his team. Your résumé hold up to a background check?"

"Of course," Alec answered. "What sort of team are we talking about?"

"Personal protection."

"Bodyguard."

"You got it. To the rich and famous. Protecting a movie star is an honorable enough job for a Clan boy, right?"

Alec wanted to snarl that a Prime was not a *boy,* but that was only his medication needing adjustment. "Depends on the movie star," he managed to joke.

"I'll get a friend of a friend to set up an appointment with Lancer for you," Shaggy said. "Maybe even today. That okay with you?"

"I appreciate it." He briefly looked the werewolf in the eye, a sign of respect, rather than challenge from an alpha male of one species to the alpha of another.

Shaggy nodded. "I'll call when I know anything."

Alec felt relieved at having set one item of his agenda in motion. He was almost looking forward to his first appointment at the very private medical facility that was his next stop. His senses, physical and psychic, were growing painfully sensitive. For example, he was uncomfortably aware of the werewolf's rising pheromone level.

Shaggy looked around restlessly and glanced at his watch. "Can't hang around and talk over old times." He grinned as he stood. "Got to get home. My old lady's in season, and we aren't getting any younger."

That explained the pheromones, but also told Alec far more than he wanted to know about werewolves' private lives. He got to his feet as well. "I have to be going myself. Good seeing you again."

"I'll be in touch." Shaggy waved a casual farewell, and was out the door faster than he'd come in.

Alec donned his jacket, driving gloves, sunglasses, and hat before walking out into the daylight. Not that long ago, he hadn't needed all this paraphernalia to face the sun. He felt like an invalid, needing it now, and hoped that the doctors at the clinic could bring him back to his normal life.

Then he could find *her.*

"Why, if it isn't Domini the Dominatrix finally sauntering in."

"I have never sauntered in my life," Domini informed Andy Maxwell, who lounged against Nancy's reception desk in the front hall.

As usual when off duty, Andy looked at her with feigned salaciousness. He wasn't really a sexist pig, but a good friend with a twisted sense of humor.

She pointed sternly to the white marble floor. "On your knees when you speak to me, slave."

Andy promptly obeyed, then looked up at her with anticipation.

Domini laughed; the silliness made her feel normal.

Nancy peered over the top of her glasses. "You two stop that."

They both knew who the real dominatrix was in the company. "Yes, ma'am," they answered together. Andy bounced to his feet and leaned against the desk again.

"Your grandfather wants to see you," Nancy told Domini.

"Right now?"

"I buzzed him as soon as I saw you get off the elevator."

The wide glass wall and door of Lancer Services' office suite gave Nancy a very good view of the long hallway that led to the gleaming copper doors of the elevators. "And you go back to your cube," Nancy told Andy, "before I tell him you asked me for a date again."

"I just came out for staples," Andy protested as Domini left the reception area. "And to flirt a little bit —"

Domini shook her head with amusement as she drew out of earshot. Andy *was* a flirt, all right, but he liked his job too much to break the old man's rule about no fraternizing among the staff. Concentrate on business or get out, that was Grandpa's philosophy.

Concentrating usually wasn't a problem for Domini, but she was having a hard time getting the image of the man she'd seen watching her out of her mind.

Domini knocked and then walked into her grandfather's office. The Old Man was on the phone, so she grabbed a bottled water out of the small fridge, took a seat in the deep brown leather chair in front of his desk, and blatantly listened to Benjamin Lancer's side of the phone conversation.

"D-Boy is just out, eh? How civilized is he? Any PPA training? Good. We can polish him up quick enough. Can he wear a suit? Okay. Send him over."

"Found someone to replace Hancock?" Domini asked after her grandfather put down the phone.

The desk was a wide, modernistic glass-topped affair; a present from a grateful corporate client a few years back. It didn't suit the Old Man's taste, but it, and the rest of the office's decor, set a low-key but expensively professional tone that reassured the company's clientele. A sleek new flat-screen computer and the telephone took up one side of the desk. The Old Man generally propped his feet up on the other side when there weren't any clients around. Nancy made it part of her job to see that the desk was clean and gleaming before any client meetings.

He put his feet up on the desk. "Looks like," was the gruff answer.

"That's a relief. A team leader type?"

"Won't know till I see him, will I?"

Domini shrugged agreement.

People came and went a lot in this business. Lancer only hired the best, and the best eventually tended to go freelance or start their own agencies. Tommy Hancock had recently taken an offer from the Secret Service, so there was a certain amount of pride, and no hard feelings, about his leaving. But replacing someone of his caliber was proving harder than usual. The Old Man had been starting to be frustrated about it. He didn't look frustrated now, which pleased Domini on several levels. Though he thrived on stress, she wished he'd take life a little easier. God forbid she should suggest it, however.

Though he didn't look a day over a very fit sixty, Old Man Lancer was pushing eighty.

There was more silver than brown in his hair and beard. His skin was tanned, and the only wrinkles that showed were deep crow's-feet around surprisingly blue eyes. She'd heard someone describe Ben Lancer's eyes as neon blue, and they were the one physical feature she'd inherited from him. There was maturity in his voice rather than age. The tone was deep, dark, and had a rough timbre to it, like the taste of good whiskey. Whiskey was also a drink he tended to overindulge in once a year, on the anniversary of losing Domini's grandmother.

With that date looming over the horizon, Domini was glad the Old Man had one concern off his mind. Especially as she might be presenting him with another one.

Since he'd sent for her, she first asked, "What's up?"

"Holly Ashe called," he answered.

Domini smiled. "Called the house? She knows I have my own place now, and my cell number even if we haven't seen each other in over a year."

She and Holly had been best friends from preschool all the way through high school. Domini went on to college; Holly went on the road. They kept in touch, though since Holly's singing career went white-hot, contact had been less frequent. There had been a lot of phone calls and e-mails when Holly broke up with her longtime lover, but that had been a year ago, when Holly was touring Europe.

"So why did Holly call you?"

"Her management's looking to beef up her security. She remembered her old friend's family business, and she wants you to be her bodyguard."

Domini slugged down half the bottle of water. "I'm sure you told her that isn't exactly how it works."

He nodded. "Took the assignment for the company. You'll go through her people to set up the details."

Domini almost dropped the bottle. "You want me to run a detail for a friend?"

Those sharp blue eyes narrowed. "I want you to do the workup and briefing for the team. That all right with you?"

When Benjamin Lancer asked a question like that, he expected only one answer. "Yes, sir. How large a detail? Duration of contract? Who's your point person?"

A slight smile creased his weathered face. "I noticed you didn't ask if you were going to be on the team."

She smiled back. "I assumed that Holly insisted that I would be."

He nodded. "Good girl."

A compliment from him was rare, so Domini basked in it for a moment. She was also relieved. Doing groundwork meant several days spent mostly in the office. That would give her more than enough time to recover from the weirdness of the last few hours. She needed to be sharp, focused, and above all, behaving like a normal human being while in the field. People's safety depended on her out there.

For a moment she hesitated on telling her grandfather about the incident, since it now looked to be a nonissue. But this profession demanded honesty, and her grandfather expected her to be honest. He'd raised her that way.

She cleared her throat. "I need to tell you something."

"I noticed your butt's still in the chair when you've got work to do."

Domini grinned mischievously. "Don't you want to see my pretty face first thing in the mornin', Grandpa?"

He glanced at his watch. "Not exactly first thing, is it? What'd you want to tell me, girl?"

"I had a dream last night. It wasn't a normal dream. It was a premonition —"

"Thought you didn't get those anymore."

"I don't talk about them, it's not the same thing."

Ben Lancer gave her a glower that should have had a trademark symbol on it, it was so definitive. "Hmmph. Go on."

"This dream was way different than anything I'd had before. It was . . ." She didn't want to say *erotic,* because she wasn't sure the word was big enough to fit the sensations that had overcome her. "Disturbing. I woke up with this need . . . a craving —"

Her grandfather's boots hit the floor with a shocking thud as he sat up straight. Those bright blue eyes held hers with laser intensity. "Compulsion?" he asked. "Somewhere you had to be at a certain time?"

If she didn't know him so well, Domini would have sworn that was fear she heard in his voice. His tone made her nervous. "Yes. How did you know?"

"How do you feel now?"

Domini shrugged. "Better. Steadier. But I was really disoriented until I got out of the market. I normally get very low-level premonitions. It's not like I *see* important events before they happen —"

"You did once, when you were three. You woke everybody up screaming, 'Shake! Shake!' We barely got out of the house before the quake knocked it down."

Domini was startled. "I don't remember that."

28

"It happened, whether you remember it or not. You said market?"

Domini took a deep breath, and went on. "The Central Market. That was where I was — okay, compelled — to go. I needed to buy fresh peaches."

"You were late for work because you needed fruit?" His disgust was palpable. He sat back in his chair. "I thought you were forced to go there to meet someone."

Again, she was surprised. "There *was* a man." Even speaking about him sent a shiver through her. "How did you know?"

He was leaning forward again, his hands flat on the thick glass desktop, studying her intently. "Tell me about him. What did he look like? Did he approach you? Speak to you?"

Domini felt thoroughly shaken now. "Forget it. I don't want to talk about it." She stood and turned toward the door.

"Wait —"

Domini bolted out the door.

"Just what I don't need," she muttered as she hurried to her own desk. "One psycho psychic in this family is more than enough."

CHAPTER THREE

"Yeah?" Domini answered the ring of the internal phone line, later that day.

"Get in here," the Old Man answered.

"Be right there." She promptly hung up and headed back to the boss's office.

He wasn't alone.

A man standing beside the desk turned when she opened the door. Though the room was brightly lit, all she made out at first was a silhouette of a man, tall and broad-shouldered, standing unnaturally still but exuding grace and strength and power all the same. Domini blinked and he came into focus, but the impression of danger did not go away.

He was not the handsomest man she'd ever seen, but he was the most — something. The word that came to mind was *strong,* not just in the physical sense. His features were so strongly defined, his square jaw and high cheekbones could have been chiseled. There was a deep cleft in his chin and he had green eyes, which she couldn't quite make herself look into directly. It would seem too much like an alpha challenge to do so.

"Domini, you're staring," her grandfather said.

"Well, who wouldn't?" she heard herself mutter. The alpha smiled slightly, which brought her back to herself with a jolt. She was so not acting normal today.

Define normal?

She ignored the thought. "You wanted to see me, sir?"

"Would I have told you to come in if I didn't?"

Her grandfather's gruff rudeness told Domini that the stranger was not a client. She'd realized that anyway. He would never be the one in need of protecting. Standing perfectly still, with a totally neutral expression on his face, he was the most dangerous person in the room — which said a lot, considering that neither she nor her grandfather were mild-mannered kittens.

So, this was the D-Boy.

"Alexander Reynard," he introduced himself. "Interesting name, Domini."

He spoke softly, and his voice had a vel-

31

vety rumble. It was the caressing kind of voice that tempted one to lean closer.

"It's an old Scottish name," she answered. "It's a term for a schoolteacher."

"Oh?" he asked. "I thought it was a variation of Domanae, which means 'mistress.'"

Domini blushed, remembering her teasing with Andy Maxwell. Had this new guy been talking to the staff already?

"Never mind what her father decided to call her," the Old Man broke in. "Domini, show Mr. Reynard around. You'll be supervising his orientation for the next week, starting tomorrow morning."

Alec watched as Domini curbed both surprise and irritation. She was busy. He disturbed her. It took great effort for him to reach through the dull fog surrounding him, to read her. It would be better to save his energy, so after a few more moments he broke off the contact.

Her gaze flicked Alec's way and darted away again. "Yes, sir," she answered her grandfather.

Mistress indeed, Alec thought. A prize. Mine.

For an instant he held an image in his mind, a vision of how in ancient days, his kind were rewarded for mighty deeds with the bodies of the most beautiful women in the world. Long before his time, of course, but he knew the legends of the good old days. No one was going to bring this woman to his bed but him, which suited him. He only wished she wasn't here right now.

But it didn't surprise him to find her here; fate loved cruel jokes. To be so close and yet utterly distant . . . He dared not touch her, or taste her, or make any claim. Not in his condition.

He was all right for now, with a cocktail of drugs pouring through his system. The doctors had dosed him with a temporary fix to get him through the interview and the rest of the day, but because of the drugs, he could barely touch the senses of the woman meant to be his. He was grateful, in a way; it was only the drugs that kept the fury of *having* to be drugged in check. Catch-22, vampire style.

While she talked to her grandfather, Alec stared at Domini as blatantly as she had at him. The old man noticed without even looking Alec's way. Alec refrained from smiling at Lancer's protectiveness, for if he did, the smile would be predatory.

When he'd seen Domini in the market, it had been her spirit more than her physical appearance that he'd noticed. Then he'd seen that she was tall and dark-haired. This close to her, he could appreciate her long-legged athlete's body, but too much perusal of all the curves and lines of her figure was not wise right now, not even when he was numbed by the drugs. Later, when he had time to slowly strip her naked and look, he would caress and taste to his utter satisfaction. For now, Alec concentrated on Domini's face.

She was not classically beautiful and certainly not Hollywood beautiful, for which he was thankful. Not blond, not a size zero; nothing had been surgically altered or injected to try to make artificial perfection out of the perfectly lean and lithe form given her by nature. She was a hardbody, which took hard work, sweat, and dedication. He appreciated that, admired it, wanted —

Face. Concentrate on her face, before you get hot and bothered and do something stupid.

Domini's eyes were amazing, bright blue surrounded by thick, dark lashes. Her chin was sharp and stubborn. Her skin, pale and flawless but for one mole to the right of her lower lip. The beauty spot added a saucy air of wantonness to a mouth that was already more than amazing. Those full, ripe lips were made to be kissed for at least several hours a day. A man could make a full-time job of worshiping that soft, sensuous mouth.

"Come on, I'll find you a desk and show you around," Domini said, jarring him back to the present.

"Thank you." Alec exchanged a long glance with Ben Lancer. Lancer's look held a warning that no fraternization was allowed, especially with his granddaughter. Alec nodded, but it was in acceptance of the risk of breaking the rule, rather than agreement to abide by it.

For Domini, the walk down the corridor that led to the warren of office cubicles had never seemed so long. She felt like she was being tailed, almost stalked. Maybe he disturbed her because she couldn't hear him behind her. The corridor was not carpeted, and he was not wearing soft-soled shoes, so why were there no footsteps? And why couldn't she hear his breathing? She was damned good; was a Delta Force veteran that much better?

Stupid question — of course he was, or she would know he was there.

When his hand touched her shoulder, Domini was shocked, literally. Sensation burned through her like a bolt of electricity. A gasp caught in her throat as she spun to face him, hands held up defensively. Only to find herself facing a mildly surprised, very good-looking man, who said, "Sorry."

She should have been the one to apologize, but she felt stupid and — scared. Something else as well, something that sent her heart pounding in her ears and the blood sizzling through her veins. She didn't know what it was, but she knew Mr. Alexander Reynard caused it.

"Cat got your tongue?" he asked after silence stretched taut between them.

Domini quivered inside at the sound of his cool, lilting voice. Looking at him made her knees go weak. And — she wanted him to touch her again.

She turned around. "Come on." It was a victory that her voice didn't shake.

A few more steps, and they reached the large room partitioned into a dozen low-walled cubicles. Here she felt on firmer ground. Here she actually could find something reasonable to say to the man.

A few people turned from their telephones and computer screens as they passed, and Domini paused each time to introduce Reynard. Most of the office area was empty, so the journey to Reynard's future workspace didn't take very long.

The cubicle contained a pair of workstations with computers, phones, and file drawers. Two very comfortable desk chairs took up most of the floor space.

Domini gestured for Alec to have a seat. She leaned against the doorway, arms crossed, and explained, "Agents share the cubes. We're not in the office much, so it's not likely you'll have company crowding you when you're doing office work."

She pointed toward the workstation on the left. "This'll be yours. Nancy will set you up with supplies and passwords and a keycard for the secure areas. We'll go through the fun stuff tomorrow, if that's okay with you." She checked her watch. "I have an appointment in an hour."

He nodded. "Fine. Fun stuff?"

"Hardware, surveillance equipment. Nothing as fancy as you're used to, I'm sure."

He gave her a genuine smile. He had dimples. "I can't talk about what I'm used to."

Ex-special-ops people always said cryptic stuff like that, if they even talked about what they'd done at all. Naturally this whetted curiosity, but Domini refused to wheedle for information that wouldn't be given. It only encouraged the spooks' sense of superiority. And this man exuded so much confidence that she definitely didn't want to stroke his ego.

So, what would you like to stroke?

Where had that thought come from?

Domini returned to business. "We have two floors of this building. Offices here, fun stuff down a flight. We have a good exercise room downstairs, but most of our people also do classes at various martial arts schools. Though we don't carry guns on our protection details, we can get you a discount at the Pherson shooting range, and we have an arrangement with Delano Defensive Driving School. You'll be put through the driving course during your orientation. Let's see, what else?

"We're a dress-down, dress-up organization with very high-end clients, so your wardrobe has to reflect their lifestyles. You'll have a generous annual clothing allowance. Nancy has a list of recommended clothing stores and tailors."

She checked out Reynard's suit while trying not to eye *him,* not entirely succeeding. "Doubt you'll need Nancy's advice. Armani?"

He fingered the well-made, dark suit jacket. "Found this on Rodeo Drive. Wanted to impress my prospective employer."

Which brought up another question that she should have considered before now. "How *did* you impress the Old Man? He usually takes a couple of weeks to vet a new hire."

Alec gestured at the cube's other chair, and watched Domini take a seat. He had managed some mental influence on the Old Man, but only enough to smooth his way into the job. He hadn't lied about his skills. Lancer could trust Alec to do the job he hired him for, even if he'd been telepathically influenced not to run the normal background check.

"Your grandfather trusts the mutual friend who recommended me for the position," he told the clearly suspicious Domini. "And I know that you're about to say he doesn't trust many people."

She narrowed her extraordinary blue eyes. "Reading my mind?"

"Lucky guess."

Alex stood, and Domini rose to face him. He offered her a hand, which she pretended not to notice. Too bad; he very much wanted to touch her again. *Needed* to, and intended to. For now, he allowed himself the merest thought of how her skin would be warm and satin-smooth against his stroking hands.

Domini's eyes widened, letting him know that on some unconscious level she responded to his desire. She blinked and stepped carefully past him, while he resisted the temptation to reach for her. He didn't know if this was a victory of the drugs or his own self-control.

"Thank you for your help," Alec told her. "So, we'll resume the orientation tomorrow morning?"

She nodded. "You'll need to fill out forms and get an ID photo before you go. I'll leave you with Nancy to take care of that. Be nice to her," she added. "Nancy's the real boss around here."

He put a hand to his heart. "I will be the epitome of charm."

"That won't work on Nancy." Domini led the way back through the offices, saying over her shoulder, "Try bribery. She makes out like a bandit during Secretary's Week."

"Roses and chocolates it is, then." Alec hung back a few steps, so he could fully appreciate the view as Domini walked away.

CHAPTER FOUR

"Does this hurt?"

"If you ask me that again, I will rip out your throat." Alec was strapped down naked on a lab table built for vampires, but that didn't make the threat any less meaningful.

The drugs had worn off, and Alec was feeling very testy indeed. His fangs brushed against his lower lip and his claws scraped against the metal table. Anger pumped through him, and his control was very, very thin.

"I'll take that as a yes," Dr. Casmerek responded calmly. "These tests are necessary," he went on. "The consequences will be far more uncomfortable if we don't find out exactly what types of adjustments we need to make."

The doctor went on about proteins and allergic reactions, while assistants continued to poke needles into Alec's sensitized flesh and attached monitors to every section of his head and body. Alec closed his eyes and tried not to struggle. He hated being restrained. No matter how much he knew this was for his own good, he still felt like a prisoner. Worse, he was helpless and defenseless, something no Prime could take for long. Instinct fought with reason, and the effort left him panting and covered with sweat.

The doctor, who was a very specialized specialist, was totally trusted by the Clans. He was completely devoted to helping his patients, but right now Alec hated Casmerek with all his might. Alec was powerless, and Casmerek in control. Never mind that Alec had surrendered the control by his own free will; he *needed* the mortal's help. That was not the way it was supposed to be.

Maybe it would be better to return to the old ways. There were many, even among the Clans, who thought this modern solution wrong and unnatural. Many argued that the drugs that helped them live in daylight, that protected them against silver and garlic and the other allergens that limited their powers, were an abomination. For thousands of years the Primes, the venerable Elders, the House Ladies, the Matri, and the sheltered young had lived in the darkness and controlled the thirst with strength of mind and willpower and devotion to duty. With the coming of modern science much had changed, but the will still existed; mental disciplines could still be applied to curb the fire in the blood and mind.

Alec realized he must have been speaking aloud, possibly even raving, when Casmerek said, "You will need to draw upon every mental discipline the Primes know until your biochemistry is back in balance. It's that mental discipline and probably sheer stubbornness that have kept you going the last few weeks. I wish you'd gotten here sooner."

"Well, I couldn't," Alec snarled. "I was in Uzbekistan."

"Which is a fact I'm sure I'm not supposed to know." He dared to pat Alec's bare shoulder, and ignored Alec baring his fangs threateningly at this gesture of comfort. "We're used to keeping secrets here, so don't worry about it, Colonel."

"Don't call me that."

He didn't deserve the title. Not when he'd had to abandon his men, his assignment, all for the selfish need to —

"You've only done what was necessary for you to do. Leaving the service when you did saved lives. You'll realize that when you're feeling better. How are we doing?" the doctor asked the techs.

"Ready to go," one of them answered.

"Good." Casmerek turned his attention back to Alec and patted his shoulder again. "We're going to turn off the lights and leave you now. All you have to do is go to sleep. Close your eyes. Rest. Dream. The machines will do the rest."

Alec heard the technicians leave the room, and Casmerek's voice faded as the doctor moved farther and farther away. "In the morning we'll have run all the baseline tests, and then we'll take it from there. Go to sleep, now," he urged in his gentle voice.

Alec closed his eyes as the lights went out, and he was suddenly alone in the dark — a monster who should be lurking in closets, or hiding in nightmares. Wherever it was he should be, he was here, and he was very afraid of the monster who was himself.

The night was punctuated by smoky torches at each corner of the temple courtyard, hung high upon the rough stone columns. The scent of pitch and burning straw carried to her through the cool air of the desert night. The deep portico beyond the pillars was far darker than the night itself. The courtyard held the light of the moon, the stars, and the torches, though they sent out gray smoke that swirled like river fog through the enclosure. This was a place of dark mystery, a place set apart, a place where a god would walk — and do whatever he pleased.

Though she saw no one, she knew she was not alone. A shiver ran through her, compounded of deep fear and a thrill of excitement. She had been chosen. Though it meant her doom — for how could one not be consumed when touched by a god? — she faced her fate with the pride of a king's daughter.

She circled the courtyard slowly, drawing nearer to the altar set in the center of the sacred place. Then she realized that the place of sacrifice was in fact a bed, more ornately carved and gilded than any bed frame in the king's palace. The bedcoverings were richly embroidered, the mattress thick and piled high with pillows.

She sensed movement as she reached out to touch a carving on the bedpost. She heard and saw nothing, yet knew which way to turn to face the Lord of Darkness.

She confronted a tall, broad figure clothed in an all-enveloping cloak and hood. She knelt but did not bow her head, showing respect but not subservience.

The cloaked figure moved silently toward her, as graceful as a hunting cat. "Did you come here of your own choice?" His voice

was soft, rich, commanding attention and response.

"I came," she answered. "That is as much as
you need to know."

The Lord of Darkness had rid the city of evil
ones that killed in the night. He had asked for
a woman as reward. It was fitting that the king
give his city's savior a daughter to honor such
great service.

They had drawn lots in the women's quar-
ters. Each of the king's six unmarried daugh-
ters had taken a turn to draw a stone from a jar,
one white stone among the five black ones.
She had drawn third, and the white stone. So
she had donned her jewels and her best gown
and combed out her long, black hair as if
preparing for her wedding. She had refused to
weep, had kissed no one good-bye, but had
gone silently with the priests who led her here,
then left her to the god's will.

And here was the god.

She should remain humble and silent. She
asked instead, "What do you want with me?"

He answered with a gesture toward the bed.
Then he dropped his cloak. By both moon and
torchlight, she saw that he was naked.

He was pale as milk, and perfect.

His face was beautiful, though the sharp
lines of it might have been carved from stone.
His expression was solemn, harsh, and very

46

sad. She could not look at his face for long, yet she could no more look away from him than willingly stop breathing. He was taller than a mortal man, as a god should be. Taller and more — everything.

He was like a statue come to life. Everything about him was sharply defined, from the rippling muscles of chest and thighs and arms to the rampant phallus that inexorably drew her gaze.

She had never known arousal before, but surely this heavy, hot, aching growing inside her must be it.

She licked her lips, hardly aware of the gesture until the Lord of Darkness's soft chuckle caressed her ears.

"Can a god laugh?"

*"A god can do anything that pleases him."
He was before her suddenly, moving with cat grace and god speed. He took her by the shoulders with a touch that surprised her by its gentleness, and drew her to her feet, brushing her body against his as she rose. His flesh was warm, and not made of stone at all.*

His fingers were skilled and quick. Her finest dress pooled around her feet within moments. It was but another moment before he picked her up and placed her on the bed. She did not realize she'd put her arms around his neck until he gently loosed her hold. He held her hands in his and kissed one palm, and then the other. The light touch sent a flame of desire through her.

Then he tilted her head up and covered her mouth with his. She had not realized what deep, fiery pleasure the touching of lips, the delving of tongues, could bring. The kiss was headier than unwatered wine, a rich feast of sensation.

It was said the Lords of Darkness had fangs and claws, so she was not surprised, and only a little afraid, when she felt sharp teeth press against her lips. The excitement of his touch overwhelmed her fear. Perhaps fear enhanced her excitement. All she knew was that she moaned with loss when his mouth left hers.

"No — !"

"Peace," he whispered. He held her face in his hands, so that she must look into his eyes. They glowed faintly in the moonlight, as any night beast's would. "This night you are mine, to do with as I please."

The look in those eyes demanded an answer, an assent. Her body was crying out for his touch. She was a spoiled daughter of the king; she wanted to demand he make love to her. She swallowed hard and gathered her wits to remember why she was here. "I am yours," she told him. "A gift for the god."

"Do you want me? Do you want my body to

cover yours? Do you want me inside you? I will have your consent."

He had gone out of his way to arouse her, and now he was asking her? "Don't be ridiculous." She grabbed his thick black hair in her fists and pulled his mouth back to hers.

This second kiss was as intense, but he did not let it last as long. "The night grows late," he whispered against her mouth.

His hands skimmed over her then, and he kissed her throat and between her breasts and suckled at the tips, and moved on to her belly and thighs. Wherever he touched he left traces of fire behind. The heat pooled deep down in her belly, making her grind her hips and arch up against him, insistent, begging for more.

Every now and then there would be a slight sting as his sharp teeth penetrated her skin, pain that was more pleasure than pain. If he took a drop or two of her blood with each kiss, she welcomed the small sacrifice for the bright bursts of joy it brought. His fingers delved between her legs, caressed and teased her until she thought she would die from the tension building inside her.

He made her wild with longing. Finally she opened to him, and lifted her hips. He knelt between her legs and looked down. She held her arms out beseechingly, and looked up a long, long way to meet his gaze.

Only she couldn't see his eyes, because he was wearing sunglasses. His features shifted as he smiled, and a glint of moonlight sparkled off his fangs.

"Reynard," she demanded angrily. "What the hell are you doing in my dream?"

"Your dream?" he answered. "I thought it was mine."

Domini sat up in bed, shaking and covered in sweat. "What the hell?" she muttered, and swiped hair out of her face. She was checking herself for bite marks when she realized it had just been a dream, and that she still wasn't quite awake yet.

Good Lord, two nights in a row of weirdness. What was the matter with her?

Domini got out of bed, and discovered that she was shaking so hard she could barely stand. Her knees were like jelly, her breasts felt heavy and tender, and her insides ached. She sat on the edge of the rumpled bed, staring into the darkness, the image of the smoky temple courtyard overlaying her shadowed bedroom.

"So that's what an erotic dream feels like."

She was edgy, weary, drained. Arousal was fading to dull ash, leaving her with a growing sense of frustration.

"It was just a dream." It had been a wild,

crazy ride, but — it was only a dream. One where she'd made love with a man she'd barely met who turned into a vampire. It was still so vivid that she could almost feel the sweet sting of the vampire's kisses.

Why a vampire? She hadn't dreamed of vampires since she was a little girl and her mom insisted Grandpa stop telling her horror stories before bedtime. Maybe she'd seen a movie billboard or television ad about a vampire movie. Maybe it was something she'd eaten. Maybe Reynard was just a spooky guy.

"I wonder if he does look that good naked. . . ." She shook her head sharply. "*Stop* that."

It was weird, it certainly wasn't the sort of dream she usually had, but it wasn't like last night's disturbing premonition. This time all that had really happened was that a lot of exotic props bubbled up from the warehouse in the back of her mind, and her subconscious went on a randy rampage.

But how was she supposed to face Reynard in the office tomorrow morning?

Calm down, girl. It was only a dream. After all, it wasn't as if Reynard was going to know what went on in her mind in the middle of the night.

Alec woke up in chains.

He snarled and howled in desperate fury,

and fought against the restraints. He had to get to her. How dare they keep him from her!

People surrounded him while he struggled. Hands held him down. Needles pierced his skin, bringing white-hot pain, bringing calm, bringing peace, bringing him back to himself.

"I had a dream," he said, recognizing who these people were, where he was, and why he was restrained. "I'm all right," he told the anxious faces. They were here to help him, but he hated them — because they would keep him from getting to her. "It was just a dream."

Someone patted his bare shoulder. It was meant as comfort, but Alec would have bitten the hand off if he could have gotten to it. These people did not know what it was like to be Prime, and in the bonding state.

Gradually, the drugs sent him back into a drifting half-sleep. The monitors and alarms died down and stopped flashing and buzzing. The medical personnel left, one by one.

Alec smiled. He had not dreamed alone. He knew where the dream came from. He had thought of the ancient customs when he was with Domini Lancer, and his drugged subconscious had built on that sexual fantasy. In his sleep he took Domini as the old ones took mortal women; tasted her and pleasured her and was very near to completing the act, when Domini became aware that she was dreaming.

She woke up — and left him hanging out to dry with a raging hard-on, nearly out of his mind.

But the fact that she'd shared his dream meant she was aware of their connection, even if only on the deepest subconscious level of her being.

"Cool." He drifted back into to deep sleep even as he murmured the word.

Chapter Five

"Good morning," a voice said

"Go away," Alec growled.

"I realize vampires are not morning people, but you need to wake up now, Alec."

He opened his eyes. Dr. Casmerek was standing over the bed with a chart in his hands. Looking past Casmerek's broad frame, Alec was glad to see two technicians unfastening all the probes and monitors and restraints. He flexed his arms and legs. The metal table was still cold against his bare skin, even after hours lying on it. At least the lighting was dim and didn't bother his eyes.

"Am I free to go now?"

"Hardly." Casmerek looked at his watch. "It's five-thirty in the morning. Sorry to rouse you so early, but I wanted time to talk before you leave. You can get up now," Casmerek added as the technicians left the room.

Alec sat up, and looked at the inside of his arms. The marks from the intravenous needles faded as he watched, and he noticed unhappily that the Clan mark on his left wrist had faded a bit further. He held his wrist up for the doctor. "When can I have this redone?"

"In a couple of weeks, perhaps. We have photographs of it on file that we can check against to see if it fades further." Casmerek handed Alec a small paper cup containing a half dozen pills of various shapes, colors, and sizes. While Alec gulped down the drugs, Casmerek pointed toward a doorway on the other side of the room. "Take a shower and get dressed. Then we'll talk in my office."

Shortly after, Alec took a seat across a desk in a room decorated in soothing shades of pale green and blue. There were no windows in Casmerek's office, but beautiful landscape paintings on the walls made up for the lack of sunlit scenery.

"Will I live?" Alec asked.

"For several centuries yet," Casmerek answered, "even without the medication. But to live in daylight during that time" — he passed a metal case across the desk to Alec — "follow the instructions on using these religiously."

Alec snapped open the case to check out

the carefully packed contents. "Pills, capsules, syringes, eye drops, skin cream."

"A supply of medicated animal protein —"

"We call it blood where I come from," Alec said dryly.

"— will be delivered to your home twice a week."

"When will I be able to stop taking the medication?"

"We have to start with the preliminary test results and go from there. Vampire physiology does its best to reassert itself every chance it gets. We're working on tracing mitochondrial DNA and gene mapping, which hold out a great deal of hope for the future, but for now, we're limited to tailoring a treatment for each individual case.

"I can't give you any firm date on when you'll be fully recovered. All we can do is take it one step at a time. Now, about last night." He looked over steepled fingers at Alec.

"We were monitoring your sleep cycle. The REM readouts went so wild for a few minutes that it was like we were recording the brainwaves of more than one person." Casmerek gave him a curious look.

"Interesting," Alec answered.

"It was a strongly erotic dream," Casmerek went on. "Perfectly normal for a Prime, of course."

"Nothing hornier than a Prime," Alec agreed.

"Was the dream about anyone specific? Someone you know?"

Primes might be highly sexed, but they protected even the most casual of lovers. They defended their bondmates to the death.

"None of your business," Alec informed the doctor.

"It is if it affects your treatment."

The bonding was an essential part of being a Prime. It was at the heart of what made one a vampire. The bond was sacred; it was as fundamental as the night.

After he'd seen Domini in the market, Alec had made a promise to himself to protect his mate from the dark part of his nature, to wait until he was totally in control of himself before he pursued her.

But he hadn't expected to meet her face-to-face so quickly. He hadn't expected to stand beside her, talk to her, breathe in her scent, and touch her skin. He hadn't expected to dream with her. Maybe he wouldn't be able to control the mating urge.

All he could do was try. He was Prime. The woman was his. He would do whatever was necessary to protect her.

Dr. Casmerek had worked with Primes long enough to know when to let a subject go. He nodded and went on. "Practicing the meditation skills you learned as a child is also vital for your treatment."

"I haven't stopped practicing them."

"I'm sure, but we've still set up a refresher course with an elder."

Casmerek was watching him closely, so Alec did not let the wariness show. "What clan?" he asked calmly.

"An Honored Father of Clan Shagal."

Alec relaxed. "The Jackals are friend to all."

"The Matri who will act as your therapist is also of Shagal. Don't look at me like you're about to bite my head off, Reynard. A mortal isn't going to be of any help if you need to talk things out. You can sit in a chair and glower at her for all I care, but you will see her."

"I have more respect for the Matri than to glower at one."

"You might think all these measures are overkill, but believe me, you are far closer to the edge than you think you are. We know what is necessary to help you."

"Fine." Alec stood, grasping the plastic handle of the case so hard he could feel it begin to crack. He'd had enough of being treated for one day. "I have to go to work now."

Domini held a white paper bag up before her as she entered the kitchen, following the smell of brewing coffee. She rattled the bag to get his attention. "Yo, Grandpa, I brought doughnuts."

Ben Lancer was wearing a white terry bathrobe. He was barefoot, and his silver hair was still damp from a shower. He'd been staring at the ocean out the kitchen window when Domini came in.

"Don't you know how to knock?" he asked, turning to face her.

He asked her that every time she dropped by, which was almost every day of the week. They generally had breakfast or supper together, if they weren't on a detail. He always pretended to be surprised to see her, though she knew the gruff old codger looked forward to her visits. They had a long-running chess competition going, and sometimes they'd drop into the game without bothering to say a word. Grandpa had also gotten her into Everquest, so they played the online role-playing game together on their laptops when either of them was out of town.

"Why knock when I have a key?" Domini

answered, as she always did. And knew the codes for the other layers of security surrounding the Malibu property.

"What if I'd had a woman with me?"

"Then both you and I would be very much surprised."

"Point taken." He poured her a cup of coffee, then sat opposite her at the kitchen island. "What kind of doughnuts?" He opened up the bag and pulled out an old-fashioned chocolate doughnut. His favorite, as Domini well knew. "You ever going to learn to cook?" he asked after he'd taken a few bites.

"I wasn't built for comfort, I was built for speed."

"Is that a way of telling me I have no one to blame for your lack of domestic skills but myself?"

"Yep."

"Well, at least you know how to shoot."

Domini and her grandfather settled into a comfortable silence, concentrating on doughnuts and coffee. Grandpa made great coffee. She enjoyed the sound of the surf pounding on the beach in the distance, and the calls of the gulls. She enjoyed the salty fresh scent of the breeze that came in the windows and the doors that opened to the deck. She loved this house. It wasn't all that large, compared to some of the mini-palaces that lined this very prime stretch of ocean-front real estate. She'd spent much of her life here, and still thought of it more as home than she did her own small house.

She always felt safe here, yet she didn't feel safe right now. She felt — like she was walking on the edge of a knife and suffering from vertigo. She was bound to fall one way or the other, and she had no idea what waited for her at the bottom. She wished she could pinpoint why she felt this way; then she could do something about it.

The old man put down his cup, looked her over, and glanced at the clock. "Not exactly dressed for work."

"I'll change when I get there. I need to work out."

She was wearing shorts, a T-shirt, and athletic shoes. She suspected he would always prefer to see her in something feminine, even while she was kicking butt. He was kind of sweet that way.

She dusted powdered sugar off her fingers and sat back in her chair. "Speaking of work, I have a question about Reynard."

"What's wrong with him?" he asked, never one to let anyone else take the offensive.

"I haven't seen enough of him to think there's anything wrong." Seeing Reynard naked in a dream didn't count — though there certainly wasn't anything wrong with Alexander Reynard in the altogether. Not that anyone could actually look that good naked, and that wasn't what her grandfather meant, anyway.

"You're blushing."

"Sugar rush," she countered. "Is there any way I can get Andy or Castlereigh to take on the new guy's orientation? I'm busy setting up the Ashe detail."

He gave her his sternest look. "This guy make you uncomfortable?"

Dream images danced through her head, and her pulse rate picked up. Uncomfortable? Oh, yes. Very yes.

"Training him gets in the way of setting up protection for Holly. I have at least three venues I need to check out today."

"Then take him with you."

She sighed. "I should have known you'd say that."

"You should have thought of it yourself."

"I did."

"Then you *are* uncomfortable around him."

Domini held up her hands in surrender. "All right. Fine. I'm uncomfortable around him."

"Glad to hear it."

She eyed the Old Man suspiciously. "What do you mean?"

"I mean that I'm uncomfortable around him, too. That boy ain't what he seems, and what he seems to be is one dangerous, in-control dude. Got the feeling he's much more than simply dangerous. Want you to keep an eye on him."

Domini was flabbergasted. "Me? If you thought he was lying, why did you hire him?"

"I wonder why I hired him so fast, myself. I acted on impulse, and I'm too old for that."

"You should have waited for a full background check. He may not be who he says at all."

"Or more than he says. Don't think he was lying; he just didn't tell the complete truth. That's not necessarily a bad thing, but I want to find out why a good friend recommended him to me on such short notice. I'm not going to completely trust Reynard until all his references check out."

"Glad to hear it." It bothered her that her sharp-as-a-laser-scalpel grandfather was questioning his own judgment. She was also relieved that he was quickly doing something about the lapse.

"Until then, I want you to keep an eye on him out in the field. You, I trust completely." He poked at the doughnut bag. "Any more chocolate ones in there?"

"I brought you three, and I think you've only snarfed down two. If you're going to have another doughnut, so am I."

What were a few hundred more calories, if it meant putting off being thrown together with the sexy and unnerving Mr. Reynard for a while longer?

CHAPTER SIX

The testosterone was so thick in the workout room that Domini could practically chew it. A group of her coworkers were having a high time flinging each other around on the floor mats. Practicing martial arts wasn't uncommon, but at the moment the place looked like a Jackie Chan movie. There was one man in the center of the fray, with at least six men coming at him from every direction, using at least six different martial arts styles. The man in the center was tossing them around as if the skilled protection agents were mere straw dummies. From the whoops and catcalls and laughter, it was obvious that the men getting beat up were having a ball.

Guys were funny that way.

Domini was impressed, and couldn't help but grin at the sight of a bunch of macho puppies taking on an alpha wolf. Her smile faltered when she saw it was Alexander Reynard making mincemeat out of Grandpa's finest.

She waited in the doorway, crossed her arms, and watched. There was nothing else she could do. The mats were in front of the door to the women's locker room, where she kept spare clothes. To get to the locker room she'd have to pass the gauntlet of male bodies, and they'd just ask her to join in. She enjoyed practicing with the male agents, but she wasn't prepared for sparring with Reynard.

Domini couldn't take her eyes off him. It was as if there was no one else in the room. He wore only an old pair of gray sweatpants and his body was almost exactly as she'd dreamed it — but not as pale, and even better muscled. The dream lover had been beautiful, but the fighter was magnificent!

He moved with tiger grace, every movement deadly poetry. His dark hair was pulled back off his chiseled face. Reynard's features were as still and concentrated as a statue's. His eyes gave nothing away, not showing by a flicker what move he intended next. He had long, narrow feet and long-fingered hands, and they moved with deadly, lightning speed as he kicked, spun, tossed, hit, jabbed, and ducked, putting down all comers. He was the most dangerous thing she'd ever seen, and the most compelling. She didn't recognize his fighting style, but he was obviously a deadly artist.

And she'd never seen anyone move that fast.

"It's unnatural."

She didn't think she'd spoken loud enough to be heard, but Reynard suddenly spun around, looked at her, and said, "It's Krav Maga."

His gaze bored into hers, green as moss, with sudden fire in their depths. His Zen-like fighting aloofness was a mask, and that fire drew her. She was across the room to the edge of the thick blue mats before she knew she'd moved.

"Krav Maga," she heard herself say in awe. "Wow."

"Yeah," Andy Maxwell agreed, coming to stand beside her. He was sweating hard, and she noticed bruises forming on his neck and right wrist. He looked about as awed as she felt. "I've been wanting to see this stuff in action." He rubbed his neck and nodded toward Reynard. "This dude is hot."

Masculine grunts of agreement issued from all around the room.

Reynard's gaze stayed on her. "Care to give it a try?"

She shook her head. "I don't —"

"You backing down, Dominatrix?" Andy questioned. "That's not like you."

"Come on, Domini," Joe Minke urged. "Give it a try." He was holding his hand over his ribs.

"Alec could use a new victim," Connor Marsh said. "He's used us up already."

None of them sounded the least bit resentful at having taken on the newest member of the firm and lost. It wasn't easy to win the respect of the professionals that worked at Lancer's, but Alec seemed to be more than holding his own, and this was only his first real day on the job.

Reynard caught her gaze again, which kept her from staring at his naked chest and washboard belly. This close to him, she caught the warm scent of his body, and the dream images rolled up out of her subconscious. For a moment she saw a glint of amusement in his eyes, and she had the horrible sensation that he knew exactly what she was thinking about.

Part of her wanted to run. Another part said, *Oh, don't be ridiculous!* and wanted to drag him down onto the thick mat. But that was the dream talking, and the discussion going on in the training room was about fighting, not fu—

"Krav Maga?" she repeated, trying to keep her mind on reality. "Where'd you learn that?"

"Army."

The unarmed fighting style had been developed in Israel, down and dirty and deadly. Krav Maga training was part of the bag of tricks favored by special forces and black-ops operators all over the world. And they didn't get much more elite than Delta Force.

Just one more reminder that Alexander Reynard was a very dangerous man, more dangerous than anyone she'd ever encountered. The knowledge sent an emotional rush through her that was part primal terror, and part primal "I want to have your babies."

Alec had been spoiling for a fight when he arrived at the Lancer offices. He'd come down to the exercise room to work off some tension, and found the group of agents there waiting to check him out. He'd have done the same with a new man transferred into his Delta unit, or with another Prime looking for Clan acceptance. He'd smiled at the other men, accepting their challenge. He fought them without arrogance and with humor, hadn't hurt any of them too badly, and the challenge gradually grew into a teaching session.

He realized now that he'd been waiting the whole time for this moment, for Domini Lancer to walk in and see him doing what he did so very well. He was preening for his mate. In a way it made him feel like a raw young Prime, strutting his stuff in the hopes a female would choose him as one of her consorts. But it was also a demonstration that told his woman that he could protect her. Or have her.

He wondered if she noticed.

To make sure, Alec gestured for Domini to take a turn on the mat.

A rush of heat that made her toes curl went through Domini as Reynard took a wide stance, knees flexed, and beckoned her toward him. His smile could have cut diamonds as his gaze swept through the group. All the other men backed away.

He looked back at her. "Come at me."

She shook her head. "I don't think so."

"Chicken," Andy called.

"Silence, slave," she retorted automatically, her attention on Reynard. What would she do if he touched her?

Fall down, she told herself sternly, and stepped onto the mat. This was a fighting exercise, and her style was aikido.

Aikido was a defensive art; the object was to use an attacker's own energy to deflect the assault. She had a second *dan* black belt in aikido.

"I'm going to die!" she squeaked as Reynard lunged toward her.

After all the years of training and practice, her response was instinctual. She countered his extended arm with a wrist block and fell away.

Or should have.

The next thing Domini knew, Reynard held her right arm up against her back, with her thumb locked in an unbreakable grip. Her chest was pressed to his, and he was looking down at her, smiling. He wasn't hurting her, but the threat was there. He could do with her as he pleased, and they both knew it.

She countered by hooking her ankle around his, which only made things worse, because he went down on his back, and she came down on top of him. His hold on her hadn't loosed a bit. His smile had turned into a savage grin. And his teeth were very sharp. They stared into each other's eyes. Applause erupted all around them, and someone whistled.

He let her go then. Domini was blushing hotter than she ever had in her life when she got to her feet. For the few seconds Reynard held her, she'd forgotten anyone else existed but the two of them.

She tossed her hair out of her face and said with strained dignity, "I'm going to change for work now." She glanced around the room at the grinning male faces. "Don't you gentlemen have places to be and things to do?"

"Took you long enough."

The humor in Reynard's voice was the only thing that kept Domini from jumping out of her skin. She didn't normally surprise easily. She glared across the room at him from the locker-room doorway. "What are you doing here?"

He gave a casual, one-shoulder shrug. Very economical of movement, was Mr. Reynard. "Waiting for you."

The contrast between the bare-chested street fighter and the conservatively dressed man leaning against the Bowflex machine was striking.

But he's bare-chested under his clothes. She could have sworn this inane thought earned her a low, dirty laugh from Reynard, except that he didn't make a sound.

He did give Domini a slow, intense, foot-to-head once-over that left her toes curling in her sandals and made her wish she'd wore more clothes.

Or less.

She'd taken her time in the locker room, getting cleaned up, putting on makeup, then swearing because the business suit she normally kept in her locker was at the dry cleaner. She ended up wearing a short, sleeveless pink-and-white-print sheath dress. It had been appropriate for accompanying a client on a shopping trip, but she'd rather wear something a bit less girly for today's assignment, which was doing walk-through evaluations of several places on Holly's schedule for the next few days.

Something less girly for facing Reynard would also be nice, although she couldn't tell from the look on his face if he liked what he saw of her bare arms, legs, and neckline. Which was possibly more irritating than an outright lewd eyeing of her assets.

And why was she standing here letting him do it, anyway?

He held up a hand. There was nothing threatening in the gesture, yet Domini felt held in place by it. "About what happened . . . We need to talk."

Domini wasn't quite sure exactly what Reynard wanted to discuss. She gave a wary shrug. "About what?"

"What happened when we fought."

"You won. Nothing to discuss."

"I have a problem with that."

Oh, lord, what did he want from her? To acknowledge how great he was? "Why? I don't mind that you beat me. No, I mind," she added after a raised eyebrow from him. "But I'm not —"

"You were scared." He took a step forward. "You went into a fight scared, already thinking you were going to lose."

"I *knew* I was going to lose. And it was an exercise," she reminded him. "Not a real fight."

He came closer, the look in those compelling green eyes more concentrated. She got the impression he was trying to see into her mind, her soul. Domini resisted the urge to step back.

"You have no reason to fear me. You will never have a reason to fear me."

She considered this, and him. Reynard was tall, dark, and dangerous to the core. She didn't know him, had no reason yet to trust him. Worst of all, he disturbed her in a way no man had ever done before.

She said, "It isn't up to you to tell me how I should feel. Now, I need to get to work."

His eyes sparked and his jaw tightened, but he gave her a curt nod. "Let's go."

"Fine." He followed her silently from the exercise room and down the hall. "You're spooky," she told him when they stepped into the elevator. "How can you move so quietly?"

He chuckled. "Maybe I'll teach you someday."

He stood too close to her for comfort, and he pressed the button for the garage level before she had a chance to. The overhead lights seemed too bright to her, the space far too small. She was used to take-charge guys; it didn't usually bother her. But with Reynard it was somehow — personal.

Was he trying to intimidate her? Impress her? Did he even notice he was doing it? Was it all her imagination? That had certainly been working overtime since meeting him.

They remained silent while the elevator moved down. She didn't look at him, but her awareness of Reynard was tactile. He might as well have been running his hands over her, with all the heat growing in her from merely being near him. Part of her wanted his touch. She couldn't help but remember what being held by him felt like, even though they'd been in a fight. Sparring with him was anything but an academic exercise.

He evoked strange, new sensations, and she couldn't afford any distractions. Why shouldn't she fear him, when he brought this — awareness — bubbling up from some deep well in her subconscious?

Protecting their clients required teamwork and respect, if not absolute trust.

She turned to Reynard and forced an affable smile. It was up to her to make this work, since she was in charge. "So, Alexander, can I ask where you're from?" She hoped he wouldn't give her any special-ops secretive bullshit.

"My branch of the clan came from France originally, but we settled in Idaho."

"Idaho? Like potatoes?"

He shook his head. "That's the southern part of the state. We're from farther north, up near the Canadian border."

"I've been all over the country, and on foreign travel details as well, but never to Idaho. But even when I travel, the clients do the sightseeing; I keep my attention on them."

"I know how you feel," Reynard said. "You know the bit: join the army, travel to exotic places, meet interesting new people — and shoot them. I've never had much chance to play tourist."

Alec hoped Domini was appreciating his effort to hold a civilized, superficial conversation. There was much that needed to be discussed, but it was too soon to talk of who they really were and what they meant to each other. Too soon to speak of souls and hearts and bodies bound by passion for eternity. That was kind of heavy for a first date.

Besides, he couldn't offer her anything yet. Not when he was at risk of going feral. There was an animal caged inside him, banging hard against his discipline and the drugs, hunting for a way to the surface. If the animal broke free, it could be years before Alec saw the light of reason again. It wasn't that a feral couldn't bond with a mortal, but the results weren't pretty. He wouldn't force himself on Domini like —

"Yo, Reynard, you in there?"

Alec blinked as a hand passed before his face. "More than you know." He gently grasped Domini's wrist, but only for a moment, as she easily circled her hand away from his. Aikido was such a graceful art.

He dug into his pocket and brought out sunglasses and his car keys. He gestured toward the burgundy Jaguar with darkly tinted windows. "I'll drive."

She frowned. "We should take a company car."

His only reply was to jingle the keys again.

Irritation radiated from her. She didn't like giving him control over any part of the situation, didn't like his taking the initiative. But it was easier to protect her if he was doing the driving. He wasn't going to budge, and luckily she decided not to push such a small matter any further. Alec could practically hear her grinding her teeth in frustration, and he civilly didn't show even the faintest flicker of smugness. He pressed the button on the key chain that unlocked the doors.

"Well," she said, looking at the dark windshield, "this'll help, since I forgot sunblock."

Alec glanced at the pale skin of her arms, legs, and throat. "You burn easily?"

She made a face. "Born and raised a child of the desert, but I turn into a french fry if I step outside in less than SPF 45."

Alec snorted. "Tell me about it." He reached into his inner jacket pocket and brought out a capped metal tube. He tossed it to her. "Try this sunscreen. My own special brand."

He hid a very sharp smile by sliding into the driver's seat, more than a little amused that they had serious sunburn issues in common.

CHAPTER SEVEN

"No, don't stop here," Domini told Reynard when he started to pull into a parking space in front of a Japanese restaurant. "They're out of wasabi. Can't have sushi without wasabi."

"Fair enough," he said, and drove on in the bumper-to-bumper midday traffic.

Domini spotted another sushi bar a couple blocks down the street. She pointed. "Let's try there."

"No parking spaces."

"Right. You want to try a drive-through?"

"What you want, I'm happy to give you."

Domini glanced sideways at Reynard's odd turn of phrase. She saw a profile of sharp cheekbones and jawline, his sculpted face made enigmatic by his dark wraparound sunglasses. "I can grab takeout on the way home. Right now we need to get a solid meal and get back on the road. We still need to stop by Kodak Center, then get the detail briefing in so we can start the assignment tonight. What do you want to eat?"

You. What Alec wanted was blood, a few warm, sweet drops drawn from skin soft beneath his tongue. The thirst hadn't hit him so hard in years. He wanted his hands on her, her body beneath his, her moans of pleasure in his ears, and her salt, copper, honey taste in his mouth.

"A burger sounds good," he answered, his hands clamped on the steering wheel.

The woman who sat beside him was a ticking time bomb and didn't know it. But he'd had decades of practice at being a very good actor. Wild men did not get sent on dangerous covert missions, and they certainly didn't lead them.

There was a very childish, churlish part of him that said she should *know* he hungered. She was his bondmate, wasn't she?

Domini is not on the menu, Alec firmly informed the beast inside him. If he tried making love to her the way he was now, the experience would terrify her and taint their relationship from the beginning. As strongly psychic as she was, she might be able to throw up mental shields around her heart and mind that he could never break through. Not that he wouldn't keep trying, and that would destroy them both.

So keep it together, he told himself. Keep your eyes on the road. Keep an eye on the rearview mirror and the blue RAV-4 that's following us. *Do not* reach over and run your fingers along her bare arm. Don't touch the hint of thigh showing below her provocatively short skirt. Don't brush your hand through her hair, or across those amazing lips.

"I need a really cold drink." *To dump in my lap.*

"Thirsty?" she asked.

"You have no idea."

Domini kept part of her attention on spotting a drive-through, and part on the realization that Reynard hadn't questioned her comment about the sushi place, which sounded strange even to her, and she *knew* she was psychic. Maybe he was simply indulging the whims of the boss's granddaughter, but he hadn't seemed to notice that what she'd said was a little odd. Was he as crazy as she was?

For all that Reynard's idiosyncrasies were fascinating, she decided to dwell on them later, for increasingly her gaze kept returning to the passenger's-side rearview mirror. Every now and then she caught sight of traffic as Reynard changed lanes and turned corners. She was beginning to see a pattern, and she didn't think it was her imagination.

"There's a Toyota RAV-4 behind us. About three cars back . . ."

"Has been for a while," he replied.

She slanted the enigmatic Mr. Reynard a curious look. "Someone from your shady past catching up to you?"

"Why would you think that?"

"It's your car."

"Ah, but they picked us up as we left the club in Westwood where Holly Ashe is doing the benefit. I spotted them again when we left the show venue in Venice. Quite a co-incidence to see the same vehicle in both locations. Ms. Ashe's concert schedule is public information. I checked it out on her website myself."

Domini seethed as she listened to his calm recitation. "You might have mentioned the tail sooner," she pointed out.

"Figured you'd notice eventually."

"If I was any good, you mean."

"I didn't say that."

"I'm here to test you, Reynard. Not the other way around."

Alec was so very tempted to get into a fight with her. Her blue eyes sparked with anger, her emotions seethed, barely under control. Her voice was cold as ice, with fire beneath it. He wanted to stoke that fire, take it higher, to its inevitable conclusion.

Instead, he calmly said, "You're a competent professional protection agent, Ms. Lancer. I come from a specialized, far more dangerous, even more paranoid world than you do. You look after people but don't expect anyone to come after you. I always expect people to come after me."

"Why would anyone come after —" She cut off her angry words and held up a hand. "Wait."

Alec enjoyed watching the thoughts flicker quickly across her face and the swift shift of emotions as she analyzed what he'd said.

"I've read through the hate mail that made Holly decide to hire better security. There's one nutcase under a restraining order, but he claims he has lots of friends that hate her as much as he does. I don't think he made that up. I'd say those letters came from several different people, and there's a pattern that makes me think they're working together. Another pattern is the theme of getting her alone. There's a song on her first CD called 'I Want to Get You Alone,' and it's referred to quite a few times in the letters. So — these people aren't interested in approaching Holly during public appearances —"

"Unless they can't get any other opportunity," he cut in.

She nodded. "Right. They want to find out where she's staying. They want to hunt her down to the place where she thinks she's safe."

"So they set up surveillance at places she'll be, places —"

"— her security people were bound to check out. And when our car was spotted at more than one of these places —"

"— they made us."

She nodded. The way they'd been finishing each other's sentences was an indication either that they shared a mind, or that they made a good team. She wasn't sure which was more frightening. "I think we'd better lose the tail," she suggested.

He smiled. "Couldn't we waste them?"

The eagerness in his tone was contagious, but Domini squashed her perverse interest in finding out how a Delta Force operator really worked.

"I think we should let them follow us long enough to get their license plate numbers, and then get the hell out of Dodge. We don't want them trailing us back to the office." She added a note on her PDA about not allowing a vehicle as conspicuous as the dark red Jaguar anywhere near Holly Ashe. "You do know how to lose a tail, right?" she asked.

Reynard gave her a very dubious glance from over the top of his sunglasses. "Let me know when you make the plates," he said, and pushed the sunglasses back up on his nose.

Alec adjusted the driver's-side mirror to give her a better view behind them. Domini held her PDA at the ready, concentrating on her assignment. The RAV-4 was three cars back, so Alec braked, shifting down into first gear. This resulted in getting the two cars in front of the blue Toyota to change lanes to get away from his slow driving. The Toyota slowed to stay with them; the person following them wasn't experienced enough at it to move inconspicuously within the flow of the traffic.

"Got it," Domini said.

The moment she spoke, Alec stepped on the gas, upshifted, and switched lanes. Then, moving smooth as silk, he switched lanes again and took a left-hand turn against a light, accompanied by squealing brakes and honking horns and cars swerving to keep from crashing. The RAV-4 tried to follow, but it wasn't a Jaguar, and the driver was nowhere near as skilled as he was.

"How very — Starsky and Hutch — of you," Domini commented as they sped away.

Alec grinned as he took the next right. The few moments of action had helped calm him. "That was fun."

"We definitely lost them." Her tone was amused when she said, "I don't think you'll need that evasive driving course as part of your orientation."

"Happy to hear it. Now, about lunch," Alec said as he brought the car to a gentle halt at a red light. "Do you think you can find us a sushi place where they do have wasabi?"

CHAPTER EIGHT

"How do you like the view?" Domini asked.

"There's a view?" Holly replied.

Alec watched as Domini pointed to the west side of the living room of the small but luxuriously appointed house. "Holly, you see those cloth things hanging on the wall? They're called curtains. If you pull them back, you can see a whole lot of lights twinkling in the valley below."

"No kidding?" Holly Ashe stood in the center of the room, her bare feet sunk almost to the ankles in the slate-gray carpet, and chewed on a fingernail. "Don't I pay people to open curtains and stuff for me?"

"Don't expect me to do it," Domini answered. "You still owe me lunch money from high school."

Ashe put her hands on her bare hips. "You were always cheap."

Ashe wore almost microscopic frayed

denim shorts and a sequined red lace bra, along with a lot of jewelry and tattoos. Domini, to Alec's disappointment, was wearing loose linen slacks and a short-sleeved embroidered peasant blouse.

"Look who's talking," Domini told her friend. "I suppose you paid a fortune to look like a tramp, too."

"Tramp?" the singer laughed.

"If I called you a pop tart, you'd hit me."

"I'd try. Do I look like Britney Spears?"

"In that getup, yes."

"You're fired."

"Your manager hired us. Not cheaply, I might add."

"Cheap is as cheap does, as your grandpa would say. Besides, that wasn't lunch money I owed you, it was drug money."

Domini thoughtfully put her hand on her cheek, then pointed at the singer. "Oh, yeah, right."

Then the two of them broke up laughing at some old private joke.

Alec smiled internally at this nonsense, as he stood impassively and inconspicuously with his back to a wall in a spot with a good view of the whole room.

The two women had been bickering like giggly teenagers, apparently enjoying themselves immensely, ever since Holly Ashe was whisked out the guarded back entrance of her hotel and into the back of the limo where Domini was waiting.

While Domini and Holly seemed very different on the surface, they clearly had the sort of friendship where they could go for years without communicating, then pick up as comfortably and easily as they'd left off. Alec found it kind of cute, especially seeing Domini's lighter side. Had she been officially on duty, she would be behaving differently, of course.

It was Domini who set the tone for this part of the assignment at the detail briefing. Old Man Lancer presided over the meeting and made all the final decisions, but they were based on Domini's assessments. The threat level against their client was deemed high enough that she'd been talked into staying at a safe house equipped with state-of-the-art surveillance technology. Ms. Ashe was to have a minimum of two agents as well as a driver on duty at all times. There would also be an agent monitoring the security equipment in a room set aside as a command post. Andrew Maxwell was named team leader.

Andy was currently outside, making a sweep of the grounds. Castlereigh was in the command post, monitoring camera, audio, and infrared equipment. Alec had been assigned as Ashe's driver, but he was handling the inside-man job until midnight. He'd been surprised to end up on an assignment his second day on the job, but no one argued with Ben Lancer — though Domini had looked for a moment as though she was going to. Alec understood quicker than she did: Lancer wanted her to keep an eye on his newest employee. Domini was working the Ashe detail, so it made sense to assign Reynard to where Domini was going to be.

Domini had come along to "hang with my friend and make her as comfortable as possible, until she gets used to having you jokers around."

The approach was working so far.

"So, you want to look at the view?" Domini asked Holly.

"Nope," Ashe answered.

"Want something from the kitchen?"

"Nope."

"Have you suddenly decided to pout, after you agreed coming here was the best way to keep you safe?"

"Yep." Ashe was looking more stubborn by the moment.

"Why?"

" 'Cause I hate not being in control of my life."

Domini moved to stand in front of her friend. "Are you scared of these people?"

"No! My management's being stupid."

Domini put her hands on Holly's shoulders. "If you're not scared, you should be."

"I don't want to talk about it."

Ashe shot a quick look toward Alec.

Domini exchanged a glance with Reynard, and they reached silent agreement about the situation without even so much as an exchange of a nod. She put an arm around Holly's shoulder and turned her toward the hallway that led off to the right of the living room. "Let's check out your bedroom."

Holly laughed. "Hey, I've been waiting for you to say that for —"

"Cut that out!" Domini dragged her friend down the hall into the spacious master bedroom and closed the door behind them. Two suitcases and a guitar case were laid on the bed. "Want help unpacking?"

Holly looked around and gave a mock shudder. "Everything's beige."

"The decorator used terms like *ecru* and *champagne.* It's supposed to be soothing." The room was the largest in the house, brightly lit, the decor intended to help keep a client calm and disguise the fact that there were no windows in the bedroom. Domini gestured to a doorway on her left. "Walk-in closet, with a huge bathroom on the other side. Bathroom's done in blue."

"I'm impressed at your knowledge of the real estate."

"The company owns the house. The best part's the state-of-the-art command center."

"Can I have a tour of that?"

"No. Can I help you unpack?"

"I'm used to living out of a bag, hon. Besides, I'm not staying."

Holly picked up the guitar case and started toward the door. Domini stepped in front of her, took the case from Holly, and set it on the floor. "You're staying for the next three nights."

Holly was smart enough not to argue with that tone, so she batted her eyelashes at Domini. "All by myself?"

"I'll be in the bedroom on the other side of the hall tonight."

Holly went back to the bed and took the bags off it, every movement stiff with tension. "I hate living like this," she muttered.

Then she settled down cross-legged in the center of the king-sized mattress, folded herself into a yoga lotus position, and closed her eyes. Domini watched as Holly's muscles relaxed and her expression became more peaceful.

Maybe I should try yoga sometime, she thought, aware that her own nerves were strung as tight as a bowstring tonight. Nothing has happened, she reminded herself. Nothing is going to happen. You aren't going to let it. Holly looked so small and vulnerable in the center of the big bed.

Domini had always thought of Holly as the brave one, because of her honesty, because of the way she went out into the world on her own, because of how she passionately embraced everything in life. Where Domini needed shields, Holly was almost skinless, recklessly open to every joy, hurt, and sorrow life had to offer. That was brave. Stupid beyond anything Domini could imagine, but brave.

Domini smiled affectionately and lay down on her side at the foot of the bed. She leaned on an elbow and propped her head on her hand. Though she seemed relaxed, she was positioned between her client and the door. Domini wasn't on duty and didn't think anything was about to happen, but why take any chances when another person's safety was involved?

Holly finally opened her eyes and leaned forward, a wicked look on her face. "Is he going to be with you?"

"What?"

"In the other bedroom. He going to be with you?"

Domini was completely confused. "Who? What?"

Holly laughed. "Don't tell me you're still oblivious? You know who I mean: the stud out front."

"Stud?"

"The guy holding up the living room wall."

"Reynard?" Domini cleared her throat. Reynard was meant to be unobtrusive, but Domini had been aware of him even though she'd tried hard to concentrate on Holly. She sighed.

"I heard that."

"Holly —"

"What's with the guy? He's so — male. Has he got like three testicles or something?"

Domini nearly squirmed with discomfort at that image. "Come on, Holly," she said. "You know I don't look at men any more than you do."

"You don't look at women, either. You've never looked at anyone." Holly pointed at her. "But this man, you're looking at."

"I'm working with him. We have to look at each other occasionally."

"You're looking at him with your body. I don't blame you," Holly went on as Domini shot to her feet. "And it wasn't me that had his attention, even though he was pretending not to look at anything. He has the hots for you."

Domini glared down at her grinning friend, then she took a deep breath and sat again with great dignity. "This is a ploy to get your mind off your own problems."

"The yoga didn't work, but no, it isn't." Holly plumped and stacked the huge pile of decorative pillows at the head of the bed until she had them just the way she wanted them, then leaned back on them. She spread her arms out across the pillows and said, "Let's talk about me."

"Always an interesting subject," Domini agreed, and settled back down on the wide expanse of satin.

"You'd look good naked on that," Holly observed.

Domini ran a hand across the champagne satin. It was marvelous to touch. "No, I'm too pale. I should be naked on stronger colors. Now, what about you?"

"I'd look good naked on this."

"I *meant,* what do you want to talk about?"

"You're in the business of protecting people from stalkers. Why are these people after me? I've never had any trouble before."

"It's your turn. Celebrities draw nutcases, and you've been lucky up until now. You managed to keep your private life quiet for a long time, but the breakup with Jo made screaming headlines in every tabloid for months. Remember when the unauthorized biography came out?"

"I didn't read it."

"I did. More pictures than words in it, going all the way back to you in diapers. There's one of you standing next to me at *my* sixteenth birthday party. There are even pictures from our high-school yearbook in it. And you remember what happened at the prom?"

"My real life's in that bio?"

"In a twisted, lying way, yes. More importantly, it didn't help that you talked about Jo doing you wrong to every media person that stuck a camera in your face."

"Against your advice," Holly added. "I was crazy then, I admit it. Passion will do that to you."

"If passion makes you crazy, then it's better not to feel it. Passion got you slapped with a restraining order to keep you from performing the songs you wrote about the breakup."

"My lawyers got that overturned. The controversy helped album sales," Holly offered. "But I guess it also got the attention of the bastards who're stalking me." She looked thoughtful for a moment, then asked, "Think Jo has something to do with this?"

"No. Jo's been checked out," Domini answered. "Are you behind it — to get Jo's attention?"

"No! How could you think that?"

Holly's outrage hit Domini like a slap in the face. She hated that her friend looked so betrayed, but she answered calmly, "I don't think it, but Lancer's is thorough. We consider all the possibilities when we take on a client. We're here to protect you — even from yourself, if we have to."

"Gee, thanks. I'm impressed." Holly shook her head. "But I'm not likely to go around raving about how I'm an impure abomination, and my kind must be stamped off the face of the earth. Not that I mind being impure, of course," she added. "You should try it sometime."

"I have. It's boring."

"Try being impure with Mr. Triple Testicles."

"Lancer's has a no-fraternization policy."

"I won't tell your grandpa."

"You know Grandpa: he'd know anyway." Domini looked at her watch, then got to her feet. It was just after midnight. The shift had

97

changed, and she wanted to talk to the new men on the detail. "Time for me to get to sleep. You, too," she advised.

Domini left the bedroom, very glad after Holly's speculation that Reynard wouldn't be waiting in the living room. By tomorrow, she'd be able to get the question out of her mind. Mr. Reynard's reproductive equipment was no one's business but his own.

CHAPTER NINE

"It wouldn't hurt you to get laid."

Alec nearly spit out the water he'd just taken to wash down his pills. He wasn't sure if he was more shocked at the elder's suggestion, or at hearing an Honored Father of the clans using such language.

"Don't look so startled," said the Matri seated beside the elder in Alec's living room. "We both sense your need. Sex would be good for you."

"It's the best way for a Prime to release tension," the elder reminded him. "Still works for me," he added with an affectionate look at the woman seated beside him. The couple were holding hands. "Of course, if you would rather kill something, that can be arranged." Elder Barak looked as though he hoped Alec would rise above the need to kill.

"Sex is easier," Matri Serisa said.

They had arrived at his front door a few

minutes after Alec got home. The regally calm woman's presence had helped ease the tension of two males meeting for the first time. Alec hadn't been able to stop a quick snarl and baring of fangs, but the Matri touched his cheek soothingly and sent cool, calming thoughts into his mind. He'd caught a hint of her age and wisdom that left him stunned — stunned enough to step back and bid them welcome when they stepped into his dwelling.

They were an elegant couple, dressed in black, both with large dark eyes and curling dark hair, the man's with far more gray in it than the woman's. She wore a gold pendant in the shape of the Egyptian god Anubis, and a carnelian ring carved with the same design on her left hand. They introduced themselves as Barak and Serisa of Shagal, and said they thought it best not to wait for the mortals at the clinic to arrange the meeting. They couldn't seem to get it through those well-meaning humans' heads that there were certain nuances and courtesies that needed to be observed. . . .

"For us to be comfortable with each other," Serisa diplomatically put it.

"To keep us from going for each others' throats," the blunter Barak added.

Though Alec gave them permission to

enter his sanctuary, he resented their appearance in his life, even if they had brought him a case of fresh blood from the clinic as a welcome present. He'd hoped they'd simply introduce themselves and then leave, giving him a chance to get used to the idea of talking to them in the diplomatic way of Clan Shagal.

But no, half an hour later, they were still here. In some ways their presence soothed his aching senses. He had not spent time around his own kind in years. He'd forgotten how the habits and rituals of vampire society were another way of imposing civilized behavior on instincts that hungered for possession and dominance.

Matri Serisa had insisted on serving them bloodwine and water. And she'd brought cookies. While bread and fruit to go with the wine and water were more traditional ceremonial foods for the ritual of getting to know new vampires in your territory, the Matri told them she had a taste for almond biscotti. Who argued with a Matri's desires?

"I thought I was supposed to practice meditation and have some sort of therapy sessions with the two of you," he told them.

Serisa's large dark eyes danced with laughter. "We're vampires, Alexander. Action *is* therapy for us. Sex is a necessity."

"We hunger," Barak said. "We need to feed."

"I'm not sure I could feed without killing right now," Alec admitted. "As for making love . . ." He shook his head. "I don't think I could keep it under control."

"Perhaps not with a mortal woman," Serisa told him. "But with one of us —" She gave a delicate shrug and the brush of a hand across her skirt that somehow conveyed a world of eroticism. "There can be a great deal of mutual pleasure when a female bends to the will of a Prime."

An image of such a wild encounter went through Alec's head and straight to his groin, but the woman he pictured struggling beneath each hard, dominating thrust was no vampire female. He rubbed his hands across his face. "I really wish you hadn't said that."

Serisa chuckled, low and enticing. She rose gracefully and came to Alec. Her thigh brushed his as she leaned close, and placed a pack of matches in his hand. A telephone number had been written on the inside of the matchbook cover. Alec stared at the neatly printed numbers as Serisa stepped back. "What's this?"

"It's the cell-phone number of a young woman of the Family Caeg. She finds herself in town and at loose ends," Serisa told him. "She's spending the evening at the local hangout."

There were three nations of vampires: the Clans, who lived among men as protectors; the Tribes, who scorned all things mortal except what they could use and cause pain to; and the Families, who chose a gray, shadowy, opportunistic way. While the Clans took the high road and the Tribes traveled gladly in darkness, the Families moved uneasily in between, friends to neither, allies to both.

Alec gave Serisa a hard look. Forgetting the respect that was a Matri's due, he asked harshly, "Why would you have me mate with a woman from Caeg?"

"Why do you think?" Barak answered. "You are needy. Family Caeg is in danger of inbreeding. You might get lucky." Barak held up a hand to stop Alec's protest before it could be voiced. "It's not unheard of to sire a child outside the Clans."

"With a mortal woman perhaps, but —"

"Do you have a mortal in mind?" Serisa quickly cut Alec off. She sensed his reactions and shook a finger at him. "Dr. Casmerek suspected as much. I forbid it. I stand in your Matri's place, and in her name I forbid your touching a mortal woman at such a dangerous time."

"You don't have to forbid it," Alec snapped. "I know I can't have her."

Yet a war was beginning to rage within him, between what he wanted and what was best for Domini. Through the battle, the siren song of the promise of an eternal bond would call and call . . .

Perhaps he should follow the sage advice of these clan elders. The Caeg woman was willing, and the conception of a child was a rare and wondrous thing. He could at least meet the woman. The night was young enough.

"All right," he told the pair from Clan Shagal as he ushered them toward the door. "I'll give her a call."

Domini's heart was hammering with terror, her palms were sweaty, her head ached fiercely, and her mind was a complete blank. *Okay. Where the hell am I?* More important, *why was she here? And how did she get here?*

The *how* was obvious, sort of. She was sitting behind the wheel of one of the company cars. The car was in park, the engine was off, and she was parked on a side street near the center of downtown Los Angeles. She knew her approximate location because the tall, elegant towers of Financial District offices and hotels loomed up in the near distance. The dashboard clock told her it was the middle of the night.

This was worse, much, much worse, than the compulsion that had pulled her out of sleep and to the market two nights ago, and the erotic dream from the night before.

I can't remember a thing. She dug into the smooth leather upholstery with her nails and pounded on the dashboard with her fists until she got the fear and frustration under some control. *Why can't I remember?*

Okay. Take it a step at a time. What's the last thing I do recall?

She remembered going into the bathroom to brush her teeth. She'd looked into the mirror and —

Seen Reynard kissing a woman reflected in the glass.

She whirled around to face the couple, and —

Here she was.

Okay. Rewind. Where was the bathroom?

At the safe house. She'd left Holly's room and gone into the bedroom she was staying in. She remembered looking at her watch before taking it off and placing it on the nightstand. The time had been 1:44 A.M. Domini looked at her wrist now. She wasn't wearing her watch. She remembered taking off her shoes, and the luxurious feel of soft carpet under her feet. Domini glanced at her feet and wiggled her bare toes. Okay, no watch, and she was barefoot. Current reality corresponded with memory. She remembered the walk to the bathroom, turning on the light, and taking toothpaste out of the medicine cabinet. She'd closed the cabinet door and looked into the mirror.

And anger had rushed over her, as red and hot as lava.

If this was passion, she didn't like it. She tried to forget about the vision, but she felt her lips draw back in a snarl and the earlier rage heated her blood.

Domini leaned back against the headrest and took long, deep breaths, making herself relax, willing the world to make sense. The exercise helped calm her, but the world refused to cooperate as far as being sensible went. The fact remained that she'd blanked out and ended up in a part of town where keeping streetlights repaired was not a high priority.

The thought of a cold beer suddenly made her mouth water, and she got out of the car and followed the craving.

Barefoot was not the safest thing to be on this particular dark side street. For a few steps the cool, gritty hardness felt good on the soles of her feet, then she stepped on a piece of broken glass.

The pain sent Domini staggering against the nearest wall, swearing under her breath at herself for not being more careful — and for being out here in the first place. She leaned against the wall and lifted her foot. She was lucky: her big toe was bleeding a little, but no glass was imbedded in the cut. She waited for a few moments until she was sure the bleeding had stopped, then moved forward again, much more carefully. She didn't know where she was going, but she knew she'd know the place when she got there.

She was looking for a bar, she supposed, since she had a taste for beer. She was glad to discover that along with the car keys, she had a few dollars folded in her pocket. No ID, though — not that anyplace open at this hour in this part of town was likely to card anyone.

Domini crossed a deserted street and limped along until she reached the center of the next block and knew she was at the right place. The low brick building was thoroughly unremarkable, and there was no sign to identify it. Seedy didn't begin to describe it. A heavy curtain blocked any light from escaping the one wide window. The door was scarred and needed painting, but the brass door handle was worn smooth and shiny with use. She could hear noise inside, muffled and faint. She almost expected someone to appear at a peephole and ask for a password. She glanced at her bare feet. Would a dive like this have a "no shoes, no shirt, no service" policy? She opened the door and stepped inside.

She'd expected the place to be dim and smoky, but she hadn't expected almost total darkness, and to choke on the first breath she took as the door closed behind her. Not all the smoke she took into her lungs was tobacco. The miasma that drifted all the way up to the low ceiling consisted of some weeds she could recognize, some she couldn't, and there were hints of candle smoke and incense beneath the more pungent herbal odors. The floor beneath Domini's feet was sticky, she didn't want to know with what. Her palms grew sticky with nervous sweat as the noise level slowly died down and every eye in the house turned her way. Danger swirled around her, more substantial than the smoke. Some of those staring eyes shone with a hungry animal glow. She caught hints of fangs glittering in the shadows. A sound like a collective gasp washed across the length and breadth of the room, and Domini knew instinctively that the hunters within had caught the scent of fresh blood.

If she turned and fled now, they'd come after her.

You're making this up, she told herself, even as her heart hammered in her ears and the primitive part of her brain screamed at her to run for her life. Domini kept her back to the door as she peered through the shifting haze. There had to be a reasonable explanation. Maybe she'd walked into a Goth hangout, or a party of makeup artists.

Or a vampire bar.

Which was a logical explanation, in a way, but not a sane one. Of course, waking up parked outside this place was neither sane nor logical, now, was it? And driving away once she came to her senses would have been the sensible thing to do, now, wouldn't it? But no, she had to follow some stupid compulsion that she knew deep in the depths of her soul was all Reynard's fault, and —

She knew Reynard was here. And that he was with a woman. Anger flared through her.

And this was her business *how?*

Domini decided to ignore her unreasonable jealousy, and what she thought she saw. The sane thing was to just get the hell out of Dodge.

But when she turned around, someone was standing behind her. He was tall, dark-haired, handsome. He held an empty cocktail glass in one hand and looked her over like she was the dish of the day. He was wearing a lot of leather.

"Hello, Blackbird," he said. "It's been a long time."

"Excuse me," Domini said, and tried to step around him. Though her back was to the room, she knew she was still being watched. The energy from all that attention felt like static electricity on her skin.

He moved with her, keeping her from the exit. He held his free hand toward her, just short of touching her. "You don't remember me? Anthony? San Francisco? 1969?"

Domini shook her head. "Never been there. Wasn't born then." She looked him over. "Neither were you, Tony."

Anthony tossed his empty glass onto the nearest table, then held both hands out toward her. "Am I drunk, Blackbird?"

"Will you get out of my way?"

Instead he leaned closer, his hands not quite touching her shoulders as he peered at her intently, drew back his lips, and sniffed. Domini saw his canine teeth extend into fangs. She backed up, deeper into the smoke.

The crowd parted and he followed, his fanged smile turning from puzzled to predatory. "A cuckoo in the nest." He chuckled.

The sound of his laughter jarred against Domini's senses. And his change *hadn't* been a special-effects trick. When she took one more step, she backed up against the bar. The vampire moved in, put his hands on her waist, and pulled her to him. His body was hard, his hands were strong, and she had very little room to maneuver.

As she leaned sideways to break the hold, she barely caught sight of the shadow as it rushed out of the swirling smoke. She was flung backward, and Anthony went down.

Domini hit the bar hard enough to knock the breath out of her. For a moment, all she saw was the smoke swirling around the ceiling. She heard shouting in a language she didn't know, animal snarls, the crash of breaking furniture, and a howl of pain. When she tried to sit up, hands grabbed her arms from behind, lifted her onto the bar, and held her. Her captor held her with bruising force, but at least she could see the fight.

Two vampires circled each other in the tight space that had been quickly cleared in front of the bar. Behind the antagonists loomed the solid mass of the avidly watching crowd, like the hungry eyes of a wolf pack glowing out of the night.

Between her and the crowd, the fighters circled and slashed with deadly grace — two intensely masculine figures of muscle, fang, and claw, one in a white shirt, the other in black leather.

There was a quick flurry of movement, a blur of black and white — and red — too quick for Domini to make out details. The dim room and swirling smoke didn't help. Then the smoke cleared away, like a curtain pushed aside. The fighters grew still, crouching statues facing each other. Domini counted a dozen racing heartbeats before the one in black — Anthony — slowly straightened. The thin slash of a cut marred his cheek. He didn't seem to be in pain as he smiled; a smile full of irony, without a hint of fangs showing.

Anthony bowed, ever so slightly, to the vampire in white. "Felicitations." Then he disappeared into the crowd and the dark.

The instant Anthony was gone, the winner sprang out of his crouch and straight at her. In the blur of speed, Domini made out fragmented details. A spot of blood like a small red rose dotting the front of the pure white shirt. A swirl of hair darker than a raven wing, a hard-set jaw, green eyes blazing like emeralds under spotlights. Shoulders wide as a mountain, hands as deadly as sharpened steel. Then the kaleidoscope of images came together into a recognizable form.

"Reynard."

Domini wasn't even surprised.

The grip behind her let go, and as Reynard lifted her into his arms, Domini swirled down into a dizzying vortex. Her head fell forward onto his chest, and everything went dark.

CHAPTER TEN

"Mine."

The word came out a rough rasp, full of as much pain as pleasure.

With his body pressed against hers, Alec held Domini upright against the brick wall just inside the dark alley. Full of the debris and stench of derelict lives, the alley was nowhere to make love, but it would do for the hard, quick sex he needed.

"Mine." He wanted her to acknowledge it. "Wake up," Alec commanded, using all the force of his mind. This brought only a faint moan and flicker of eyelids.

His. Won with blood; to be claimed with blood.

Alec held his prize tightly, her arms above her head, her slender wrists grasped in one hand.

With his other hand, he pushed her clothing aside to reveal belly and breasts as soft as white velvet. Her lithe body was warm, pliable, waiting to be covered, filled, possessed. His hand roamed freely; his lips brushed her throat where the pulse beat strong and steady. His mouth lingered at this spot, breathing in the scent of her, savoring her spirit while his hand caressed her breasts, then strayed down until his fingers pushed her thighs open and slipped between her legs.

Domini woke with a shocked gasp when he began to stroke and tease her soft, sensitive flesh. She bucked, but he held her mound pinned against his palm, his fingers working inside her, coaxing the beginning of pleasure from her.

Pleasure is mine to give. Mine to take.

When Alec felt her respond, he lifted his head to look into her eyes, deep into her soul, into her thoughts.

Mine. Only mine. Forever.

Domini's world was made of heat curling through her, of eyes of green fire branding her, steel grip binding her, a voice dominating, demanding acknowledgment, submission. A heavy, hot weight covered her, pressing into her breasts and stomach. And —

Inside her.

A mouth covered hers, hard, overwhelming. A prick of pain touched her lips. A taste of copper slid across her tongue and was gone.

Blood for blood, a voice whispered in her mind. *Always.*

Not her blood, she realized. His. The pain his, but he'd shared that with her as well. He'd bit his lip before he kissed her.

Confusion warred with the fire licking through her insides. She was helpless, totally without control; fear sang through her heightened senses. But her tongue danced with his and her hips swayed to the tune his fingers played inside her. She could not help herself. She'd never known that being out of control could be so —

Exciting?

The confident voice in her mind was like velvet over steel. A sheathed knife, beautiful but holding the potential for violence.

Exciting?

There was no mistaking the edge, no denying the demand for truth.

Yes!

I excite you. As no other has, or ever will. Truth.

He had her soul under a microscope. There was no escaping his overwhelming will. Nothing to give but truth.

Yes.

Good.

His silky, smug pleasure infuriated her. Anger helped counter the spell, helped bring her back to awareness. He was not the world.

I am your world.

Bullshit.

Alec was so shocked, he stopped kissing Domini. "What?"

It was a mistake. It brought him out of their shared mind, closer to awareness. Their gazes locked, and Alec no longer saw only himself reflected in her eyes.

"What are you doing?" she demanded.

"Fucking you."

"Oh, no you're not!"

"Despite evidence to the contrary . . . ?"

His voice held dark humor, darker determination. There was magic in his eyes. Domini fought off the urge to look into their swirling green depths. That way lay the molding of her will into anything he wanted of her.

She squeezed her eyes closed and said, "Get off me. Get away from me." She fiercely imagined herself free of him; willed it. If magic was real and he had it, then so must she.

"*This* is real."

Domini heard him as if from a great distance as he continued touching her. She tried to block out the sensations, but ripples of pleasure kept rolling through her, building . . .

"Stop it. Stop it. Stop it!"

He didn't. It just got worse. Better.

Alec loved the mastery of forcing pleasure on her, but his own need clawed at him. Enough of games; it was time to claim his own pleasure.

His hands left her for a moment as he reached for his fly. She was still trapped with her back pinned tightly against the wall, but her hands came down fast. Her fists would have slammed into his temples if his reflexes weren't faster than any mortal's.

Alec grabbed Domini's shoulders. "Don't try to attack me."

"Don't try to rape me," she snapped back.

Rape? This wasn't — he'd won her — she was his —

"What would your mother say?"

Where fists had failed, her words hit hard enough to box his ears. How did she know exactly the right question to ask?

"Damn you!" he snarled — and stopped being a Prime in heat — barely.

What *was* he doing? What was he thinking? His Matri would exile him, or worse, for taking a mortal woman like this. Yes, she was his, but he'd already vowed not to force himself on her. How soon he'd forgotten that vow.

Though not without provocation.

He took her by the shoulders and shook her. "What the hell were you doing with Tony Crowe?"

"What were you doing with that woman?" she shouted back. "What was I doing in that bar?"

"What woman?"

"The one — the one —" Domini blinked and shook her head. "The one I saw you with."

"You didn't see me with any woman."

Maia Caeg had been long gone before Domini showed up. One kiss had told them both that nothing would come of the meeting, and the incident had only added to his building frustration. Frustration that wasn't getting any better.

"In the mirror," Domini answered. "I saw you in the mirror." She knew her words made no sense. Nothing made sense. Her mind and body were alive and singing and singed by an inner fire, and she didn't know where she was, but she was nearly naked, and the reason was ridiculous. "Why the hell should I care who you kiss?" she added, puzzled.

Alec was shocked that the connection was already so strong on her side. They were nowhere near to being bonded, yet she knew

119

when he was with another woman and re-acted accordingly. He might have been smugly pleased if this weren't so dangerous for Domini's sanity. Considering his condition, it was no doubt his fault — some kind of psychic leakage, messing with her head as well as his. Not good for him; certainly not good for her.

But she wasn't ready for an explanation yet. He wasn't ready to tell her she was hopelessly entangled with a vampire trying to fight off madness and feral impulses. He was dancing on a knife edge and had her dancing with him. He couldn't let these incidents go on.

The need to protect her was even more basic than breathing or the call of blood. So he'd handle it. Somehow, in their day-to-day life, he'd keep his distance, keep his cool.

But first they had to get out of this alley and into what she needed to think of as the *real* world, until he could properly bring her into his.

Keeping his hands on her shoulders, he leaned far enough to let her adjust her clothing. He needed the contact; he needed to touch her — but also needed to keep her from running. When she was done, Alec picked Domini up and carried her out of the alley. He turned left when he reached the street.

"Where are we going?" she asked

"Your car."

Domini was weary beyond belief; so weary that she was beyond fear. Her limbs and eyelids were growing heavier by the moment. It might be from the fading adrenaline rush. She suspected it was from Reynard.

"You're messing with my head."

"Not at the moment."

"Then why am I so sleepy?"

"You've had a long day." Or maybe it was because he was practicing a mental exercise for calm, and she was reacting to it.

Or — and he smiled hopefully at this thought — maybe the smoke was getting to her, now that he no longer was hooked into her mind. She'd been in the bar for some time, and she'd breathed in a lot of the drugged air. The place was kept pumped full of drugs that affected mortals for a reason: to make any humans believe they'd imagined any strange things they saw, should they be foolish enough to stumble into the very private establishment.

"You're stoned," he told Domini. "This is very good for both of us."

"I wasn't stoned a minute ago." Her voice was slurred, but her indignation came through loud and clear. "I do not do drugs . . . okay, maybe Ecstasy once in high school, but we were at a rave and I didn't know what Holly handed me when I told her I wanted something for cramps . . . and I've just told you more than you want to know . . . haven't I?"

"Not necessarily. Here we are." He'd followed her scent back to her parked car. "Keys."

When she didn't respond, he gently set her down, to lean on the side of the car while he dug into her pockets for the keys. Once he found them, he opened the door and tucked her into the driver's seat. He got in on the passenger side and found Domini slumped over, her forehead resting on the steering wheel.

"Can't go to sleep yet," Alec told her, and propped her up. There were thoughts and memories he had to make sure were planted in her mind before he could let her rest. He took her chin and turned her head toward him. "Open your eyes. Look at me."

Domini blinked a few times, then her gaze held steady on his.

Alec smiled at her, careful that not a hint of fang showed. It wasn't going to be easy to invade her thoughts, even with the drugs, but it had to be done. He kept up a steady,

122

gentle pressure on her natural mental barriers, waited until her pupils were fully dilated, her breathing slow, deep, and steady. Then he said, "You were at the safe house. What did you tell them when you left?"

The answer came slowly, with no expression in her voice. "Nothing."

"You're sure? No one questioned you?"

"I left. Didn't talk to anyone."

Good. A clean palette to start with. There were bound to be questions from the protection team when Domini returned. "You're going to go home to set your VCR. Tell them you forgot that you wanted to tape something."

"What?"

He had expected her to simply comply with the command, but why would Domini make it easy on him?

"A basketball game," he told her. "Tell the team leader that you remembered you'd miss the Sparks games this week while on the detail, and wanted to set your VCR for all of them."

"I don't follow the Sparks. I'm a Clippers fan."

"You follow the Sparks now. You love the WNBA."

"I love women's basketball."

"Then set the tape for it."

123

"I don't have a VCR."

"Everyone has a VCR."

"I have TiVo."

"Fine, then set that."

Alec fought down impatience, drawing on the same meditation techniques used to keep the hunting instinct at bay. He needed to be patient, gentle, persistent, convincing. He should be proud of her level of resistance, not irritated at her literal attention to detail. God was in the details, right? So was a successful brainwashing. They'd get through this, no matter how long it took.

"After you set the TiVo," he went on, "this is what you are going to do . . ."

CHAPTER ELEVEN

"Are you supposed to be here?" Ben Lancer asked.

Though it was a joke with them, this morning Domini wasn't in the mood for her grandfather's gruff ways. "Just once, you could show you're happy to see me."

He turned from the kitchen counter and gave her a narrow-eyed look. "What'd you bring for breakfast?"

She held up two white paper bags. "Bagels, cream cheese, and lox."

He gave a cursory nod. "Then I'm happy to see you. You look like shit — and you're supposed to be at the safe house this morning."

Domini set down the bags and got out plates and knives. "Holly won't be up until noon or later. I'll be there when she needs me." She took a seat at the kitchen island and began slicing bagels.

She wanted to rush into his comforting arms and ask him to make the dreams go away. She didn't know what was the matter, but maybe Grandpa could make it all better. Or maybe, since she was a grown-up now, she needed to figure things out on her own. Either way, she wanted the comfort of being with him this morning. He was the only family she had, the only sure thing in a shaky world, and her world was getting shakier all the time.

It wasn't just the odd visions and weird dreams. Something was in the air, something that told her her world was about to change forever. A feeling that she was about to fall off a cliff, and she'd either crash and burn or figure out how to soar like the condors she loved. Her parents had crashed and burned — and she'd never know why she hadn't seen that coming. She couldn't see what was before her, but she could sense . . . *something*.

Or maybe it was just her overactive imagination. Whatever it was, she liked her calm, ordered, controlled way of living. Ever since her parents' death, her grandfather had made her world stable, structured if not safe. He'd never let her think the world was safe. She wouldn't even have moved out of the house if he hadn't made her. She'd learned to appreciate a certain amount of independence, but she feared drastic change. Okay, maybe she feared growing up, and that was stupid. It didn't change the fact that she needed her grandpa.

The Old Man wouldn't mind being needed, he just wouldn't want to her to go all mushy on him. The Lancers hung tough, even when they thought they were going crazy.

Actually, she *was* feeling better about the going-crazy part this morning. Maybe the world was unstable, maybe she was confused and melancholy, but a voice whispered deep in her head that she wasn't insane. It was as if a weight had been lifted from her last night, even as she had another long, complicated erotic dream. With vampires. Again.

The vividness of it — not even counting the sexual aspects — had stirred up old images, old memories. Snatches of stories? Overheard conversations?

"Grandpa?" she asked as he set a coffee mug in front of her. She sounded like a plaintive kid, and he raised an eyebrow as he took a seat opposite her.

"What?" He took a sip of coffee and a bite of bagel.

"I had another dream last night. Not a compulsion or a premonition, just a dream."

She *had* felt the need to run home to record some basketball games, but that was only because she'd forgotten to earlier. Domini wished she hadn't dropped off to sleep on her couch afterward, when she should have returned to Holly. But Holly had been perfectly safe then and now; Domini had called to check before coming over to the Malibu house. She felt vaguely irresponsible, but maybe not as guilty about it as she should. Which in itself was bothersome.

"If it was just a dream, why are you staring off into space with that worried look on your face? And why do you want to talk to me about it?" he asked.

Domini drank down her grandfather's excellent coffee, not sure why she was stalling. She wasn't quite sure what she wanted to know, or why she needed to ask him. She was afraid to hurt him. He was a tough old bird, but he was also a fragile old man, about some things.

Domini finished her coffee, then put the mug on the counter. "Does Blackbird mean anything to you?" It was an odd question, a snatch of conversation pulled up out of a dream, but so oddly familiar and —

"Course it means something to me." The old man's voice was steady, but his vivid blue eyes held painful shadows. "You know that."

She did. It came back to her now, though she hadn't heard the word in years. Domini closed her eyes for a moment, damning herself. She'd hurt him, damn it all. She had no right to —

"What's this about?" he demanded.

Domini held up a hand, and shook her head. "Nothing. I told you I had a dream."

"Premonition."

"No. It's — stuff coming up from my childhood, I guess. Mixed up with grown-up stuff." An explanation hit her suddenly, and she laughed. "You know, I bet it's from seeing Holly. Being around her makes me feel like a kid again. Makes me remember — stuff."

Domini didn't mention the part Alexander Reynard played in last night's dream, or the dream the night before that. There were some things one did not share with one's only living male relative. Or with anyone else, come to think of it. She couldn't imagine even telling a shrink about watching Reynard in a fight where the combatants had fangs and claws. Or the rough sex after.

It had only been a dream. One so vivid, her body still felt used, still felt unfulfilled. The tang of hard, coppery, hot kisses was still in her mouth. Her lips were tender, and —

She looked at the bruises on her wrists.

"What you staring at?" her grandfather asked.

She held up her wrists to show him. "I'm always getting bruised at the aikido dojo, but I can't remember when I got these." Someone had obviously grabbed her hard and held on for a while. The finger marks felt almost like a brand. But she was a fast healer. "I've got a pair of cuff bracelets I can wear if they haven't faded by tonight."

"Tonight's the ceremony?"

She nodded. "The venue's got tight inside security, but we'll still have three people on the red carpet. Andy Maxwell's running the team. Reynard's on point."

His usual frown deepened. "Who made that assignment? Reynard hasn't been on board a week yet."

"Andy's decision. He trusts Reynard."

Those bright eyes hit her like lasers. "Do you?"

Domini's reactions to Reynard were in total chaos. She took a deep breath, as though California air held enough oxygen to actually clear her head, and said, "I trust his professional expertise."

She remembered how almost eerily still and watchful Reynard was on the job. She remembered him standing unobtrusively in the living room of the safe house, his stance seemingly relaxed. Yet there had been such concentrated protectiveness emanating from him that even Holly had picked up on it. Holly described his intense vigilance as a macho thing, but Domini read it as understated confidence that nobody and nothing got past him. Ever.

Her own reaction to Reynard in all his glorious Delta Force grandeur was complex, and no part of a professional discussion with her boss. "He's competent to do the job."

"Point it is, then," Ben confirmed the team leader's assignment. "Where will you be tonight?"

"I'm on flank."

The Old Man snorted. "Which means you get to wear a pretty dress and walk the red carpet with our principal."

"Well, no one would think Reynard was Holly's date, would they?"

"Point taken. You don't mind?"

"Why would I? Remember, we went to the prom together."

"But not as a date," he reminded sharply.

Domini hid a smile. Ben Lancer wasn't narrow-minded, but sometimes his generational biases showed.

"Not as a date," she agreed. "But neither

of us were interested in any of the boys in high school."

"At least Holly had an interest in someone," he said. "While you —"

"Grandpa."

"I wouldn't mind having great-grandchildren."

"I can still provide those." An image of Reynard flashed unbidden into her head. She shook it and said, "There are several ways to have babies without too much personal involvement from the sperm donor."

"I don't want to raise another baby," he answered. "You'll need a man around to help you with that."

Domini did not want to have this conversation. She finished the last bite of her bagel and got to her feet. "I'd better head back to the safe house. There's always the chance Holly might wake up before noon and need me."

Domini felt a tad guilty at leaving. For disturbing her grandfather, for his disturbing her, and because she'd been less than truthful with her excuse for leaving.

She would head over to the safe house in a while, but right now she planned to head directly to her aikido dojo. Maybe an hour spent practicing her martial art form would help center her disturbed spirit and work off

132

the restless thrumming of her body.

It didn't help her mood when the first car she noticed as she pulled into the road was a blue Toyota RAV-4. It was sheer paranoia to think it was the same car that had followed Reynard's Jaguar, but that didn't stop her from keeping an eye on the little SUV in her rearview mirror. Traffic was heavy, so she couldn't make out the license plate. The RAV-4 soon disappeared from sight, but she didn't relax until she was sure she wasn't being followed.

"I hear you had a date last night."

Alec held onto his temper and gave Dr. Casmerek a steady, direct look. He was sitting on a table in one of the clinic's examining rooms, his shirt off, and the doctor had just administered the second of three painful shots. Vampire skin was tough.

It was six-thirty in the morning, and he hadn't slept. He did *not* like the mortal prying into his business. But Alec also knew Casmerek wouldn't have brought up the subject casually.

"The Caeg woman and I didn't get it on, if that's what you want to know."

"Hmm," the doctor responded, and picked up the third needle. "I suspected Barak and Serisa would try to fix you up.

That wasn't the liaison I was referring to."

Alec did not ask what the physician was referring to. The complicated drug regimen had him feeling almost like his old self, but even his old self didn't take lightly to inquiries into his private life.

He held his arm out for the last injection, a serum formulated after the clinic staff studied the results of his tests. Alec hoped this witch's brew worked, otherwise, like vampires in the past, he'd be a victim of the daylight.

Not a victim, Alec corrected himself harshly. It was not a weakness to be a vampire. Daylight was merely inconvenient. They'd lived without it for thousands upon thousand of years.

I could live without the light; I don't have to put myself through this. But then I wouldn't be the man I want to be. Couldn't fulfill my Clan vow with the totality I want to give.

"Tony tells me it was quite a party." Casmerek interrupted Alec's thoughts, punching in the needle.

Alec glared, the sort of glowing, red-eyed supernatural glare designed to bring a mere mortal to his knees.

Casmerek didn't even look up. His gaze remained steadily on what he was doing as he slowly guided the plunger down on the injection.

Alec supposed he was grateful for the doctor's meticulous care. "Tony a patient of yours?"

"No." Casmerek finished the injection and put the used needle into a sharps disposal container. "But he knows you are." He held up a hand before a question could explode from Alec. "Anthony Crowe was a police detective —"

"Was?"

"He currently runs his own private investigation business, and oversees our security here. He still thinks and acts like a cop. Tony makes it his business to know when Primes are in town, and why. He didn't expect you to challenge him for a mate. A mortal one," Casmerek added, with a significant look.

"It's not what you think." At least it hadn't turned into the sort of orgy Casmerek thought it had. "I saw Tony hitting on a mortal woman who'd wandered into the wrong place. He didn't pay attention when she wasn't interested. We foxes are more chivalrous than the crows. I got her out of there, hypnotized her into thinking it was all a dream, and took her home."

"No sex?" Casmerek sounded deeply suspicious.

Alec shook his head. He loathed having to

135

explain himself like a horny half-grown boy to his Matri, but he needed Casmerek's help. "I followed doctor's orders." Though he had come far too close to the edge.

"Then why did you tell Tony —"

"Macho Prime stuff."

"Hmmm." Casmerek stepped back. "You can get dressed now."

Alec got up from the table. "How am I doing?"

"I'll let you know."

"What does that mean?"

"It means that you continue to follow the regimen you're on, and we'll do tests in a couple of days to see if that cocktail I just gave you has any effect."

Alec wanted Casmerek to tell him that he was fine now, that all the allergies — or whatever they were that made a vampire vulnerable — were under control.

Before putting on his shirt, Alec checked the tattoo on his wrist. "I don't think the ink's faded any more."

"Doesn't look like it," Casmerek agreed. "Don't be so impatient, Alexander," he cautioned. "The process might be slow, but it does work."

How could he help but be impatient? The mate he'd been waiting for all his long adult life was within his hands' reach, and he couldn't touch her. Shouldn't touch her.

Would touch her.

His fists tingled and clenched tightly at the memory of touching her warm, yielding —

"Forget about it," he muttered. When the doctor gave him a curious look, Alec said, "I'm going now."

After Alec left the building, he made himself look toward the sun cresting the barren hills to the East, without the benefit of sunglasses. He couldn't do it for more than a few seconds, but he counted it a victory of pure stubbornness that he accomplished it at all. Then he put his sunglasses on and went to his car.

As he stood by the door of his Jaguar, the sensation of being watched struck him. Alec stood frozen in place, letting all his physical and mental senses roam. They weren't as sensitive as usual, due to all the drugs in his system, but his perceptions were still far more acute than any mortal's. Even in the daylight his sight was excellent, though nothing compared to his night vision. His hearing matched any owl's, and he was brother to the wolves when it came to smell. His reflexes were as incomparable as Deja Thoris. On top of that, he came equipped with strong telepathy, a modicum of mind control, and the occasional dose of second sight.

And the clinic has its own security, he reminded himself. The best in the world, since it was run by vampires. All of whose senses were more acute than his were at the moment.

This knowledge didn't keep Alec from standing perfectly still, his palms flat on the roof of the Jag, while he breathed and listened. After a minute or so, he concluded that the prickle of warning was probably a side effect of the new drugs in his system.

Someone dancing on my grave. He got in his car and drove home, since he wasn't due at work until late afternoon. *Plenty of time to gulp down a pint of O-positive and get some sleep.*

CHAPTER TWELVE

"My feet are killing me," Domini complained as she and Holly stepped aside for a waiter carrying a tray of hors d'oeuvres. The food looked great, but little of it was being eaten. Ah, the Hollywood obsession with staying a size zero.

"Well, look at what you're wearing," Holly whispered back. Their heads were close together so they could hear each other over the loud buzz of conversation. The media room in the recording executive's mansion was huge, yet crowded. The decor was black marble, gray granite, and stainless steel, all sharp angles and calculated coldness.

Domini followed Holly's glance down to her shoes. She was wearing ankle-strap high heels to go with her short black lace dress and matching bolero jacket. Holly was dressed with the studied casualness her image consultant had put together, but neither of them stuck out in this crowd of media and recording people.

"*You* get to dress like a rock-and-roll slut in jeweled Keds," Domini pointed out. "I'm wearing Prada. But it's not the shoes' fault my feet hurt; I've got a cut on my big toe."

"Want me to call over Mr. Testicles to kiss it and make it all better?"

Domini successfully fought the urge to glance across the crowded room to where Reynard lingered by the open patio doors. She kept her attention on the succession of people who approached Holly, while Reynard concentrated on an overview of the room. No attack was expected; they just wanted to get Holly used to having a team around her during social situations. It would help her feel more relaxed and secure when she faced the gauntlet of the crowds of media and fans later in the evening.

"He's on duty right now; he can't kiss anything," she answered Holly.

"He's staring at us."

"He's protecting your ass."

"He'd rather have yours. When he isn't looking at me, he's looking at you," Holly went on. "And he looks at you a lot different than he does at me."

Domini couldn't help but glance Reynard's way this time.

Holly laughed. "Made you look."

Alexander Reynard didn't appear to know that either she or Holly existed, which was exactly how it was supposed to appear. He wore a tux and held a champagne glass full of ginger ale in one hand. He stood at an easy slouch, seemingly listening to a perky, petite young blonde in a backless red dress.

Frankly, the man looked like a movie star. It wasn't only his sharply defined good looks that set him apart. There were plenty of handsome men here, but Reynard had that indefinable charisma. He wasn't *doing* anything, but he wasn't being unobtrusive, either. There was utter confidence and cool in the way he carried himself. It was attracting attention, mostly of the female kind. Domini supposed Reynard's polish came from knowing just how silly this sort of affair really was, compared to a black-ops military operation.

She took a sip of her own ginger ale and brought her attention back to Holly as a couple in matching tattoos and body piercings approached.

It turned out the pair were record producers, and Holly was delighted to see them. Domini stood back while the trio engaged in a technical discussion that would have left her reeling in boredom, had she actually paid attention to it.

After a few minutes the producers wandered away, and Holly turned back to Domini. "So, you finally have the hots for someone, don't you?"

Domini sighed. "You have no mercy."

Holly laughed. "Hell, no. Not when I have a captive audience."

It was Domini's turn to laugh. "Captive? Do you know how much you're paying me by the hour?" A television celebrity passing by paused and gave Domini an interested look. She glared, and he kept moving.

Holly cackled. "Look what you've done to my reputation."

"Serves you right for picking on me."

"I'm not picking, I'm . . . concerned."

"You're meddling. You always meddle with my love life when you're between girlfriends."

Holly put a hand on Domini's shoulder. "I want you to be happy."

Domini leaned over and said quietly, "Sex is not necessary for happiness."

"We've had this discussion before." A slow, wicked smile lit Holly's face. There was steel in that smile, and a hint of the burning charisma the tiny woman could use to mesmerize a crowd of thousands. "This time," she went on with utter confidence, "this time, my friend, you are only going through the motions of being indifferent to lust." She gestured toward the other side of the room. "You want him." Holly brushed her fingertips down Domini's arm. "You're heating up just thinking about him."

Domini jerked away from Holly's touch. "Stop it."

Don't stop, Alec thought, growing warm himself. Not when you're at a really good part.

He was completely unashamed of using his psychic ability and sharp senses to eavesdrop on Domini and Holly's conversation. Ashe's safety was his duty, and Domini was his lady. Each life was his to cherish, one for this moment and one for eternity, and he put all he was, body, mind, and soul, between them and any danger. He had no trouble focusing on their conversation while keeping watch.

When he'd begun listening in, he was fascinated and a bit flattered — Mr. Testicles? — at the way the conversation was going. How could he help being interested in finding out what Domini thought of him?

He wondered if Holly had any inkling about how psychic her combination of charisma and empathy was. He guessed that Domini and Holly's friendship was based in part on the talents that set them apart from the normal world. They'd grown up as the strange and out-of-sync ones, but they were also the ugly ducklings who'd turned into swans. In Domini's case, anyway; Ashe was more of a bird of paradise.

He understood about being different, but perhaps not as completely as the two young women did. Vampire young, precious and rare and cherished, were sheltered from any contact with the mortal world. He'd gone out into the world as a young adult, and decided he liked associating with the mortals his people protected. A vampire didn't *need* the medicines that brought the daylight life, but for those like him who wanted to do more, experience more, the drugs were essential. He desperately craved the full life that only the drugs could offer. To see his beloved by sun and candlelight, if nothing else.

He continued to watch the room and to flirt with the young woman hitting on him, while he listened for Domini's response to Holly Ashe.

"You want him, don't you?" Holly whispered to her friend.

Ambivalence swirled through Domini's mind. "I don't know what I think —"

"Feel."

144

"Feel about Reynard. I don't know *the man. He's good at what he does, but I have absolutely no clue about his background or what he likes."*

"You don't have to know someone to want to screw them. Lust does not require an exchange of résumés."

"I'll admit to having erotic dreams about the man. That's a first for me."

Alec was gratified that Domini had to fight very hard not to look at him.

"Not a bad start," Holly said. "You gonna jump him?"

"Of course not."

"Why the hell not?"

Holly's disgust tickled across Alec's senses, and he couldn't help but smile.

"Because I have no intention of losing my job," was Domini's answer. "I've got too much time, training, and loyalty invested in Lancer Services. Grandpa'd bounce me out of the company as fast as he would Reynard if I got caught fooling around with him."

"You could always find another job."

"But I can't find another grandfather. No way will I betray Ben Lancer's trust. Besides, Reynard hasn't shown any interest in me."

"But you want him to. Even I can tell that Mr. Testicles is a prime example of the breed."

Alex smiled. *How right you are, my little friend.*

The conversation between Domini and Holly was interrupted as their hosts, Emmett and Joni Brakie, approached Ashe and asked to speak to her in private. Ashe nodded. The power couple frowned when Domini stayed in step as they hustled Ashe off, but all they dared to do was frown when Domini gave them a hard, no-nonsense look.

That's my woman, Alex thought, and swiftly followed the group through the thick crowd.

Domini caught a flicker of movement out of the corner of her eye when Emmett opened the door to a private room. A quick sweeping glance showed her that nothing was there, but warning prickled along her skin. She waited to be the last person in the room, and made sure the door was securely shut before crossing a wide expanse of plush blue Chinese-patterned carpet to stand near Holly. In direct contrast to the spare, modern decor of the media center, this room was full of old-fashioned luxury. Blue velvet curtains hung from tall windows, and tall crystal vases of white calla lilies lent a subtle scent to the air.

Holly headed straight for a shiny baby-blue grand piano and immediately began playing something by Chopin. She stopped after a few seconds and turned an accusing look on her host. "Brakie, when's the last time you had this thing tuned?"

Emmett Brakie shrugged. "I don't come in here very often." He waved her toward a pair of blue brocade couches that faced each other across a low white marble table. "Come have a drink."

Joni Brakie was standing behind a bar in a distant corner of the room. "Wine?" she called.

"Mineral water." Holly glanced at Domini and murmured, "Got to keep my head in the shark pool."

Domini gave a faint nod and followed Holly across the room.

"We've been thinking," Joni Brakie began as she took a seat next to Holly on the long couch.

"About your tour schedule," Emmett said. He sat down on the other couch, but leaned forward across the wide expanse of tabletop. "We think you should add a few dates."

"To support the new single."

Emmett picked up the ball from his wife. "Airplay's not as strong as we'd like."

"Maybe add some more in-store appearances," Joni went on. "We have some charity events lined up."

"Here in Los Angeles," Emmett said.

"This week."

"We know your schedule's already tight, but —"

"Hold on," Holly finally interrupted, much to Domini's relief.

Domini was prepared to protest the security problems the Brakies' plans entailed, but she needed to know her client's opinion before she could voice her own.

"I'm not interested." Holly held up her hands in front of her. "I'm not even the person you should be talking to about this."

"You are the one who needs to make these decisions," Joni insisted. She put her hand earnestly over Holly's. "You don't want your career to lose momentum, do you?"

"We want to support you. Push you into the spotlight."

"Cutting back on your schedule right now is the last thing you need," Joni said. "It's against the bold, brave image you've been building."

"Your coming-out was bold, and —"

"I was never in." Holly cut Emmett off once more. "People are threatening to kill me," she reminded the owners of her recording company.

"People threaten to kill me all the time." Emmett waved her protest away. "Dealing with crazies is the price of fame. Consider it a compliment."

Domini spoke up. "We prefer to think of it as a threat."

"We'll add extra security for you," Joni said to Holly.

Domini knew that was a promise the Brakies had made for other artists, and had followed through in the most desultory fashion. Which was one of the reasons Holly's management had called in Lancer Services.

"We've always treated you right, haven't we?" Emmett asked, a touch of hurt in his voice.

Holly flinched slightly at his tone. "Yeah. I know."

"We'll take care of you," Joni promised.

"Ms. Ashe, it's time to go."

Reynard's calm, commanding voice sent a shock through Domini's entire body, and she whirled to face him. Where the hell had he come from? She hadn't heard him come in.

A chill crawled up her spine, and she watched silently as Reynard approached Emmett Brakie, who'd risen from his seat.

"We aren't finished —" Brakie started.

But Reynard looked deeply into the music mogul's eyes, and Brakie grew silent. Joni Brakie stepped up to touch her husband's arm, but she was caught by Reynard's glacial green gaze as well.

"You are finished with Ms. Ashe."

They stared at Reynard. Joni smiled faintly, as though appreciating Reynard's angular good looks. Emmett's expression was rapt, as though he was about to learn the secret of obtaining ultimate power.

"Any interference with Holly's current schedule might jeopardize her safety. You don't want that."

"We don't want that," Joni repeated.

"We don't want that," Emmett echoed.

Reynard gave a slight nod. "Good." Then he turned to Holly and gestured. "Come."

Holly looked almost hypnotized, but relieved. "Happily," she said.

Joni and Emmett Brakie sat back down on their big blue couch. They were holding hands.

"What the hell?" Domini muttered. "What did you do?"

As Reynard shepherded Holly out the door, he threw her a brief glance over his shoulder. The power in that look was scalding. She had to fight to turn away from the fire in those eyes, and to fight against the sensation of that power probing against her mind.

"It is time to go." His voice was soft, persuasive, tinted with immense assurance.

She wanted to slap him.

"Where did you come from?" she demanded as she followed closely behind him and Holly through the crowded mansion. "Nobody came into that room after I entered. I was watching."

"I did."

Her senses rebelled. She would have known. She would have seen. All she'd felt out of the ordinary was a breeze. That couldn't have been him, moving too fast for anyone to see, even though that's what she half believed.

"What'd you do to those people?"

"I'll tell you sometime."

The party continued around them as they headed for the front door. He didn't push anyone out of the way, but Reynard was as efficient as Moses parting the Red Sea at getting people to move aside for Holly. Domini would have admired it if she weren't so freaked about what had happened in the music room.

"Nothing untoward happened," he said as they stood outside and waited for Holly's limo to be brought up. He wasn't looking at her, but he spoke in the same tone he had with the Brakies — as if all he had to do was tell her something to make it so. "Something needed to be done. You didn't seem to be in any hurry to stop those fools."

She bristled at the implication that she hadn't been doing her job, but she didn't let it distract her. "Don't try to tell me that you learned hypnotism in the Delta Force."

"Of course not. I was merely firm with them. People like the Brakies aren't used to taking orders. It makes for a nice change."

"You should have knocked before you walked in." The protest sounded lame even to Domini, but she was disturbed, maybe even frightened. There was something very *wrong* with Reynard's behavior. Maybe it could be explained away, but . . .

He turned his head just enough from scanning the cars moving in the wide brick drive to show Domini a faint smile. "We're on duty," Reynard reminded her. "This is no time to argue."

That, she couldn't argue with. Damn it.

Their two cars pulled up as she tried to think of something scathing but nonargumentative to say, and Reynard handed Holly into the back of her limo.

"Later," Domini snarled at Reynard before following Holly into the limo.

"I'm sure." He closed the door and went to join Andy Maxwell in the lead car.

CHAPTER THIRTEEN

He'd been showing off, which was *not* the sort of thing a vampire was supposed to do. Alec admitted that part of it was trying to impress his girlfriend, but not all of it. He'd hated standing by and seeing Holly Ashe being put in jeopardy from within as well as from without. Her so-called friends were no more interested in her welfare than the strangers who threatened her life. He'd watched Domini become more and more concerned, and waited for her to say something. When she didn't, he acted on impulse and instinct. He felt good about that.

He doubted Dr. Casmerek would approve.

The key to survival was subtlety, as any Prime in control of his powers knew. Walk in the Light, Work in the Darkness, as the saying went.

But what fun was there in being a vampire if you couldn't show it off sometimes?

"What're you smiling about?" Andy Maxwell's voice came through the receiver in Alec's ear.

"Enjoying my work," he answered through the headset mike.

They stood on opposite sides of the walkway, just inside the black velvet rope that marked off the magic territory where the stars treaded a red carpet. The noisy crowd of fans was at their backs. A swath of media announcers, camera crews, paparazzi, and publicists made a human barrier between the security men and the famous folk slowly making their way toward the auditorium entrance. Alec and Maxwell were watching opposite sides of the area outside the ropes, but caught the occasional glimpse of each other.

"Not just looking at the beautiful people?"

"Can barely see them from here. Our girls are up," Alec said as he spotted Domini and Holly.

Holly was being interviewed while Domini stood back and watched. Domini was wearing an earpiece, artfully concealed in her large jet bead earrings, so they could contact her if there was any trouble. A herd of gorgeous women occupied the densely packed length of the carpet, but none of them were as beautiful to Alec as Domini Lancer.

Where many had style, she had substance, purpose instead of ambition. Then there was the matter of those long, sexy legs, meant to be wrapped around him, that swan neck, and the mouth made for ravishing.

"Does she have any idea what she does to a man?"

"None whatsoever," Maxwell answered.

Alec had no doubt Andy Maxwell knew he was talking about Domini. "Good." He had no doubt Maxwell took the warning.

"Don't fall," Maxwell warned back. "It'll hurt when you land."

Too late, Alec thought. "I'll keep that in mind."

He turned his full attention back to the mass of bodies piled tightly together on the other side of the velvet ropes. He had continued his visual scan while he talked to Maxwell; now he opened his mind, as well. He didn't try for thoughts, but dove into the roar of emotions like a swimmer jumping into pounding surf. The world went white for a moment, then Alec came through the blinding cacophony and swam above the flow.

It was amazing how much anger, hate, envy, and greed swirled like veins of lava through the superheated longing, lust, and admiration. The fans loved their celebrities, and were equally eager to eat them alive. The urge to both adore and sacrifice the object of adoration was nothing new to the human psyche, and Alec recognized the lack of personal animosity that fueled most of it. He was looking for genuine threats, trying to focus on anyone whose hatred was targeted specifically.

It took several passes through the shifting levels of passion before he brushed against a blaze of loathing so raw and angry, it sent a wave of nausea through him.

Alec drew his mind back and put up mental shields instinctively. Once he was wholly back inside himself, he lowered the shields just a little, enough to inch back toward the hatred. This time he used his eyes as well as his mind to search for the source.

When he found it, it wasn't at all what he expected.

The old woman was so bent and withered, she could be a hundred in human years. She looked as ancient as some of the most senior Matri, and had much of the stubborn strength and force of will as the Mothers of the Clans, as well. She was vitally alive, and it was clear to anyone with psychic eyes that it was the hate that kept her going. There was no magic in the ancient one, but there was a whole lot of mean.

She was surrounded by three men, all much younger. They clearly existed to do her bidding, and reminded Alec of ferocious leashed dogs. None of them matched the photos he'd seen of the man who'd threatened Ashe. The hounds' gazes scanned the crowd, as protective of the old woman as the Lancer security team was of Ashe.

The ancient one's glare was as hot and as straight as a laser beam. Alec followed her intent gaze, and it was no surprise that the look was directed at —

Not Ashe.

But Domini.

"What the —" Alec muttered the words even as he moved.

"Trouble?" Maxwell's voice asked in his ear.

"Having a closer look at someone," he answered, calm and cool. Though Alec followed instinct, by long habit he made mortals think he was following by-the-book procedure. Mortals and civilians liked to think there was logic to the world.

"Not a deal," he added as he moved stealthily closer, weaving unnoticed into the clog of publicists, reporters, and camera crews that filled the area between the carpet and the velvet rope.

It was very hot among the lights that had

been set up at close intervals for interviewing the celebrities. The heat hit him hard, the stab of the lights even harder. Artificial light shouldn't have sent the stab of pain through his skull, but the pain was there, disorienting and nearly blinding.

Somewhere along the line, he must have forgotten to take a pill or a potion. He swore, pulled out a pair of sunglasses, and pushed on.

Something nasty tickled the back of Domini's neck, scratched at her nerves. There was the sensation of being tapped on the shoulder by a wicked claw. The feeling spun her away from Holly's side, looking for the danger at her back.

As she turned, the first thing she saw was Reynard, pale as sculpted marble under the lights, and cool as the distilled essence of the Rat Pack in Armani and designer shades. One instant he was on the edge of the interview area; the next, he was a few feet away. She filed the incongruity for later and kept turning. Whatever he was to her, Reynard was no threat to Holly.

Domini faced the noisy crowd. It was difficult to see beyond the brilliant lights. She made out packed bodies, reaching hands, blobs of faces. Auditorium security patrolled the perimeter, watchful but showing no signs of concern. There was no evident physical threat; just a feeling.

She squinted and followed that ugly, dangerous feeling, narrowing her focus to a spot where she saw a little old lady, wizened down to the size of a cricket and tough as old leather. Domini couldn't see the woman clearly, but that was her impression.

"Hate in her heart and venom in her blood," Domini muttered.

"What?" Holly asked, turning away from an interviewer.

"Nothing. We should head inside now," Domini answered calmly, trying to block off the psychic input.

ABOMINATION!

The word exploded in her head with the force of a bullet, black and boiling and sickening. Domini staggered back, blind with pain, and came up hard against a rock-solid wall of flesh covered in silk.

Strong arms came around her. A voice whispered, "I'm with you. You're safe."

The darkness cleared from her vision, the pain evaporated like fog in sunlight. She was aware of Reynard's scent. His arm circled her from behind, his presence alert, protective, with leashed fury held just under the surface. She realized he had mental barriers up that put a guard between her and the attacking voice.

These impressions were insane. So was her impulse to turn in to his embrace and rest her head against his heart.

Domini took a breath and opened her eyes. All the insanity was over in less time than it took anyone to notice. It probably looked like she'd stumbled and he'd caught her, which was exactly what had happened. Holly was the star, and all eyes were directed at Holly, not at her companion or the man who'd come up behind her.

Domini moved away from Reynard, and they both took a step back while Holly laughed and answered one more question.

"I thought I saw something," he said to Domini's inquiring look. "It was nothing," he added after sweeping a look across the crowd.

It was true. There was nothing obviously threatening in the area. Nothing physical, she thought. But something real.

It was only an old lady with a bad attitude, no matter how ugly it felt.

But Reynard had known. He'd felt the invisible threat.

He'd moved like the wind; he'd spoken inside her head. It was as real to him as it was to her.

Or maybe he'd seen her flinch or change expression, and he'd reacted — but Domini didn't believe it for a moment. Giving him a hard look, she whispered, "What are you?"

His body was still, his expression bland, his eyes unreadable behind the dark glasses. Maybe he counted on her telling herself it was all her imagination.

"Time to take Ms. Ashe inside." He stepped back. "The car will be waiting as per procedure after the show."

She nodded stiffly, annoyed but grateful he'd reminded her that there was a routine to follow, a schedule to stick to, a client to protect. She needed to hang on to that until she could be alone.

Domini took Holly by the elbow. "Show time," she said, steering her friend past the last interviewer. "Let's go."

CHAPTER FOURTEEN

It was two in the morning and Domini was finally off duty, in her own home, in pajamas, with a glass of wine in her hand.

ABOMINATION.

The word still echoed in Domini's mind, worsening her splitting headache and a horrible sense of disorientation. She'd tried aspirin, she'd tried meditation; now she was curled up on the patio swing, sipping a glass of merlot and looking up into the light pollution that hid the southern California stars. She had twelve hours off, and she wanted to enjoy them.

ABOMINATION.

The word rolled over and over, wanting her to worry over it like a sore spot in her brain. She didn't know why it should be such a puzzle. Most of the time her psychic gift manifested itself by showing her little sound bites of the future. The last several days, her oddly wired mental faculties had been acting up. So, she'd picked up a particularly strong emotion from an old lady who didn't approve of Holly Ashe's lifestyle. It was a simple, straightforward enough explanation, even if it did require a belief in telepathy and other psychic phenomena.

But it hadn't felt like it was aimed at Holly.

It had felt more like a stab in her own heart. Like she'd been branded. Marked.

Domini shivered, but made herself give a cynical laugh. "Right."

A coyote howled, and she heard it slinking through the dry bushes. She took a sip of wine, closed her eyes, and tried to savor the cool night air. It was quiet up here in her fairly secluded little canyon.

It would be lovely to go to sleep, but when she closed her eyes, images from tonight's detail began to replay in her head. With Reynard smack in the center of every move she made, every place she looked, every decision and thought. And that damn word still buzzed viciously underneath.

Technically, tonight's detail had gone perfectly. Holly had breezed through the party and the awards show without any incident. Now she was at the most trendy club in town, with a fresh protection detail discreetly keeping her company. She'd wanted

Domini to come along clubbing as a friend, but Domini had opted for home. Tomorrow morning she could write up her report of almost perfect procedural actions. But should she also talk to her grandfather about Reynard?

"By the way, Grandpa, the guy's not only a spook, he's spooky." It sounded not only flippant but stupid — and were black-ops commando types the same thing as spy spooks?

She finished the wine and noted that her headache was finally fading.

Abomination.

"Not me, lady," she muttered. "I'm just a working girl trying to get by."

And at least the shout had eased off to an insidious whisper. A silly word for the twenty-first century, anyway. It reeked of fire and brimstone, with satanic overtones. Very apocalyptic. Very melodramatic.

Come to think of it, the word appeared in several of the hate letters sent to Holly.

But the old lady never actually spoke the word, Domini recalled. No overt threat was made.

It wasn't your imagination.

Damn, it, Reynard, get out of my —

She cut off the thought and sat up straight. She'd only had one glass of wine, right? She took deep, calming breaths and listened to the night all around her. The coyote whimpered once in the bushes, then silence came down to gently enfold the yard. Domini tensed, mistrusting the silence. Then she got up and went into the house.

Alec stayed very still, refusing to pet the scruffy critter that was licking his hand. *Children of the night, get lost,* he thought at the coyote, but it paid him no mind. The thing was half domesticated already, and found having a Prime in its territory more interesting than terrifying.

Alec waited on one knee in the deep shadow of a bush to see what Domini would do next. No lights came on in the house. After a couple of minutes he began to hope that she'd gone to bed. If she had, it would make his patrol easier.

He rose to his feet, and a second later the back door opened. Domini came outside, carrying an object in each hand. When she lifted one of the objects to her eyes, he realized they were night-vision binoculars.

She scanned the yard before he had a chance to hide.

"Busted," he said to the coyote, and stepped to the center of the yard so Domini could get a good look at him. The animal followed him and sat down at his feet, leaning its weight against his leg.

"Good evening," Alec said to Domini. "Nice place you've got here. Nice Glock," he added, seeing the 9mm pistol at her side.

"Why are you here?"

He took a step forward. "I'm here on business. We need to talk."

"In the middle of the night? In my backyard?"

"They want you, not your friend." Alec spoke the words calmly, but her shocked response rocked through him. Shock, yes, but not surprise, at least no more than on a superficial level. "How did you guess I was in the yard?"

"Realized the coyote was upset. They have a den —" She peered hard at him, at the form at Alec's side. "What are you doing with my — with that animal? Get away from it, it's wild."

"Barely. You've been feeding it, haven't you?"

"They have cubs. What am I supposed to do, let them eat Mrs. Gregory's cats? Those cats mean the world to Mrs. Gregory. But babies have to eat, so —"

"You take the predators' side." Alec found her attitude sweet. But then, a predator would.

"If they were feral dogs instead of coyotes and went after domestic critters, I'd shoot 'em. Feral animals are confused and crazy. They don't know what the hell's going on."

He could sympathize. "Making them more dangerous than a truly wild thing."

"Yes. And how did you distract me into this conversation?"

"I'm not sure," he admitted. "But I like getting to know something about you." He gestured the animal away and took a step closer to the patio. "People who work together should be friends." He continued to inch forward as he spoke.

"Only on Sitcom World," she answered. "This is Planet Earth."

"This is Los Angeles," he countered. "Not quite the same thing. Of course, after spending twelve- to twenty-four-hour days with your coworkers, I can see why you'd want some distance from most of them."

"Most? How about all?"

He smiled. "You don't want to keep your distance from me."

His voice was soft, persuasive, and exuded complete confidence.

"You drive me crazy, Reynard."

"Lancer, I haven't even started."

Domini figured maybe it was the wine. She must have had more than one glass; otherwise why would she be standing here, carrying on an inane conversation?

Maybe it wasn't the wine. Maybe it was Reynard. He did things to her.

"What sort of things?" he asked in a velvet whisper, suddenly standing in front of her. It took him no effort to take the Glock from her. "Like this?"

Alec knew he wasn't playing fair with the one person in the world he ought to face on level ground, but the game had gone on long enough. Besides, her shiver of fear when he took the gun was arousing.

He put a hand on her shoulder, not allowing her to step back. Her skin was smooth satin stretched over supple muscle. His thumb found and caressed the point where the pulse beat quickly in her throat. Her gaze shot to his, panic warring with anger in her bright eyes. Excitement coiled like smoke through all her other reactions. Her vulnerability was ruthlessly tamped down within the space of a breath, but the predator in Alec took dark pleasure in it.

He let her spin away from his touch and held the gun out to her when she turned to face him again, several feet away. "Haven't I already told you that you have nothing to fear from me?"

Domini hadn't believed him the first time

he said it. She certainly didn't want to believe him now. Except . . .

She snatched back the gun. Then she made sure the safety was on and set it down beside the binoculars on the swing. Her skin still tingled warmly where he'd touched her. Looking at Reynard, standing there gorgeous and half smiling, Domini was aware that she wanted him to touch her again. She'd never wanted anyone's hands on her before. She clasped her hands behind her back to deny the other thing she wanted: to touch him.

He gestured toward her back door. "Let's go inside."

What the hell. It was obvious that she couldn't make Reynard go away until he wanted to. It was also obvious to her that she didn't want him to go, even though she should. That was probably obvious to him, too.

"Come on in." She turned and scooped up her stuff before opening the back door. "You want a glass of wine?" she offered over her shoulder.

"I don't drink . . . wine," he answered, following too close behind her. "But I could use a beer."

CHAPTER FIFTEEN

Two references to *Dracula* in less than an hour, Alec chastised himself as he took the beer Domini handed him. *That definitely puts me over my weekly vampire cliché limit.*

"What are you smiling about?" Domini asked.

"Telling myself bad jokes." He glanced at the label on the beer bottle and saw that he was holding a microbrew apricot ale. "Chick beer," he complained.

"If you want a Bud, you'll have to go back to that bar where —"

Alec watched as Domini's eyes filled with confusion. He watched while the memory almost surfaced. "What?"

She shook her head, her dark hair swinging around her pale face. "Nothing."

"You sure?"

He half wanted her to remember, to know that she hadn't been dreaming, that the world was crazy but she wasn't. And that he'd had his hands on her, had very nearly taken her. Damn, but it would have felt good.

Wrong, but good.

He noticed a bruise on her wrist, and remembered that she'd worn a silver bracelet with that sexy black lace dress earlier tonight. It had covered the mark he'd left on her, which brought a twinge of guilt. Alec wondered if she'd subconsciously known he wouldn't have been able to touch the bracelet. In his current condition, his people's allergy to silver was in full force.

"Living room's this way," Domini said after a drawn-out silence.

She sat in the room's one chair and left the couch for him. Alec took a quick look around as he sat.

The furniture was light brown leather, the coffee and end tables carved pine. A flat-panel television screen and other electronic equipment on steel shelving took up one wall. A desk with a computer and other office equipment took up another. There was a bookcase near the desk, with framed photos and a couple of blown-glass paperweights on the top. He recognized pictures of her grandfather and of Holly Ashe, and assumed the photos of a couple were Domini's parents.

The walls were neutral beige, decorated with vibrant Navajo wall hangings and a painting of condors soaring over a desert canyon. Another bright rug covered the middle of the Spanish tile floor. She switched on a halogen floor lamp that was too bright for his taste. His eyes really were giving him a lot of trouble tonight.

"You okay?"

"Fine." He made himself stop squinting and focused his attention on Domini.

Domini thought he looked tired. He'd been up as long as she had, and there was weariness in his eyes, and edginess as well. A dark fuzz of beard shadowed his square jaw and highlighted the cleft in his chin. A form-fitting black T-shirt stretched over hard muscles, and dark jeans molded his thighs. It took an effort to tear her gaze away from Reynard's powerful body, but when she did, she saw that he was giving her the same sort of once-over. And she remembered what she was wearing.

Alec liked her cotton knit shorty pajamas, which were red with white polka dots. The top was low-necked, held up by thin ribbon straps, and the bottoms were very short indeed. He watched with growing pleasure as a slow blush crept across her pale cheeks and long throat. The blood just beneath the surface of her soft skin called a sweet invitation to him. It took a great deal of effort not to lick his lips, and it took more not to pounce.

"I never thought of you as the polka-dot type," he said, stretching an arm out on the back of the couch.

She sat up straight, which made the pajama top dip lower on her breasts. "There's a great deal you don't know about me." She eyed him with renewed hostility. "I don't know anything about you."

"I'll tell you anything you want to know," Alec answered, and meant it.

There was much he shouldn't tell her yet, but if she wanted the truth from him, he would give it to her. He wouldn't volunteer a thing, of course, and she'd have to ask some very specific questions — questions no one was likely to think of in this modern age. But if she asked them, he'd answer. Whether she'd believe the answers . . . Well, his part was to offer truth. Hers would be to find belief. She was going to have to believe, eventually. But it would be better for them to come at it together, slowly, when he was in complete control of himself once more.

Tonight Alec felt like an animal was trying to claw its way out inside him. He'd forgotten to take his scheduled medication earlier in the day, and taking a double dose before coming to patrol Domini's house might not have been such a good idea. If he'd been at top form, Domini wouldn't have noticed his presence.

And he wouldn't be sitting here having a beer and enjoying the rush and thrum of lust he got from simply looking at her.

"What do you want to know?" he asked her.

"Why are you here?"

"I wanted to make sure you were safe."

She looked at him with complete and utter consternation. She also looked — touched. Something went soft in her eyes, in the tautness of her shoulders, and the tilt of her head. She didn't realize it, but Alec did, and it pleased him more than he could have believed possible.

Of course, the softness was quickly replaced by the annoyance of a modern woman well aware that she could take care of herself, thank you very much. Girls who grew up with Lara Croft, Captain Janeway, and Xena, Warrior Princess, for role models didn't take well to the idea of being rescued by brave, brawny men. The attitude could be hard on a man's ego, especially on a man who'd been born around the turn of the twentieth century.

"Chivalry is dead, have you noticed?" He

took a sip of beer.

She instantly picked up on what he meant. "I don't mind men opening doors for me."

"Just stay out of your way when you come through carrying riot gear."

"Exactly."

Alec stood. "I obviously shouldn't have come."

She reacted just as he hoped, by jumping to her feet, disappointment in her eyes. She managed to sound firm when she said, "No, you shouldn't have. But since you're here, you're not going until we've talked."

He smiled. "You don't want me to go." The anger that shot from her energized all his senses. "Okay, I played you," he told her, and didn't apologize for it. He smiled instead, which served to fuel Domini's annoyance. Which fueled him. The woman made him hot. "There you are, a tower of indignation in polka-dot pajamas. Maybe not a tower," he amended, coming closer. "Towers don't have such nice bumps . . . and curves."

Domini saw something wild in Reynard's eyes, so wild they almost glowed. The way he looked at her sent heat lightning blazing through her. His smile was sharp, predatory. She felt as if he were about to eat her up.

He was Reynard the fox, cunning, clever, beautiful, and dangerous. The danger drew her as nothing ever had before.

Domini felt her senses spinning as the wildness in Reynard lured her toward him. At this moment, she couldn't avoid him if her life depended on it.

While her eyes stared into his, she held out a hand and discovered she was close enough to touch his face, to draw her fingertips down his throat. Beard stubble teased against her palm, sending shocks of heat through her. The texture and scent of his skin skirled around her. His gaze held her. She could see herself reflected in green depths. And deeper down, there were flames.

Reynard's eyes closed when she touched him, and he let out a low moan. The sound broke the eye contact and the spell long enough for her to drop her hand, to take one long step backward.

She was trembling so hard she nearly fell back into the deep embrace of the chair, but she tried to make it look voluntary. Why wasn't she just throwing him down on the couch to have her way with him? Her heart hammered in her chest and her insides boiled, while she fought not to let the turbulence show.

"Sit down. Talk," she managed.

Reynard gave an elegant shrug, suddenly looking cool and unconcerned, as though he'd never made any suggestive remarks or touched —

Okay, he hadn't touched her; she'd touched him. And she'd been tempted to touch him a lot. She'd come damn close to breaking company policy.

Alec tucked his hands out of sight when he sat down. He'd managed to keep his fangs drawn back, despite the pain the effort caused him. But his claws had inexorably dug into his fisted palms while he fought the need to take her then and there. One touch from her was all it had taken to nearly send the madness over the edge. His control was thin, his body and soul demanding the taste and total possession of her. But he couldn't let it show, couldn't act on it.

Why not? the demon inside him wondered, silky and seductive. *She belongs to me. She wants me.* He sighed. *She'd be terrified of the real me. Here I sit with my own blood on my hands, and my fangs trying to pop out to sink into her flesh. All I want right now is hard sex and hot blood. A vampire's supposed to seduce his lovers, earn their trust, calm their fear; share passion, give pleasure. I want to mark, to possess —*

"Reynard? You okay?"

Alec swung his gaze toward Domini, forced his attention to focus. "No."

He shouldn't have had the beer. Dr. Casmerek had told him not to drink, right? He couldn't remember any of the doctor's myriad instructions right now. He didn't think the treatment was working. Alec turned over his left wrist and stared at the fox tattoo. Was it still fading?

"I'm tired," he said before looking back at Domini.

"Been a long day," she agreed. Then she blinked, and a gasp caught in her throat.

"What?" Alec asked.

"Nothing," Domini managed to answer.

A premonition had just streaked through her. In the vision she'd watched Reynard answer his cell phone, heard a voice on the other end say, "Your appointment at the clinic needs to be rescheduled. The serum formula has to be adjusted."

What clinic? she wondered. What serum?

Somehow she knew it would be dangerous to ask.

"How long have you known you were psychic?" he asked after the silence drew out between them for a while.

Domini went stiff. Her fingers dug into the arms of the chair. "How did you know I —"

"The sushi incident was the first clue."

For a moment she struggled to remember what he was talking about. "Oh, right," she finally said. "The place that was out of wasabi." Thank God he hadn't picked up on her vision about him and his medical problems. She waved a hand, trying to be casually dismissive, but the movement was stiff and jerky with nerves. "Probably just my imagination. I have a very active imagination."

"So do I," Alec answered. He managed to smile without showing any extra-sharp teeth. "Someday we'll try our imaginations out on each other."

He enjoyed the faint outrage that swept through her as she puzzled that out. "Was that a come-on?"

"A statement of intent," he told her. "But let's concentrate on the conversation we're supposed to be having, or neither of us will get any rest before we have to go back to work."

Domini pressed her fingers to her temples for a moment and said, "You've finally said something I agree with. How long have I known I'm psychic?" she went on. "All my life. It's no big deal, no woo-woo talent. Nobody's going to offer me a syndicated television show where I talk to the dead for money, or anything like that."

"I'm rather partial to the pet psychic lady on *Animal Planet.*"

"Me, too," she admitted. "Apparently I

could do that as a kid."

"Bet you still do," Alec said, recalling her relationship with the coyotes. "But not consciously."

"Right."

"Your skepticism is charmingly postmodern, but it gets in the way of your psychic development."

She made a gagging sound. "Don't make me throw up on you, Reynard."

"You should be happy that I appreciate your gifts, instead of making such a vile suggestion."

She couldn't help but smile. "Vile? What an old-fashioned word."

He smirked. "Didn't know that Delta Force operators have large vocabularies?"

"To go along with your large egos?"

"All sorts of things are large on us D-Boys."

Domini recalled Holly's speculations about Reynard's testicles, and firmly kept her gaze away from his groin. "What's my being psychic got to do with anything?" she asked

"What's it got to do with Holly Ashe's stalkers, you mean? Does Ashe know you're psychic?"

"We grew up together."

"So maybe they used her to find you."

"They? Who?"

"I don't know yet," Alec said. "But there was something familiar about the old woman."

Domini leaned forward, a rush of excitement going through her. "You saw her? You — heard — her?"

"I saw her. You're the one who heard her. It was directed at you, and you flinched like she'd slapped you hard. There was telepathic communication between you."

She shook her head. "Not between. It was only her. She — hated."

"That was obvious. What did you hear?"

Domini collapsed against the chair back. "Abomination." The word still left a bad taste in her mind. "She called me *abomination.*"

"Ugly word. Why abomination?"

"Obviously she thought I was Holly's girlfriend."

He shook his head. "No. It was *you* she hated, not a lifestyle." He leaned forward, gaze boring into hers. "Why?"

"Damned if I know," was all she could answer, even though part of her wanted to proclaim that his opinion was nonsense. Nonsense she half believed, maybe because Reynard wasn't freaked by her being psychic — which was freaky enough in itself. She swiped a hand across her forehead. "I am so confused."

Reynard rose to his feet.

Domini was almost too weary to appreciate the smooth play of tight, toned muscles as he moved. But she was only sleepy, not dead, and looking at him was a pleasure, albeit a muted one at the moment.

"You're getting sleepy," he told her.

She yawned, then shook a finger at him. "You trying to hypnotize me? Won't work."

His smile had a secret, knowing quality to it. "You might be surprised."

"Don't want to be surprised." She yawned again. "Wanna sleep now."

"I didn't see anyone when I did the sweep of the area. You're safe enough tonight," he said.

She didn't bother to argue. "Good night, Reynard."

"Not going to see me out?"

"No."

"Or kiss me good night?" She didn't answer, and he walked to the door. There he paused. "About the coyotes — I know someone who takes an interest in wild canines. He'll relocate them to a safer habitat. He's called Shaggy. I'll have him get in touch with you."

Touched by Reynard's concern for the animals, Domini smiled as he left. "Fine."

CHAPTER SIXTEEN

"He was *petting* the coyote. How weird is that, Holly?"

Domini took a sip of orange juice and gazed out over the terrace, the pool, and a hedge of waxy green hibiscus with vivid orange blooms to the city below. Only a faint morning heat haze obscured the vista.

Holly swallowed a bite of toast, then said, "Maybe the coyote recognized an alpha male."

"Maybe." She couldn't deny Reynard's aura of masculinity. "But what's even weirder is that I didn't notice it at the time. It didn't seem strange until I woke up this morning and remembered everything that happened."

"I think it's *interesting* that he showed up to see if you were all right."

"You want to say that you think it was *romantic,* but you're afraid I'll hit you."

Holly tossed her hair out of her face, the movement setting several dangling earrings tinkling together. "You can't hit me. I'm surrounded by bodyguards."

Domini glanced at her friend's long scarlet nails as Holly sipped her coffee. "I wouldn't attack anyone with claws like those. I could get hurt."

Holly held them out in front of her. "Too bad these have to come off before the show tonight. Can't play guitar in these fakes." She picked up her cup and returned her attention to Domini's quandary. "You sure it was a coyote? Not a stray dog or something?"

"I'm sure. I'm also sure that wild animals do not approach humans. The critters that hang out in my neighborhood will take the food I set out, but only when I'm not around. They're cautious. What's Reynard got that drew a wild animal to him?"

Holly snorted. "I think we've been over that ground already."

Domini sat back in the green metal patio chair. A pair of doves settled on the blue-and-yellow Moroccan tiles that edged the pool. As she watched them bob around searching for food, she wondered why she was here, having this conversation with Holly. She knew why, of course, but she didn't like facing her own cowardice.

What would Grandpa say if he knew about last night? Technically, nothing sexual had gone on between her and Reynard. But she'd wanted it to. Was thinking about it against company policy? It certainly made her feel guilty and confused.

"But does lust count?" she murmured.

Holly overheard her and said, "Normally I'd say yes, but I have no idea what you're talking about. Except Mr. Triple T., that is."

Domini let out a disgruntled laugh. "I wouldn't be surprised if he does have three testicles. The guy is so weird."

"How weird?"

"So weird that I automatically accept that he accepts my psychic abilities."

"I accept it."

"You've known me since day care. Reynard's a stranger. A weird one."

"What can you possibly find weird about a handsome, competently dangerous male who accepts your gifts and worries about you? So he pets wild animals — isn't that just the testosterone attracting them?"

"I think you mean pheromones."

"Which is why you did our chemistry homework for both of us. And speaking of chemistry . . ."

Holly didn't look as teasing as she

sounded. "What?" Domini asked, then answered the question herself. "You're getting back together with Jo."

"I ran into a mutual friend last night. Not mutual anymore, really — she took Jo's side," Holly said. "So I wasn't expecting anything nice when she came up to me in the club, but what the hell, I had a bodyguard. So when she started talking, I let her. Only she was friendly. And finally we got around to talking about Jo, and I let slip how I miss her sometimes, and — and she said that Jo misses me, too. And that Jo's worried about me because of all these threats. And this friend gave me a phone number. And I gave her a phone number. And maybe I'll call."

She shrugged, pretending it didn't matter, though her eyes were glowing with hope. "Or maybe Jo'll call. Maybe we were stupid and let all this fame crap get in the way. She's a big-time artist and I'm a big-time artist, only we come from different worlds. I'm from Malibu, and she grew up in the Hamptons, but East Coast–rich and surfer-girl-rich sensibilities aren't exactly the same. But maybe we've matured and —"

"You are getting back together with Jo." Domini spoke the words slowly and clearly. She took Holly's wrists, made sure her friend

186

was looking at her, and repeated clearly, "You are getting back together with Jo."

"How do you —" Holly's eyes went wide. "Oh!" She grinned. "You *saw* it?"

Domini nodded. "Just now." She sighed with relief. "Which means that now you'll stop nagging me about my lack of love life."

"You don't lack one anymore."

"I —" The protest died on Domini's lips as the thought of Reynard caused warmth to flood through her synapses. While Holly eyed her with amusement, Domini said, "Okay, I'll admit to being in lust with him. I don't like it, but I will find a way to cope."

"Sex works."

Domini shook her head. "The guy's weird."

Holly said seriously, "He cared enough to come by your house to see if you were safe. That's nice."

Domini chose not to argue. Reynard was one of the people responsible for protecting Holly, and he had exhibited nothing but professional behavior.

Okay, to her eyes he moved too fast, saw too much. It was like the guy had super powers — and calling it Delta Force training didn't wash with her. But she shouldn't be discussing a fellow Lancer employee with their client. She wasn't going to undermine Holly's trust in Reynard's effectiveness just because she suspected the guy was —

That was the problem. She didn't know *what* he was. Never mind the *who,* it was the *what* that preyed on her mind.

"I need to get to the dojo. Nothing like an aikido class to clear the mind," Domini said, and looked at the fading bruises on her right wrist.

The marks on her left wrist were gone, but the print of fingers and thumb were still quite clear on this arm, though pale yellow now. At least the faint rash silver sometimes gave her had cleared up as soon as she'd taken the cuff bracelet off last night. Odd that the allergy had acted up, since it hadn't bothered her for a while.

Domini stood to go. "I need to do some research. And office paperwork," she added with a sigh.

Domini's first stop was by Nancy's desk in the reception area.

"Hi." She leaned her arms on the high countertop. "Quite the star-studded night, last night."

Nancy looked up with a grin, happy for a bit of celebrity gossip. "Who'd you see? What did they wear?"

Domini chatted about the rich and famous for a few minutes before asking, "The Old Man in?"

Nancy shook her head. "Lots of meetings outside the office today."

Domini looked disappointed. "Too bad. I wanted to see him. Could you let me know when he comes in?"

"Sure."

"But call me on my cell when you spot him. I'm going to be all over the office today."

"No problem."

With her back now covered, Domini walked away from the reception area and straight to Benjamin Lancer's office, where the computer she wanted to use was located. Fortunately her grandfather's office door wasn't locked, so Domini didn't have to do anything more nefarious than slip inside. Hopefully this wouldn't take long.

She supposed she should feel guilty about snooping on Reynard, but she didn't. She needed to know more about him. Maybe she could have gotten a look at his paperwork from Nancy, under the pretense that she was handling Reynard's orientation, but Nancy would have made sure the Old Man was briefed on Domini's request. And she wasn't ready to discuss Reynard with him yet, even if Grandpa had asked her to keep an eye on him.

Mostly because she was afraid she'd spill her guts about being attracted to the man. She wasn't sure where such a conversation would go with Ben Lancer. He might come down hard, angry and hurt, on the "no fraternization between my employees" side. Or he might go all soft and sentimental and remind her he wanted great-grandchildren. Either way, somebody was likely to get fired. She didn't want it to be her. And she didn't have any proof that it deserved to be Reynard.

"Yet," she muttered, and proceeded to break into the password-protected personnel files. It took her only three tries to figure out that her grandfather used *Domini* as his password, which made her squirm with guilt but didn't stop her.

There was basic information on Alexander Reynard in his file. Very basic. His full name had no middle initial; his last employer, U.S. Army; rank, colonel, retired. No mention of Special Services or Delta Force, of course. Date of birth given as July 14, 1968, Coeur D'Alene, Idaho. His address, home and cellular phone numbers. No references were listed. No one to contact in case of emergency. Health records were blank, including the company's routine drug-testing results.

Since he'd only been with the company a few days, she *could* assume that the results from his medical exam and tests weren't in yet. But she didn't. He shouldn't be out in the field without those results being logged.

It wasn't like Nancy not to enter data immediately. It wasn't like her grandfather, Andy Maxwell, or herself to vet someone without proper background documentation. Why had he left the army? Who were his references?

What the hell was the matter with all of them?

Some kind of voodoo? Mass hypnotism? What *was* it with Reynard?

Totally dissatisfied, Domini shut down the computer and went to her own workstation. She checked her e-mail and phone messages, then wrote and posted the log of her last shift on the Ashe detail. She read Andy Maxwell's log, and was annoyed that Reynard had only sent a short e-mail from his home computer rather than fill out the proper form.

"Not company policy, D-Boy," she muttered with a certain malicious glee. But Andy was team leader on this assignment; it was up to him to deal with personnel problems.

It was also disappointing to realize that

when she objectively wrote down the actions taken to protect Holly, she couldn't find any way to see Reynard's behavior as sinister.

And why do I *want* to get him in trouble? she asked herself. Because he terrifies me, she admitted.

There was something — unnatural — about him. And he wanted her to know it, she was sure of it. If he went away, she wouldn't have to follow her curiosity and the lure of her fascination about what was hidden in the shadowy heart of Alexander Reynard.

Now, there was a melodramatic thought — but she couldn't laugh. Reynard was disturbing. Distracting. Damn sexy.

Maybe that was the dark heart of her fear. He'd walked into her comfortable, contented life and just — shattered it.

And they hadn't even done anything yet. She rubbed her bruised wrist as she wondered what would happen if they ever got around to kissing.

Domini shook her head and forced herself to concentrate on her job. She got out Holly's file and reread the threatening letters, the police reports, and psychological profiler threat assessments, concentrating on finding any evidence or pattern that might jibe with Reynard's theory that Holly wasn't the intended victim. It was ridiculous, of course, to think that someone was using Holly as a cat's-paw to get to her. But —

That ugly voice still throbbed in her head. The old woman's vicious stare cut into her soul. Domini shuddered, then jumped as the phone rang.

"Lancer. What?"

"You okay, Dominatrix?" Andy Maxwell asked. She must have sounded shaken when she answered the phone.

Domini took a deep breath, then said calmly, "I was reading all the icky letters sent to Holly. Put me in a bad mood."

"With good reason. My bad mood comes from still waiting for the police to share the DMV information on the car that followed you and Reynard."

Followed me? The thought sent a chill through her. Or followed Reynard?

"We provided them with the plate numbers and were promised full disclosure on anything to do with Holly Ashe's stalkers," Andy continued. "I'll give them another day, then I'll ask the Old Man to make a call to LAPD."

"We having an afternoon briefing for tonight's detail?"

"On-site briefing at seven — that's what I called to tell you," he answered. "Alec can't make it into the office today."

"Can't?" The word dripped sarcasm. "Who's in charge of this detail, Andy? Listen, Reynard's —"

Reynard's mouth came down hard on hers. Fangs sharp as ivory daggers grazed her lips. His tongue invaded her mouth as his words invaded her mind.

Mine! Mine! Mine!

No! Her protests were growing fainter, will draining out of her like blood from a wound. Please!

Her begging only drove him on. The kiss forced on her was harsh and demanding, tasting of coppery blood. Tasting of defeat. The vampire's lust pounded through her, emotion as real and hard as the cock pounding ruthlessly inside her. There was no escape, only a storm overwhelming her. Driving total possession into her flesh, her blood, and being. She was spread out beneath him like a sacrifice. Her skin was smeared red with her blood, and his.

"The guy's got a toothache, Dominatrix." Andy's words, sounding thoroughly disgusted, brought Domini back to herself.

She shook so hard, she could barely hold the phone to her ear. She blinked, trying to bring her vision back into focus. What the hell was *that?* Her insides ached as if she'd —

"Domini? You okay, Domini? You having some kind of attack?"

"How did you know? There's a vamp—"

"You having an asthma attack or something?" Andy's concerned voice cut across her words.

"I'm — all right." Domini wiped a hand across her forehead, and was surprised to find sweat instead of blood.

Blood. The memory of it was so strong she could almost smell it. Almost taste it. Blood and sex — why did she keep dreaming about Reynard as a vampire? Only this hadn't been a dream. Yet it hadn't felt like one of her premonitions, either. What the hell *was* it, then?

A dose of paranoia? A really sick, perverted one. Something that had slithered up from some dark well of her own imagination. No matter how much Reynard freaked her, she couldn't blame him for this.

She forced her mind back to things she *could* blame Reynard for. "Why the hell isn't he coming in today?" she demanded of Andy.

"I told you, a toothache. He needed a quick trip to a dentist. Cut him some slack; he'll be on duty tonight."

"How do you know that?"

" 'Cause he said he'd be there."

Domini took a moment to calm down, to relax her tight muscles. To remind herself that she hadn't been violated in any way. *Think about taking care of Holly. Concentrate on the job and nothing else. Forget about Reynard. Let him go.*

She didn't know how she was going to do that.

"I'll see you at seven. Good-bye." She hung up.

CHAPTER SEVENTEEN

"Perhaps screaming would help." When both Alec and Barak gave Serisa a dark look, she added, "Not you, of course. Perhaps if you made someone else scream —"

Alec heard the Matri's voice filtered through the layers of pain and violent, feral urges that made up his existence now. He could not lose control. Not for one instant.

"It hurts." He could admit that much.

Alec knew he was in his own house, but he couldn't remember when the elders had arrived. He couldn't remember why. He forgot about them as a picture of Domini flashed through his mind, like a glimpse of a photograph being tossed on a fire.

She was in danger. From some unknown source. More immediately, from him.

He had to get to her.

He had to stay away.

Don't think about her now. Can't think about her now.

Must have her. NOW!

Barak stooped next to where Alec knelt on the floor.

"Look me in the eye, Prime." Barak spoke evenly, calmly. Alec hated him for his control.

His eyes were closed again. He didn't want to open them, but he did, for every word between two male vampires could be considered a challenge. There was too much light, and it burned like fire, but Alec met the challenge and looked Barak in the eye.

There was no pity in Barak's gaze, nor was there any mockery. So it would not be necessary to attack him. Damn — it would be good to attack something and hear it scream.

What a hell of a day this had been. It started with a phone call; he recalled that intermittently. He'd arrived home from Domini's, slept a little, then woken and paced, his headache growing worse with every second closer to dawn. None of the pills or injections helped. Maybe he'd taken too many. Maybe not enough. He remembered the taste of medicated blood, and how it had made him sick.

Just after dawn, someone from the clinic called to calmly tell him that his appointment was canceled. There was no explanation, but there was the bad news that the serum wasn't working. He was told that he might experience feral hallucinations.

Maybe that was why the elders came . . .

He recalled that he'd behaved almost normally for a time after the call, even though pain leaked deeper into his body with the rising of the sun. He'd drawn every curtain, blocked off every source of light, but the pain still grew. He'd meditated. He worked through it. He thought he'd even remembered to call the office and make some excuse for staying away. He thought —

"Your eyes are open, but you're not looking outside your own troubles."

Concentrate, Barak's voice whispered in Alec's mind. The whisper had steel in it. *You haven't lost control, but the fear of losing it is what's driving you toward the edge. What is the worst that will happen if you lose control?*

The image came immediately into Alec's mind. Into Barak's view.

His mouth came down hard on Domini's as his words invaded her mind. Mine! Mine! Mine! The kiss was harsh and demanding, tasting of coppery blood and sweet domination. Desire pounded through him as he pounded ruthlessly into Domini. Driving into soft heat. Driving total possession into flesh, blood, and being. She was spread out beneath him like a sacrifice. Her skin was smeared red with her blood, and his.

Mine. You are mine. Know it. Love it.

Mine. Want me. Forever. Love it.

She cried out, pain and torment mingled with the desire he forced on her. She writhed beneath him, struggled, submitted. Her mind was conquered, her body rose to meet his brutal thrusts. He roared out his pleasure, reveled in mastery, took her. And took her again.

Mine. Forever mine!

It was beyond Alec's power to shield his dark, feral desires from Barak's knowledge.

Ah. I see.

The thought was a soft sigh in Alec's mind, almost like a blessing. It banished the ugly images for now. Alec sensed no disgust from the elder, no judgment. He only sensed Barak's sympathy.

You understand?

I have known this fire.

It is evil — to want what I want — the way I am now. I cannot —

You fight nature — but I understand why. The timing is shit for a mortal bonding, but fate frequently screws with us.

Alec almost laughed, but any trace of humor fled when he felt Barak withdrawing from his mind. He hadn't wanted the intrusion, but he hated being alone within a mind that felt ready to shatter like glass.

"You'll hold it together," he heard Barak say. "For her sake."

Serisa sighed. "He's obsessing about the mortal I forbade him to see, isn't he?" She did not sound pleased. "Still, he needs a woman right now." After a thoughtful pause, she went on. "He needs to share blood, and passion; needs the fight, the conquest, and domination. He needs the strength that comes with the night, and he needs to be a Prime. Perhaps even a mortal woman would be able to bring him through this. One who understands the risks —"

"Not just any mortal woman will do."

There was a long and pregnant silence from Serisa before she said, "Damn. His timing is shit."

"So I have informed him, my love."

"Then we should bring her to him."

"No!" Alec cut into the conversation. His mouth throbbed. He had to talk around the aching fangs that had drawn down to graze his lower lip. "She's too gifted. Too fragile. I will protect her from myself." He glared at Serisa, though his eyes felt like burning coals. "I will protect her from you."

Serisa knelt on the floor in front of him and touched his shoulders lightly with her strong, long-fingered hands. Even though she was not of his Clan, even though she'd angered him, she was still a Matri. A Matri's touch brought reassurance. Her words were to be listened to.

"I admire your attitude, child." She brushed her fingers through his sweat-soaked hair. "I truly do. But you must understand what is happening to you. You've had a bad reaction to the first serum Dr. Casmerek formulated for you. The reaction is causing your body to go through an experience you've been through once before. One you don't consciously remember."

Her hand moved from his shoulder down to his groin. Agony speared through him from the spot where she touched. He was hard as a rock, and hadn't even realized it.

"Puberty is not fun for our kind," she said. "The transition from adolescent to Prime or to mature female is excruciating. It is the feral time. We forget it, can blank out the anguish when we're young. Unfortunately right now you are a Prime, fully aware of what you are going through."

"Fortunately," Barak added, "you can fight the need."

Serisa gave Barak an annoyed look. "I don't see why he should have to."

"Because he wants to," the elder answered

his bondmate. "My duty is to help him control his feral urges."

"My duty is to keep him from suffering. I will not see him scarred because he is at war with himself. The drugs that let him function in the light are his enemy today. A defender of the children of the sisters deserves all the help we can give him."

"Then take me to the clinic," Alec broke in. "Get me to Casmerek."

The older couple exchanged a look.

"What is it?" Alec asked. "What's wrong?"

"The clinic is closed for the day," Serisa answered. "All outpatient appointments are canceled. All vampires on staff who aren't part of the security team have to stay away."

"There might be a security problem," Barak explained.

"Nothing is known for sure yet," Serisa said. "But the clinic's staff is very cautious."

Alec leapt on this information. Security was something he understood, something he could focus on. Besides, he knew. "The place is being watched. I felt it the last time I was there."

Through the haze of pain caused by the room's dim light, Alec saw the older vampires exchange a worried, skeptical glance. They thought he was hallucinating, didn't they? Anger spiked through him.

It made the claws spring from his fingertips, and he let out a furious hiss as he scraped deep gouges in the floor on either side of where he knelt. Glancing down, Alec saw that these were not the first marks he'd left in the brightly polished hardwood floor. The incongruous thought that his landlord was going to have his hide for this damage flashed through Alec's aching head, and he almost smiled.

Alec forced his attention back to the clinic. He needed something he could concentrate on besides the pain. Besides Domini.

"Hunters," he said. "The clinic's being watched by hunters."

"We have a truce with the hunters here in California," Barak said.

"Unofficial, of course," Serisa added. "We haven't bothered them, and they haven't bothered us, for several years. It could be a bloodbath for their people and ours if they stepped over the line after so much time."

"Who else is a threat to us?" Alec asked. "The Families are neutral. The Tribes don't approve of the medical research done for the Clans, but they're too pragmatic to risk endangering a resource they might need. Only hunters hate us."

"It's not as bad as the old days," Barak said. "They understand now that not all vampires are the enemies of mortal kind."

"Not all of them," Serisa said bitterly. "Are you forgetting we lost a son to their worst fanatics? The ones that call themselves Purists?"

"I will never forget losing Joshua," Barak told his bondmate. "I can still hear him screaming as he burned, and the later screams of the Purists when I tracked them down. They paid. I won't hate all vampire hunters because of them. I will avoid them if I can, fight them if I have to. But not kill them, even the Purists. You know that."

Serisa nodded. Then she spoke to Alec again. "We keep track of the local hunters, as they try to keep track of us. If they're watching the clinic for some reason, we'll find out about it. And take care of it." She took Alec's face between her hands. "Right now, let's concentrate on taking care of you. Barak, bring Alexander's medicine case and the dosage instructions. It's not the medicines that have messed him up, but the serum. I still think he needs several nights of tempestuous sex, but if he won't, he won't."

"You don't have to talk like I'm not here."

She patted Alec's cheek and smiled. "Petulant. Good. That's better than vicious. And you're alert enough to worry about the clinic and not just your own needs. Between meditation and the drugs, we're bound to make it better."

Alec made himself believe her. He had no choice.

"Let's get started," he said. "I have to be at work at seven."

CHAPTER EIGHTEEN

"Well, don't you look like death warmed over, Mr. Reynard?" Domini said when Reynard sauntered across the crowded parking lot behind the club.

The lights mounted on tall poles at each corner of the lot were bright and white, causing Reynard's long, lean shadow to spear out behind him. Had he lost weight overnight? He certainly looked lean and mean in the tight jeans and body-hugging black T-shirt, but there was a hollowness to his already austere features. She thought he looked tired under the swagger. Seeing him put her on edge. Worse, it made her worry about him. The dichotomy was so disturbing, she couldn't help her tart comment.

His reply was equally snide as he reached the black SUV parked next to the rear entrance. "Thank you for your concern, Ms. Lancer."

On closer inspection, she added, "You're looking extremely pale and pasty as well."

"The lights do nothing for my complexion," Reynard said as he joined her in leaning against the hood.

Large men in shirts with SECURITY stenciled front and back patrolled a perimeter between the fans and the Lincoln Navigator parked next to the rear entrance. The Lancer team was spaced around the SUV. Domini and Reynard faced the growing crowd while they talked to each other.

"And you're wearing sunglasses at night again. Why is that?"

"Trying to fit in with the milieu."

"I don't see anyone else in sunglasses."

"It's the best I can do to appear cool, as I have no interest in body piercings or full-body tattoos. This place look like the set of *The Fast and the Furious* to you?"

She swept a look around the lot. "No rice rockets. More girls."

"I suppose."

Alec wondered if his effort to sound laconic was working. Domini had sniped at him the moment she saw him. He sniped back. Vampire courtship. Snapping and snarling could come next. And after that . . .

This exchange could prove dangerous.

Duty. Discipline. Responsibility. He lived by

these standards, but right now, his insistence on fulfilling his obligations as Prime and Lancer operative was maybe not the best idea he'd ever had. Help from the elders and pure stubbornness had gotten him here. But now that he was here, he was having trouble looking Domini in the face. His feral imagination had gone into overload today, and the harsh fantasy images he'd conjured not only haunted him, they embarrassed him.

But he couldn't bear not to be with her. It was ridiculous, since his head told him she'd be safer with him elsewhere, but he kept returning to her side.

Did she really need protecting from anyone but him? Was he imagining a threat to her to legitimize being near her?

Domini had hoped Reynard wouldn't show. Was her belief that he was hiding his true nature and intentions her way of denying . . . what? Desire? Fear of losing control? Fear of losing herself in the throes of passion?

She scoffed at such an old-fashioned notion. Who said passion required loss of control, of self?

Holly. And not just in her songs; Holly lived with total commitment to her emotions. Domini had watched her fall in and out of love with complete abandon and frequent heartbreak ever since they'd hit puberty. Domini had helped pick up the pieces plenty of times, and it was never pretty. Crazy thing was, Holly never gave up on falling in love.

Lust, passion, and desire were not safe, and they didn't make for sane behavior. Domini had enough trouble with staying sane on a normal day-to-day basis. Add passion to the mix, and —

"Our principal's still in the car," Reynard said, jolting Domini out of her reverie. He checked his watch. "Why?"

"On the phone," Domini answered. "She wanted privacy for the call."

Holly was talking with Jo. Domini shook her head. Talk about not giving up on love. If the media got hold of this —

"Isn't Ashe supposed to be onstage in a few minutes?"

Domini noticed the members of Holly's entourage pacing restlessly on the other side of the SUV. Her road manager looked very unhappy.

Domini shrugged. "We go into the club when Holly wants to."

She wasn't going to complain about a client's screwing up a schedule. That was Andy's job, if he thought the delay posed a security threat. She did notice a pair of the club's bouncers glaring at them from their post by the rear entrance. She offered another shrug to the beefy bouncers, then her attention returned to Reynard.

"Can I ask you a question?"

He crossed his arms. They were long and sinewy, and the stance emphasized the width of his shoulders. She was used to hard-bodied, hard-edged men, but none so impressive as this one.

"You can ask."

Domini took a quick breath and blurted out, "Do you believe in vampires?" She didn't think it was a stupid question to ask. She thought it was a dangerous one.

It got her a sardonic look over the top of his sunglasses. His eyes were very bloodshot. "You mean, like do I believe in things like tooth fairies and Bigfoot?"

"Do you?"

"I absolutely do not believe in Bigfoot."

She noted that he hadn't answered the question. He moved closer to her, with uncanny speed that no longer surprised her. He was no more than an inch away from her when he spoke. "How about you? What do you believe in?"

"I absolutely do not believe in tooth fairies."

"Vampires do," he said. "They go through

two sets of baby teeth, so they really clean up on the money-under-the-pillow thing. In fact, many vampire college funds are started with tooth-fairy money."

His facetiousness amused her against her will. Added to his looks and the sizzle of strong sex appeal, the combination was frighteningly potent.

"Do you believe in vampires?" he asked her.

"I used to dream about vampires when I was a kid," she admitted. "I've been dreaming about them again the last couple of days. Ever since I met you."

Domini couldn't tell how Reynard took what she said, not with his green eyes hidden by sunglasses and the angular structure of his face bleached out and oddly shadowed by the bright white light overhead. He *looked* like a vampire, damn it! Not that he could be; the dream images were only her subconscious's way of warning her of —

He brushed his fingers along her cheek and throat, not quite touching, yet still sending hot and cold shivers through her. "You're afraid I'm going to possess you, is that it? That I'm going to suck the life out of you?" His voice was low, and very angry.

Domini took a step sideways. He turned, watching her, but giving her distance. She crossed her arms. "Something like that."

He stepped back. His voice was angry ice. "I am so flattered."

Domini turned her back to Reynard and made a survey of the area. The crowd of fans surrounded the building and spilled up the block in both directions, but this early in the evening they were pretty well behaved. The tricky part would be getting Holly out of the club later, not taking her inside.

She felt Reynard's gaze on her, and looked over her shoulder. "What are you looking at, Mr. Reynard?"

He quirked an eyebrow and looked down over the top of his sunglasses. "Ms. Lancer, I can't help but notice that you have a buzzard on your butt."

Domini was wearing a short skirt that rode low on her hips, and no doubt a bit of the tattoo at the base of her spine was showing. She brushed a hand across the small of her back. "It's a condor."

"Interesting," Reynard murmured. "Do you have something similar on the front?"

"You'll never know, Mr. Reynard."

He moved up behind her so close that she could feel the heat of his skin. "Really?" he murmured, lips close to her ear. "I don't think you want to bet on that."

Domini shivered. No. She didn't.

Andy Maxwell came around the front of the SUV, and he was not looking happy.

"What?" Domini asked.

"You recommended the club hire extra security from Tanner for the evening, right?" She nodded. "Those people walking the security line and the extra bouncers aren't from Tanner. The club management contracted with Dennis Weader instead."

"Damn."

"Problem?" Reynard asked.

"Could be extra work for us," Andy told Reynard. "Weader the Weasel doesn't run the most professional security firm in town."

Domini snorted. "He hires itinerant steroid-abusing bodybuilders and the occasional ex-con," she elucidated. "He's not particular about checking references." She gave Reynard a hard look, but he didn't react to her implication.

Holly emerged from the back of the SUV just then, and Domini was relieved to get the show on the road.

"You going to ask me how my romantic life's going?" Holly asked as Domini fell in beside her.

"You're grinning like an idiot. I don't need to ask."

Domini linked arms with Holly, making sure her friend was between her and the back wall of the building. Andy was in front, with Reynard taking the rear. They set a brisk pace. Holly's posse was already filing through the rear door.

Holly swiveled her head to give Reynard a look. "How's things going with Mr. T.?"

"It's only a few feet to the door. We'll talk later."

"You're no fun."

Blatantly listening, Alec said, "That's what I've been telling her."

He appreciated Holly's chuckle and Domini's dirty look, but his attention was drawn to the bouncers on either side of the door. He slipped the dark glasses off to get a better look. Ashe's people obscured his view, but he got a better look as Domini and Holly reached the entrance. The bouncers turned toward them to shield the women further. The one nearest Domini looked at her intently. There was something familiar about the man's profile . . .

The guards who'd flanked the old woman in last night's crowd! He would have seen it sooner if he'd been on top of his game.

Domini caught a glitter from the corner of her eye, and she saw the knife in the door guard's hand when she glanced sideways. She immediately gave Holly a quick, hard shove into the building.

The man lunged at Domini before she could step inside. At her — not Holly. The realization shocked her, but training made her instinctively block the blow and spin out of the line of attack. But there were too many people around them, pressing in on all sides. Caught in the bottleneck around the entrance, she stumbled into someone.

The impact bounced her back toward her attacker, who slashed again. There was nowhere for her to go, and this time the knife grazed her arm. Blood arced out on her hiss of pain.

Someone shouted. Someone else screamed. Bodies bunched up and milled around Domini. She lost sight of her attacker, then he pushed the person between them aside and was on her again. As she blocked another blow, she saw his eyes blazing with fanatical hatred.

"Abomination!"

Alec heard the attacker snarl the ugly word through the cries and shouts as he tossed a dozen people aside to get to Domini. He smelled the scent of her blood — if she had more than a scratch on her, the bastard was dead. No. The bastard *was* dead, period.

The blade was flashing down a third time as Alec finally reached Domini. He pushed her aside and grabbed the attacker's wrist. The man screamed as the bones were crushed, and the knife dropped from his lifeless fingers. Alec considered using it, but rejected it in favor of using his bare hands.

He pushed the man to the ground and dropped down beside him. Alec pressed a thumb into the man's broken wrist, and took great satisfaction at hearing the bastard howl.

"What's going on? Where's Domini?" a voice said.

Alec swore under his breath and looked up to find Maxwell looming over him.

Where *was* she?

He made sure the attacker was unconscious before he sprang up and looked around. Shadows and light played havoc against his aching eyes. People were getting to their feet, pressing forward. The one person he needed was nowhere in sight. Noise and waves of too many strangers' emotions pressed against Alec's strung-out senses.

He turned around in a blur. "Domini!"

And saw her, a crumpled heap in the shadows against the wall. Where he'd pushed her.

He was there instantly. "Domini?"

Maxwell followed. He reached them as Alec gently turned her over. "Is she okay?"

Alec sighed with relief as he felt the life

rushing warm through her veins. He ran his hands over her, through her hair. "A bump on her head," he told Maxwell. "No broken bones." The cut had already stopped bleeding, and Alec gathered her close in his arms.

Maxwell knelt beside them. "Ashe is safe inside. What happened here? How many were there?" He glanced back toward the parking lot. "We've got a lot of bruised people calling 911 on their cell phones."

Alec frowned, knowing that the police and EMTs would be arriving any minute. That was not the way he wanted this played. He looked at Andy Maxwell, eye to eye. After a few moments Maxwell's pupils dilated, his expression went lax. "Go inside," Alec ordered. "Look after Ashe. I'll take care of the situation out here. Go," he ordered.

Maxwell rose to his feet. "Take good care of Domini," he said, and did as Alec said.

"I will."

But first, he set her gently down and returned to the attacker. He extended a claw and slashed it down the man's forearm. As blood flowed, Alec bent forward and took a long, deep breath. The man stirred, then opened his eyes. Alec looked into them, saw the dawning recognition, and the fear.

"I have your scent now," he told the man. "And you the mark of prey. We'll play later."

He heard police sirens approaching, so he backed away, scooped Domini's limp body into his arms, and disappeared through the crowd.

CHAPTER NINETEEN

Far in the distance, Domini heard a telephone ringing. It rang and it rang, and she really wished it would stop, because it made the aching in her head worse.

Miraculously, her wish was granted. But then the ringing was replaced with the sound of a voice. She didn't recognize the voice, but it was familiar, and curiosity made her want to listen. Wanting to listen made her want to wake up, but she figured that would only make her head hurt more. Besides, being awake meant thinking. Nameless fears and dark memories floated in the back of her mind, and she preferred they stay there. If she woke up she'd have to face them.

Though reality phased in and out, the voice went on, and she couldn't help but strain to hear.

"Yes?" Alec's voice was rough, and he was

feeling rougher when he grabbed the telephone receiver. He'd been scrambling through the medicine case open on the kitchen table when he couldn't take the annoyance of the ringing phone any longer. "Who and what?"

"Anthony Crowe," came the answer. "We have Purists in town."

"Tell me about it."

"They tried to break into the clinic. I don't want anyone anywhere near the place until I personally give the all-clear."

Alec recalled that Tony Crowe provided security for the clinic. Crowe also had taken his sarcastic comment literally. "I know about the Purists. We had a run-in with one a couple of hours ago."

"We?"

"He attacked my woman. Not *me,* but my woman. I didn't nail him, but I can track him," he told the local Prime. "You have a problem with that, Tony?"

"I'm not territorial, and no other Prime or the Matri's Consort will object to your protecting your woman. I'll spread the word for you."

"Good. Thanks."

"Wait," Crowe said, and paused a moment. "You're with a mortal, right? I remember her."

Alec fought down a growl at the interest in the other Prime's voice. "We've had that discussion."

Crowe laughed. "Nothing like the jealousy of a bonding Prime. As to your lady, why would the Purists — ?"

"I have no idea." After a thoughtful pause, Alec said, "Maybe you can help. You're the private dick."

"I've been known to be public about it. But I was young and blood-drunk at the time. Have you asked her why she was their target?"

"Not yet; she's unconscious. She knows nothing about us. Or them. I'm sure of that. But they have something against her. Can you look into it? Just in case I don't get a chance to ask when I track down the one who bled her."

Vampires took a fatally dim view of anyone causing their loved ones blood loss. Blood was sacred, the blood of a lover a sacrament. And blood paid with blood. The mortal vampire hunters were well aware of vampire beliefs and taboos. They desecrated these beliefs with hatred and contempt whenever they got the chance.

"I'll see what I can do," Crowe answered. "In fact —"

"What?"

"Never mind. I just recalled something. It's probably not anything, so I'm not saying until I check it out. But why don't you ask your lady if the word *blackbird* has any meaning for her? I'll be in touch."

Though she lay on the couch in the living room, Alec became aware of a slight change in Domini's breathing, of her consciousness focusing. She'd been drifting in and out of wakefulness for a while, he realized, but awareness of her state had only grown gradually in him.

"Fine," he answered impatiently. "Thanks, Tony."

Alec put down the handset, gulped down a quick selection of pills, and hurried toward the living room.

"Well, don't you look like death warmed over, Ms. Lancer?"

Domini sat up slowly, then gingerly lifted her aching head to discover Reynard leaning against a doorframe, arms crossed over his chest. The room was lit only by a few pillar candles on several tables. Reynard was wearing a white Oxford shirt tucked into dark slacks, with the sleeves rolled up over his forearms. The expression on his face was concerned.

"Why am I at your place?"

"You weren't injured badly enough to take to the emergency room." His nonchalance was grating. He sauntered into the room and took a seat beside her. Very close beside her.

Domini slowly turned her head enough to look at him. He brushed his thumb across her forehead. She was caught between the urges to lean forward and back away. She wasn't sure whether accepting or rejecting the comforting warmth of his touch would be cowardly. Getting up would probably make her dizzy, if being so near Reynard didn't do it to her first. She felt grungy and rumpled, and resented that he'd been able to shower and change while she'd been out. Well, at least they both didn't smell like the grimy residue of a back alley.

Alley? No, not quite. They'd been in back of —

"How's your head?"

"Aching." She automatically touched the small bump just above her left temple. "What hit me?"

"A wall."

"A whole wall for one little lump?"

"I put ice on the lump," he told her.

She didn't even have the strength to stiffen in alarm when he put his arm around her. She didn't go so far as to rest her weary head on Reynard's shoulder, but she did lean it on the long, strong arm across the back of the couch. She closed her eyes, breathed in clean masculine scent, and tried to piece together the events that had brought them to this spot. She supposed that she must have been struck, but —

"Do you have any memory at all of what happened?"

She kept her eyes closed and murmured, "I'm thinking about it."

"Want me to fill you in?"

"I hope it doesn't come to that."

"You're not feebleminded."

"But feeling pretty feeble at the moment."

She felt the soft chuckle ripple through him all along her side. It was pleasant to be so close to him. She didn't know how she could be so suspicious of this man, yet so comfortable with him sometimes. Why did being so close to Reynard come so easily; why did wanting him bubble just under the surface? Probably because she'd been knocked on the head. People with head injuries were not responsible for —

"How's your arm?"

"My arm?"

"You were scratched."

"Oh. That explains why it stings. Didn't notice until you mentioned it. It's not important."

"Really?"

She didn't mistake the dangerous edge to his tone, but she was distracted by another thought. There was something important she was missing. Some responsibility. What responsibility was she forgetting?

"Holly!" She sat up straight as alarm bolted through her. "Good God, where's Holly?"

He glanced at a wall clock. "Probably off-stage by now. Though I believe her sets can go on for several hours if the mood takes her."

"You mean — she's at the club? But she was —" Memory flooded back. She jumped to her feet, ignoring the momentary dizziness. "Attacked. There was a man with a knife. I didn't —"

"Holly wasn't attacked. You were."

"— protect her," Domini finished over his words.

She rubbed her hands nervously across her face while her stomach tied itself up in aching knots. She was an idiot. A fool. A complete fuckup.

His hands landed and locked on her shoulders, and he pulled her to him. She looked up to meet furious green eyes.

"Shit happens!" Reynard exploded. "If there's one thing I learned in the army, it's that no matter how hard you plan and prepare, sometimes the op gets blown to hell. You were set up, Domini, ambushed. People you thought you could trust turned on you. You couldn't see it coming. None of us saw it coming. You did nothing wrong. When you saw the knife, you got Ashe out of danger. You put her inside the building, well out of harm's way. It was *you* the bastard went after. You. Do you even know why?"

Domini was acutely aware of being held in a steel grip, of the fact that they were standing so very close together. She was even more aware of the strong emotion that sang through him, into her. The air thrummed around them, grew heated.

She blinked and found her voice through the crackle of tension. "I really wish you'd stop moving at the speed of light," she told him. "It's disconcerting."

He drew her even closer. She could swear she saw fire dancing in those hypnotic green eyes. "You want disconcerting?" He kissed her.

It was a big mistake. A terrible mistake. And Alec reveled in it.

Bad idea, Domini thought. Very bad idea. Her arms came around him. Her mouth opened beneath his. *Very good kiss.*

His hands moved over her. Hard warrior's

hands, but his touch was almost tentative, in exciting contrast to his harsh, hungry kiss. Reynard touched her as though she were fragile, some precious creature made of glass. It only made her want more.

Tentative or not, those hands were quick and clever. Her short little skirt was pooled around her feet within moments. She laughed against his mouth, and felt it send a shiver through him.

His hands skimmed up her hips, up her back, and under the thin knit top she was wearing. *The man has practice in unhooking bras.*

He cupped her breasts, then his head moved down to cover a nipple.

Practice in touching. Practice in tasting.

Her back arched as she let out a sharp gasp, and she barely noticed when he drew them both down to their knees. The wood floor was smooth and cool. She was melting. It was like nothing she'd ever expected.

He caught her surprise and wonder, caught the thought that she'd never expected to be so aroused. He was not her first lover, but the first who sparked passion. It was a sweet thing to his pride, and it also hurt him to learn that she'd been so disappointed before.

"Never again." He whispered the word

against her breast, too low for her to hear. It was hard for him to keep from taking everything he wanted, to keep the possessive animal at bay.

He loved the way her body felt, velvet skin curving over firm muscle. He stroked her — oh, so carefully — holding back. Holding on.

"This isn't safe," he told her when his mouth came back to hers.

"No," she whispered. "But it's helping the headache."

"I won't hurt you." The words were intense, like a vow.

He tried to pull back, but she held on tight. She saw concern cross his face, so fierce it looked like pain, but she wasn't about to let him get away. She wasn't going to let this stop.

She grabbed Reynard's shirtfront and pulled. Buttons popped. Once his chest was bare, she moved to kiss his throat, then farther down. While his hands fisted at his sides, her fingers kneaded his shoulders and long lean back, smoothed down to his narrow waist. His scent was pure erotic perfume, sharp and clean and —

And she was suddenly aware of her own sweat, and the grit of dirt on her skin and in her hair. "I'm filthy. How can you stand me?"

His eyes were half closed, and gleamed like a cat's. Candlelight suited him, the shadows softening the stark lines of his face. But nothing softened the coiled tension in him; the shadows only seemed to bring that out more.

While he knelt there watching her with those burning cat's eyes, Domini rose to her feet and pulled her shirt and bra over her head. She'd never known such power, knowing that he couldn't take his eyes off her, that she was making him sweat, making him hard. She couldn't take her eyes off him, either. She could barely breathe for wanting him. Lust sang through her, heat rose in her, and she couldn't help but run her hands down her body, reveling in her own desire.

She remembered the dark dreams she'd had recently, how all the images of monsters had tangled up her thinking about the real man, in her fears about bad sex. She threw back her head and laughed at such foolishness.

Domini stepped back and held out her hands. "Come on, I won't hurt you," she said. "Where's your shower?"

It wasn't just a shower, it was a perfect-for-sex shower, a double-sized cubicle with a seat and mirror tiles and lots of water nozzles set to spray in all directions. He hadn't let her turn on the lights, but there were candles in the bathroom, too. The reflection of their lights glowed on the tiles like stars through mist. By the time he was naked, steam was rising from the water jets and he followed her inside. The shower gel she cupped in her hands was scented with juniper. It glided smoothly over both their skins.

Skin slick with water and fragrant soap, Domini wrapped herself around him, immediately guided him inside her, and exploded with her first orgasm, too consumed with need to want anything but more.

She could eat him alive and still not have enough.

Alec moaned as she closed in around him, a hot, tight, sweet, engulfing pressure. The force of sensation when he entered Domini set him reeling. Her orgasm slammed into his senses, lightning-swift and hot. He collapsed, falling back onto the shower bench, bringing her with him. Streams of hot water pulsed against his skin, flowed over them. The pleasure was almost painful, the desire almost too consuming. She rode him in a white-hot frenzy.

Alec held on to her and let it happen. He couldn't take control. He couldn't lose control. He buried his face between her breasts and rolled with the thundering rhythm of her heartbeat. The blood surged powerfully beneath her skin, hot wine spiced with sex. Alec craved and craved and fought the craving.

No teeth! No teeth! No teeth!

The mantra was accompanied by a pulsing ache where fangs tried to extend into his mouth. He tasted blood on his tongue, but it was his own. He wanted to howl like a maddened wolf, but only panting moans of pleasure escaped him. The woman pounded against him, driving him deeper and deeper into her, wild, relentless. Her orgasms shot through him like bullets, only making matters worse, better, totally beyond bearing.

After an endless glorious time, Alec couldn't take it anymore. He grabbed Domini around the waist and tumbled them out of the shower. They fell, soaking wet, onto the cool tiles of the bathroom floor. He rose above her and moved into her in swift, hard strokes that quickly brought them up, up, and explosively over the edge.

For a long moment, Alec went white blind with the blended sensations. Then the world went dark, and after a moment's panic he realized his eyes were closed.

"It's all right," he rasped, stroking the drowsy Domini's wet hair. "Everything's all right."

She stirred a little, caressed his cheek, and gave a long, satisfied sigh. "Everything's fine," she agreed drowsily.

Alec reached into the shower to turn off the water. Then he helped her to sit up and grabbed towels. When they were reasonably dry, he hauled her over his shoulder and carried her into the bedroom. She made no protest when he laid her on the bed and fell in beside her. She might have been asleep before she hit the mattress. Just as he was, a second later.

CHAPTER TWENTY

Alec felt much better, even though he hadn't slept for long. So good that he wanted to howl in triumph at the moon, to mark a notch in the bedpost with a claw, to laugh, and to cry out — and to sleep. Deep, dreamless, restful sleep called to him. He hadn't felt so good in weeks. Some of the tension was drained from him, some of the pain. Even some of the fear of madness had eased, from having kept the animal side of his nature at bay for now.

Maybe Serisa had been right. He desperately needed physical release. He desperately needed Domini, and he had managed, at least this once, to make love in the mortal way. He still wanted, craved, the sharing of blood, the mating of mind, soul, and flesh — but if he let himself go now, the dream images would turn to ugly reality. He sighed.

When he did, Domini shifted position.

Her hair brushed across his chest, tracing a line of pleasure across his sensitized skin. He reacted with a gasp, and a deep chuckle.

She was nearly asleep, but she stirred at the sound. "Did I tickle you?"

It was something like a tickle, he supposed, though he wasn't sure exactly what being tickled felt like. He longed to explain how his kind experienced sensation differently than their mortal cousins, more intensely. But he couldn't explain with words; he could only explain by taking her there. A normal mortal could not share the intensity, but a bondmate was no normal mortal.

"You could call it ticklish," he told her.

"So now I know one of your secrets," she murmured, and settled back to dozing.

And I know none of yours. For it occurred to him that Domini did indeed have secrets, at least one, and it was deathly dangerous.

It was a secret he needed to know if he was going to protect her. Going into her mind to find out what he needed would be the easy way, especially in her relaxed state. Easy, but not ethical. He'd invaded her mind once already, out of desperation and the need to protect her, and he knew damn well that doing so had been wrong, even though it had seemed like a good idea at the time.

What did he know about Domini

Lancer? He held her close. He knew that she could see the future in fits and starts, but she thought that was all she could do. She worked hard, lived alone, had a soft spot for wild animals like condors and coyotes that many others thought of as scavengers and pests. She loved her grandfather and had at least one good friend. She had magnificent breasts, he added as she shifted against him again. And she smelled great.

Alec determinedly turned away from thinking about Domini's physical attributes. "You awake?" he asked.

"No," she answered.

"Talk to me," he urged. "Tell me about yourself."

He felt her float a little closer to full consciousness. He liked the way she felt, drifting like that, her thoughts as well as her body at rest. It soothed his own tense spirit.

"Tell me about your family," he suggested. "Brothers? Sisters? Parents?"

"No. No. Dead."

She didn't feel so relaxed now. Pain welled up from under the satiated contentment, like a little rift of lava finding the surface of the earth.

"How did your parents die?"

Domini stiffened beside him. She took a

tight breath and said, "Five-car pile-up on the freeway. They weren't the only ones who didn't walk away."

"Were you with them when —"

"No." Definitive. Angry. "I didn't see it coming, either. I was surfing when my parents died. Having a good time when I should have —"

"Psychics frequently never see anything really important about their own futures," he said. "It's a defense mechanism; it helps to keep you sane. If you know the hard stuff that's coming, you're more likely to freeze than try to avoid it."

"Bullshit." She freed herself from his arms, sat up, and turned to look at him.

"It's a gift, Domini."

"Curse. It's getting worse all the time. And what the hell do you know about being psychic?"

He sat up and propped his hands behind his head as he leaned against the headboard, to keep from grabbing her. She had no idea how arousing she was, naked and burning with anger. "I'm psychic," he said. "In a different way than you are, but I'm the last one who'd call you crazy."

"That's not reassuring, Reynard."

Her reaction sparked answering anger in him. He grabbed Domini, using the swiftness she found so disconcerting, and pulled her close. "Suddenly we aren't friends anymore?" His voice was a low whisper brushing across her lips.

She grew hot with fury, and he grew hard against her.

"We aren't —"

He had her beneath him in an instant. Within seconds, he proved to her that they were more than friends. He made love to her swift and hard, and it burned off the anger in both of them, turning it into quick, satisfying lust. She writhed eagerly beneath him, rose to meet him, and they came together in the same explosive instant.

Alec lay, stunned, on top of Domini for a long time. Slowly he became aware of her fingers brushing tenderly up and down his back, and through his hair. He didn't think she was mad at him anymore.

He didn't blame her for the anger, not when he'd stirred up an old, deep pain.

Alec finally rolled off Domini and off the bed. He put on the clothes he'd stripped off earlier, then pulled a long shirt out of a drawer and draped it over Domini's naked belly.

"I see that you only have the one tattoo."

"Uh-huh." She lifted her head a little from where she lay delightfully spread-eagled on the mattress. She touched the shirt. "What's this for?"

Alec looked down at her hungrily. "While I appreciate the view, it's far too tempting to see you like that. Get dressed; we need to talk."

"Don't want to talk." She held a hand up, languid as a cat. "I want to —" she sighed. "Sleep, if nothing else. Too tired to —"

He took her wrist and pulled her to her feet. He drew her close for one hard, possessive kiss. When he stopped kissing her, Domini collapsed against him, her head on his shoulder.

"That was supposed to stimulate you."

"You've stimulated me enough for one night."

He rubbed a hand up and down her back and cupped her behind. Then he moved away from her before an erection could take his mind off of anything but having her again.

"If you won't let me go to sleep, can I at least sit down?"

"Fine." Alec eased her down on the edge of the bed, then made himself take a seat in the chair. Touching her would not help him stay clear-headed.

"How's your head feel?"

Domini was confused. Muscles in areas

she hadn't used for a while were strained and aching, but not in a bad way. The man was hung like the proverbial horse. It occurred to her that she hadn't checked the number of testicles he sported when she had the chance. Holly would be disappointed in her lack of observational skills.

"Holly," she muttered, putting a hand to her forehead. "Now I remember why I had a headache."

"Had," Reynard repeated. "Good. It's gone."

"I'm a fast healer." She glanced toward a clock on the bedside table. "Is that A.M. or P.M.?"

"A.M."

"Damn." She gave him an annoyed look. "Reynard, do you always stay up all night?"

"Frequently. Why did someone try to kill you?" He stabbed a finger at her. "Don't try to pretend he was after Holly; Holly was the decoy used to find you. How? Why?"

"I figured that out."

Alec sat back in the chair, crossed his arms, and stretched out his long legs. Domini noted that some of the candles that lit the room had burned out. She was rather glad of the semi-darkness; the candlelight lent an intimacy to the scene that made it easier for her to confide in him.

"I went through all the letters the stalkers sent her again," she told him. "This time I focused on the number of times the word *abomination* was used. It only appeared twice, both times in reference to Holly's childhood. *Abomination from birth* was one term. *Abomination's child* was also used. The first time I read the letters, everything seemed like the ramblings of a vicious, deranged mind. Coming at it from a fresh angle, it occurred to me that maybe, just maybe, they weren't talking about Holly, but about someone she's known all her life." Domini twisted her hands tightly together. "Me."

"But you didn't really believe it until someone came at you with a knife."

"I didn't really believe it even then," she admitted. "That's why I didn't react fast enough. It shocked the hell out of me, and I froze."

"Because you can't think of any reason why anyone would attack you?"

She nodded. "Or why anyone would set up an elaborate smokescreen to get at me. If someone wants to harm me —"

"Kill you."

She acknowledged the brutal truth with a nod, even as a cold shiver went through her. "I'm easy enough to find," she finished.

"Why go to all this trouble? How'd they connect me to Holly? No, wait." She lifted a finger. "I think I know that one."

He tilted his head sideways. "Really?"

"An unauthorized biography of Holly was published recently. I'm mentioned in it."

"Any photos?"

Domini thought this a strange question, but nodded. "I'm in a couple of photos a high-school classmate sold to the sleaze who wrote the book. But why would anyone come after me because of pictures from when we were teenagers?"

He shrugged. "I don't know. Just throwing out questions. There are people in this world who take great pains to stay in the shadows. This sort of cloak-and-dagger plot is their style."

She gave him a hard look. "So speaks the black-ops operative?"

He nodded. "Does the word *blackbird* have meaning for you?"

"It was my grandmother's nickname." A knot fisted in her stomach. "Why?"

"I have no idea. But a private investigator I asked to look into this asked me to ask you."

"Why would he — ?"

"I don't know. I'll be sure to ask him when he checks in."

Domini rose and began to pace the room. Fear raced through her. "Maybe this has something to do with my grandfather. Maybe they're trying to hurt him through me."

Alec felt her worry, and wished he'd never brought the subject up. He should have spent the night hunting down the one who'd attacked Domini, instead of making love to her.

Tomorrow, he thought. I'll find the bastard tomorrow night. Dawn wasn't far off and his eyes were beginning to ache, even though the sun hadn't yet inched over the horizon.

He rose from his seat and stepped in front of Domini, cutting off her restless pacing. He took her in his arms and looked into her eyes. "Don't worry. There's nothing we can do right now. Everyone's safe for now."

Domini nodded. Alec didn't like using the hypnotic tone on her, but she needed rest as much as he did. He turned her toward the bedroom, eased her down onto the bed, and slipped in beside her. He aroused her, then made love to her as the candles burned out one by one. By the time he could feel sunlight pressing against the thickly insulated bedroom curtains, Domini was sleeping peacefully in his arms.

With her beside him, despite the pain, Alec found peace enough to quiet the beast inside and to sleep himself.

CHAPTER TWENTY-ONE

Domini woke up remembering that she'd had a dream where someone called her Blackbird, but she couldn't quite remember when. Not last night, she thought. Last night? What time was it now?

She opened her eyes and looked at the bedside clock. "Is that A.M. or P.M.?"

"P.M.," Reynard answered.

"Oh, my God!"

An arm like a steel bar came over her when she tried to sit up. The body beside her was firm, warm, and scented with sleep. The room was dark but not unfamiliar. The bed was comfortable, and she felt like she'd shared it with this man all her life.

It didn't surprise her that she'd slept through the day and into the night. With everything that had happened, she'd been totally wasted.

"How's your head?"

Domini thought about it for a minute. "Spinning."

"You're dizzy? Are you in pain?"

She smiled at the concern in Reynard's voice; it sent a pang of joy through her to know that he cared. Oh, dear.

"Confused," she answered. "Chagrined. No physical pain." She tried sitting up again, but his arm was immovable. "I ought to make some calls."

"Already made."

He smiled, which sent a flutter through her. She had to clear her throat before she said, "You talked to my grandfather? You told him what happened?"

His gaze darted away from hers. Was he blushing? "Not exactly," he replied. "I called the office, and got us both a sick day."

"Bought us some time," she said. "Before we get fired."

"You needed the rest."

"I needed the job." Wanted the job. Loved the job. Had believed she'd never break any of the company rules.

She needed to talk to her grandfather. What surprised her was that lust had so easily overridden her ethics. She'd never thought passion could catch her off guard like that. Now she had to face her grandfather's disappointment. Damn, she hated hurting the Old Man.

Had it been worth it? With a man she didn't know — but every couple started out strangers to each other, didn't they? A formal introduction wasn't needed before the primal mating urge took over and screwed up your life.

Well, she certainly knew Reynard in the biblical sense now. And the urge to continue knowing him wasn't nearly satisfied; the primal craving still burned in her. If she let it loose, they wouldn't get out of bed for a long time yet.

Domini sighed. The longer she put off facing Benjamin Lancer the worse it would be for both of them.

"Can I get out of bed now?"

Reynard sat up and leaned over her. There were dark circles under his eyes and his cheeks seemed a bit more hollow than usual, but he still looked gorgeous to her. He dipped his head to brush his lips over hers.

Domini fought the thrill that went through her. Losing the fight, she ran her hands through his hair and pulled him into a deeper kiss.

Domini closed her eyes and soared, but the niggling of her conscience kept her from completely losing herself. It made her turn her head away and relax the fists she'd pressed against his naked back. Even though she wasn't directly looking at Reynard, she was acutely aware of his disappointment. After a moment, he rolled to his side of the bed. She wanted to follow him, to reach out to him. To —

"Passion sucks," Domini muttered, and sat up.

She was on her back again in an instant. Reynard loomed over her out of the darkness, holding her down. The combination of anger and hurt in his eyes stunned her.

"It's all right to fall in love, Domini." The intensity in his soft whisper was more painful than a shout. "Most people want to fall in love."

Spoken by Reynard, the word sounded big, deep, complicated. It had never occurred to her that anyone would fall in love with her. She was barely coming to terms with the concept of lust, and here was Reynard using the big L word. Guys weren't supposed to be the first one to bring that up, were they? Was Reynard telling her she was in love with him? Was he in love with her?

People didn't fall in love in less than a week.

People fall in love in less than an instant.

Some people fall in love before they even meet.

"I've been looking for you all my life," he said. "You've no idea how long that's been."

His words hit Domini with a double punch that sent her reeling. *He loves me. He's a telepath. He loves me. He's talking inside my head. He loves me. He can read my mind. Can you read my mind?*

Yes.

And he had for days; she realized that now. She'd heard him — talking inside her head. And she'd been answering. It had seemed so, so — natural.

He had told her he was psychic. It wasn't his fault she hadn't paid attention, hadn't asked the right questions. Any questions.

Yet his being in love with her was almost more frightening than his being a telepath. No, not almost. She could get her mind around the concept of his having psychic talent. She didn't want him to be in love with her. Did she? Not that he'd actually told her he was in love with —

I'm in love with you.

She glared. "You're not going to make this easy, are you?"

"Love isn't easy." He gave a short, bitter laugh. "Even lust isn't easy, not when it's a consuming passion."

248

"Passion." She sighed. "Reynard, I'm not even used to the *idea* of passion. It's never happened to me before." With anyone else she would have been embarrassed to admit this, but she owed him the truth. Wanted to give him the truth. "I don't trust you," she pointed out. "I don't even know if I like you."

There was a menacing glitter in his green eyes when he said, "You don't have to like me. But do you love me?"

She was speechless, and afraid. His angular face was the only thing she could see in the dim room. His scent was on her skin, his taste in her mouth. The heat of his body covered hers, and his hands held her down. And her awareness went deeper than fear; it went into the core of her; it pounded through her heart, quickened her pulse, and heated her blood. Her body and her soul whispered that she *wanted, wanted, wanted* him and no other, and her mind was not involved in the equation.

He was a part of her. She couldn't imagine herself separate from this need. Was that love?

"I want to fuck your brains out," she finally answered. "Repeatedly. Is that a good enough answer for now?"

His expression turned bitter, but he said,

"If that's all you can give me, I'll take it. For now."

Domini realized that they'd both used the word *now.* Which implied that they both assumed a future for them, a time together that stretched beyond last night, this bedroom, this moment.

"What am I getting myself into?"

"Life," he answered. "You haven't been living until now."

"Which implies I didn't exist before you came along and got into my pants?"

"Yes."

He didn't sound smug, or arrogant. He sounded sure.

Domini's heart gave a quick, hard lurch, then it melted. She should have been furious or insulted, but instead she —

"Damn it, Reynard, don't do that to me!"

"What?" He touched her cheek. He drew a finger down her throat and chest and came to rest over her heart, where he pressed gently. "Make you feel loved?"

She gulped in air. "Yeah — that."

He shook his head, and dark hair swirled around his sharp and shadowed face. "I can't help it."

Pleasure swept through her, as strong as the passion that drew her to him. The man made her feel, more than anyone ever had.

"It's not the emotions that scare me," she confessed. "It's — there was this pattern to my life. Comfortable. Secure. Now I feel like there's this kaleidoscope under my feet — no set pattern, no —" She shook her head. "Can we stop talking about this now? I need to get up. Go to the bathroom, get dressed, check my voice mail. You know there's —"

"Life outside the bedroom," he finished for her. "Yes. And I could really use a shower."

She sniffed delicately. "You and me both."

He rose to his feet and held out a hand. "Care to join me?"

She laughed and shook her head. "We both know where that would lead." She waved toward the bathroom. "Go ahead." She switched on a bedside lamp and waited until Reynard went into the bathroom before she got up. This gave her the opportunity to study his truly fine backside, and to get out of bed without having him around to look at her. She didn't know why she was suddenly shy about being naked, but she was. She needed clothes on, so she could think about something besides sex. The same way Reynard had done last night, come to think of it.

Maybe they had some things in common, after all.

She pulled on the long T-shirt from the

night before, then padded into the living room, flipping on light switches and lamps as she went. Candlelight might be very romantic, but it wasn't what she wanted right now.

In the living room, she gathered up her abandoned clothes and sat down on the couch. She extracted her cellular phone from the pocket of the miniskirt, flipped it open, and discovered the battery was dead. Domini swore. So much for checking her voice mail. Though she could probably find a phone in the kitchen. She vaguely recalled hearing Reynard talking to someone in there while she was lying in here, recovering from the incident outside the club. Or maybe she'd dreamed it.

"Incident?" She gave a faint, ironic laugh. Someone had come at her with a knife.

And Reynard had saved her, brought her to his home to recover. He had been looking out for her all along. He'd suspected someone was after her, had watched her house, and hired a detective.

She was touched by his concern. Annoyed by his intrusion and his assumption of command over her actions, but maybe that was a D-Boy's idea of a romantic gesture. He was used to being a protector, to being in control and taking independent action.

Maybe she should cut the guy some slack. He told her he loved her, and showed it by protecting her. How could she resent that? She had trouble trusting him — but wasn't that based on dreams, imagination, and a couple of weird visions? Were dreams and visions proof of anything? Other than that she'd been half-crazed with fear of having sex?

It was all *her*, wasn't it? Not him. He hadn't done anything that wasn't kind, caring — loving.

The realization brought a dreamy smile to her lips.

"He attacked my woman. Not me, but my woman. I didn't nail him, but I can track him. You have a problem with that, Tony?"

Domini sat up straight, the smile wiped off her face as the words bubbled up out of her memory. She'd been lying here, half in and half out of consciousness. Reynard was in the kitchen, and she'd overheard him talking to someone on the phone. The detective he'd hired?

"He called me his woman." She sighed, and for a moment the gooey pleasure of being claimed by him almost overwhelmed the memory of the other things he'd said.

He'd called the man Tony. Tony was the detective. Tony had told him to ask her about Blackbird.

She'd had a dream where a man named Tony called her Blackbird. A very vivid dream with vampires in it.

Domini got up and headed into the kitchen. She hoped Reynard kept Pop Tarts or at least frozen bagels around, be cause if he expected "his woman" to go all domesticated on him, he had disappointment in his future.

When she turned on the overhead lights, the first thing she saw was the metal brief-case lying open on the kitchen table. The case was full of pill bottles.

"Drugs," she said, moving to the table to take a closer look. Was Reynard on drugs? Was he dealing drugs? Why *had* Colonel Reynard left the army? She picked up a round bottle that contained large, clear capsules. Turning it in her hand, Domini saw the prescription label. She didn't recognize the name of the drug, but Alexander Reynard's name was on the label, and a doctor's name was also listed, along with the dosage.

Her heart rose and sank almost at the same time. She was relieved that whatever Reynard was taking was legally prescribed by a physician, but she was concerned that he needed to take medicine. Almost panicked that he needed so many different medicines.

What kind of illness required this much treatment?

There was only one she could think of. She wanted to reject it, but the word AIDS rose in her mind. It left her shaking, with fear, with anger, and compassion. Was Reynard HIV-positive? Was the virus in his blood? Was that the true symbolism of her blood-drenched visions?

Had he had unprotected sex with her and not told her?

Domini shook her head fiercely. No. She couldn't believe that of him. Something else had to be wrong with him. He *couldn't* have some fatal disease; she couldn't bear it. Not when she'd just found him.

What could be wrong with him? She remembered that he was sensitive to light. What caused that? Porphyry? Some horrible chemical or biological weapon he'd encountered while defending his country?

Why hadn't he told her? Was there anything she could do to help?

Still worrying, she opened the refrigerator door.

Stacked plastic bags full of neatly labeled, bright red blood took up all the available space on every shelf.

Domini's skin went cold. She didn't believe it at first. This was some sort of nightmare; another hallucination. She could not — *could not!* — be seeing what she saw.

Blood.

Why would Reynard keep blood in his refrigerator? There had to be a logical reason; something to do with his medical condition.

I know why he keeps blood. I know why he moves so fast. I know why he needs such strong sunblock. I know why he pets wild animals. I know why he reads minds.

"I know." Her heart hammered wildly in her chest; she felt hollow with the fear that raced through her. "I know," Domini repeated, and stumbled backward and to her knees. She needed to get up. She needed to run.

"I see you found my stash."

Reynard's voice was soft, pleasantly conversational, and it utterly terrified her.

All she could do was look up, and it was a very long way from where she crouched on her hands and knees, but she made herself meet Alec's gaze.

Only to discover that he was wearing sunglasses in the glare of the kitchen lights. She couldn't look him in the eye, even though she tried. Bastard.

"You're a vampire," she said, even if saying it got her killed. "You really are a vampire."

"Yes," he answered, completely conversationally. "I probably should have told you sooner."

CHAPTER TWENTY-TWO

The bright kitchen lights increased Alec's blazing headache, but he left them on. The light would make Domini feel safer. He moved closer to her, slowly and carefully, hands held out empty before him. He didn't think she took any notice of how nonaggressive he was being. She stared at him, but he wasn't sure she was seeing.

Her emotions, on the other hand, beat at him. She was screaming inside her head, and he could hear it.

But it wasn't with fear.

He reached a hand toward her. "Domini . . ."

She rose to her feet slowly, gracefully, quivering with fury. "I'm not crazy."

"You're not crazy."

"You're a vampire."

"Yes," Alec affirmed again. This did nothing to calm her. Anger flared like neon fire in her bright blue eyes.

"I'm not dreaming this, am I?"

He inched closer and cupped her cheek. "Sweetheart, you haven't dreamed any of it."

She took a sharp breath. "None of it?"

"None."

"You let me think I was *insane?*" Her fist connected with his jaw.

"I can expl—"

"You sent me visions of vampires, didn't you? *Made* me see things."

"Not on purpose! We share —"

"You damn near raped me in a back alley, and made me think it was a dream?!"

Alec's guts twisted with guilt. "I —"

She threw another punch at him, sending his sunglasses flying. Before Domini could try again, Alec had her wrists in a tight grip. "Stop it," he ordered, and twisted her around, holding her back to his chest with her arms crossed in front of her. The intimate embrace wasn't just defensive; he needed her close to him, needed her touch, even though it increased his awareness of her pain and anger. He needed to share those hard emotions, to love all of her even while she hated him. The hate would pass. Or so he prayed.

He closed his eyes against the light. He opened his mind to hers, though he faced a storm, and spoke directly to her, thought to thought.

Listen to me. Just listen. I never meant to impose my — delusions — on you. Never meant to hurt you.

It was real! she silently yelled back. *The bar. The fight. Your winning me. Your hands on me — in me!*

Real, he admitted. *My hands are on you now. Am I hurting you?*

You're holding me prisoner.

I'm keeping you safe.

From what?

Yourself. Me.

Keeping you *safe from* me.

That, too.

Domini could feel Reynard's smile. It was the oddest sensation. It was pleasant, soothing, like a balm on her burning thoughts. She had to fight the urge to calm down, and she fought it by trying to feel beyond Reynard's smile, to probe deeper into the mind touching hers. There was an instant, less than a heartbeat, when she stepped through a door, into fire. Saw the twisted face in the flames.

The door slammed on her faster than she'd found it.

No! You can't — see me — know me like I am now.

259

There was anguish in his thoughts, real fear and shame. Fear for her. Shame at what she'd seen.

Why not? Domini demanded.

Remember the bad dreams you've had? Those were my bad dreams, too.

Domini didn't understand what she'd seen deep inside his mind; it had been too brief, too intense, to take in. But she remembered the dreams.

We'll share so much, Domini. All the good things. You have my promise. Later, when I'm more myself.

How much more yourself could a vampire be? she asked. *Showing fangs? Turning into a bat or a wolf, sucking blood? Ripping out throats and —*

"Spare me the gory details, please."

He sounded so exhausted, Domini almost wanted to hug him. "Spare *you?* You're the scary one."

"I never set out to frighten you."

How could he say that? And sound so very sincere? There was a fire inside this creature. Chained violence, she realized, horrible dark urges trying to get out. He had a grip on her that was unbreakable, arms like steel binding her close to him.

"I'm at your mercy," she reminded him. The fact that she had to remind him seemed almost ludicrous.

He kissed the side of her throat. Domini stiffened, waiting for the sharp prick of fangs, the spurt of blood. What she felt were soft, warm lips, the brush of his breath against her skin. It felt good, and it set her shivering, partly with anticipation of pain, partly with longing.

Damn it! How could she still desire him, knowing what he was? *I've been screwing the living dead, for God's sake!*

Reynard pressed his hips closer to her, and she could feel that one part of him certainly wasn't dead.

Neither is the rest of me. "I was born a vampire. I've never been a mortal. It doesn't work that way. Not with Primes. I should have told you about myself sooner," he went on. "Or not at all. We shouldn't have become lovers yet, even though it was meant to be."

"Meant?"

"We were born to be mated," Alec said. "Bonded. To be together for as long as we both shall live. I understand that you can't feel it yet, not with the way I am now. And I don't blame you for fearing the monster inside me; I shouldn't have approached you so soon. But fate led me to you, and you to me. Remember the market?"

Fear fisted Domini's heart. "The dream —

261

compulsions? It was you? You called me there?"

"I was drawn to you. You to me. That's how a bond begins. We happened to be in the same area at the same time, close enough for our dreams to touch."

"Right."

"No, that's how it really works. I wasn't looking for you. I came to L.A. to take the cure —"

"Cure? You guys have a vampire Betty Ford Clinic? You're trying to stop being a vampire?"

"I can't stop being a vampire. I don't want to. My body is rejecting the medicines that let me live in the daylight world. I don't *need* to live in daylight, but I want to."

"All that stuff in the case — that's anti-vampire medicine?"

"You aren't listening to me, are you?"

Domini tested his hold on her, but though his grip wasn't painful, there was no breaking away from him. They were locked together until Reynard decided to let her go. "I'm paying attention," she said. "How can I not be?"

"Because you won't let me get past your preconceived ideas of what a vampire should be."

"There's a monster inside you," she reminded him. "Isn't that what a vampire is?"

They were so close that she felt his shrug all through her. "Let's talk about us."

She knocked her head back against his shoulder. Maybe she couldn't hurt him, but she could still express her anger. "Us?"

He remained infuriatingly calm and patient. "You already know I love you, even if you won't believe it. As for that beast inside me — yes, I fear what I could do to you, and I fight it. I'll never hurt you. And soon you'll realize that you can have no other lover."

She didn't *want* any other lover. She hadn't wanted him, to begin with. Even before she knew he was a vampire, she knew he brought too much complication to her life.

No — he brought color to what had been a black-and-white life. Once you saw in color, how did you live without it?

"No other lover sounds terribly romantic," she said.

"Doesn't it?" His cheek brushed across hers. It was freshly shaved and smelt of soap, all normal and nice. "I am a romantic. All Primes are."

Her skin tingled where he'd touched her. It would be easier if there was at least a whiff of rotting corpse or evil about him.

"Prime. What's that?"

"Prime male of my Clan. Prime of the Fox

Clan," he answered, and there was pride in his tone, arrogance. "Alpha male, you'd say, only much more so. We're a testosterone-intensive species, we vampires. Our men more male, our women the ultimate in female."

She couldn't believe it, but a bolt of jealousy went through her. "Vamp girls are the ultimate in female, huh? Then why'd you pick me?"

"It was meant to be."

That seemed to be his answer to a lot of things. "I don't believe in fate."

"You can see the future."

"Yeah, but . . ." Okay, he had her there. "Only sometimes."

"The ability will improve and stabilize after we've been together for a while. I'll help you free all your mental abilities. And —" He kissed her throat again, and the back of her neck. It set her quivering. "There are many ways I'll teach you to feel, to excel."

Good lord, but she was dancing with the devil here. He made such sweet promises: of love forever, of carnal delights, of knowledge and power. "Tempting," she admitted. But that was the devil's job, wasn't it? "Will you let go of me now? Please?"

"Will you run?"

"Would I have a chance if I did?"

"No."

"Then I won't try to run." *Not yet.*

Alec heard her thought, but he loosed his hold and stepped back. He didn't expect trust and belief to come instantly. Not with a beginning like this. He almost wished he hadn't walked into Lancer Services a few days ago. But if he hadn't, he wouldn't have been there to protect Domini from the Purists.

And he still didn't know why the most fanatical group of the vampire hunters were after her. The fact that the Purist used a knife meant that the grudge was very personal. Why?

Her safety and the reasons why he needed to keep her safe were really the most important matters for them to deal with right now.

She'd backed away from him, all the way across the kitchen. She wasn't checking the room for exits, but she was deliberately not looking at him, either. She was trying to physically and mentally distance herself from him.

He had a terrible headache again, some of it from the angry energy she'd poured into him. Her fear hurt him; it also enraged that part of him she called monster. The monster wanted to throw her across the kitchen table and take her, to force blood as well as sex on her. Once she tasted him, she wouldn't be so superior, so disparaging. She'd crawl on her knees to beg the monster for one drop more of what only a vampire could give.

The monster, of course, was the damned pubescent part of him that he had to keep in line. He absolutely could not risk sharing blood with Domini while the beast was so close to breaking free. The pills were only so much help. If a new serum wasn't developed soon, he was going to have be locked away from civilization until his body made the adjustment back to the nightside of life on its own. But how could he abandon Domini when she was in danger?

"Where's Dr. Casmerek when I need him?" he muttered.

Domini jumped, and pivoted to face him. "What?"

He didn't answer but moved slowly, every movement as nonthreatening as he could make it. He picked up his sunglasses and turned off the kitchen lights. "That's better."

"I can't see in the dark," she protested.

"It's after dawn." As she glanced toward the lowered shades over the kitchen's window, he added, "I don't have to look outside to know when the sun rises. It's a vampire thing," he replied to her skeptical look.

"I don't want to know about vampire things."

"You must know something about vampires," he told her. "Otherwise vampire hunters wouldn't be after you. That's who tried to murder you. They're called Purists."

She shook her head. "I've never heard of them. Until a few minutes ago I truly believed vampires were fictional, the stuff of horror movies and bedtime stories."

Alec glanced at her over the top of his sunglasses. "Bedtime stories? You must have had an interesting childhood."

"My grandfather likes horror stories." She twisted her hands together nervously.

He walked toward her. "I think you're keeping family secrets."

She backed up as he approached. "I don't know any family secrets. I mean, I don't have family secrets. The Lancers —"

"Blackbird."

"You keep my grandmother out of this!"

"I think I'd better ask your grandfather about this woman."

Domini stopped retreating and stood facing him squarely, her hands on her hips. "Oh, no, you don't! It's too close to the anniversary of when he lost her. He doesn't — he's never dealt with the loss. I won't have you upsetting him."

She looked like a tigress, and Alec smiled fondly at her defense of the old man she loved. But his judgment was that the man didn't need or want protecting.

"You're the one who needs protecting, Domini," Alec reminded her. "It would hurt your grandfather as much to lose you as it did to lose his wife. You don't want to see him devastated by loss again, do you?"

Domini's lips compressed, and her nostrils flared with an angry breath. She shook her head. "Oh, you're good, Reynard."

He held his hands out in front of him. "I know." He looked her over and said, "While I think you look delightful wearing nothing but my shirt, I think your grandfather would prefer it if you were showered and dressed. Even in what little you were wearing last night."

He was sure she'd accept any excuse to put off his confronting the Old Man. And Alec wanted her out of sight long enough so that he could take this morning's prescription cocktail without having her there. While he intended to share his life with her, he was still a Prime, unwilling to show any weakness. Even the weakness of downing a few pills.

"Go on," he urged when she hesitated. He offered her a smile, and further incentive. "Then when you're ready, I'll let you drive the Jaguar."

CHAPTER TWENTY-THREE

The drive to Malibu through heavy morning traffic was a grim, silent affair, with Domini growing more nervous by the second. Once at the house, she dragged out every step toward the door.

There, she turned on Reynard and demanded, "Don't you have to ask permission to enter a dwelling or something?"

He answered by twisting the doorknob until the lock broke and pushing her into the house ahead of him. Breaking in so casually set off a very sophisticated alarm system, one that he found and almost instantly shut down. The skill had nothing to do with being a vampire, Domini supposed. More than likely, breaking, entering, and securing a residence was training he'd gotten from the United States government. At the moment, she didn't particularly approve of this use of her tax money.

Once the alarms were neutralized, Reynard sighed, and some of the tension went out of him. Domini realized that the morning light must be bothering him badly, despite his sunglasses and sunblock.

She tried to curb any feelings of sympathy and headed straight for the kitchen. She hoped to somehow warn her grandfather . . . but he wasn't in the kitchen for her to warn.

The room was empty, and for some reason this frightened her. Maybe she'd really been counting on him to rescue her. Grandpa'd always been there for her before.

"There's no one here," Reynard said, after he drew the blinds to shield the room from the bright light coming through the deck doors facing the ocean. "We're alone."

There was an empty stillness inside the house, easy enough for Domini to detect once she filtered out the outside sounds of the ocean, the wind, and the gulls. Where was the Old Man?

Her first thought was that something had happened to him, but there was no sign of any struggle. All looked normal: there were dishes in the sink, the dregs of coffee in a mug, and breadcrumbs on a cutting board. A glance at the clock on the microwave showed her that it was later in the morning than she'd thought.

"He's at the office," Reynard concluded. He put a hand on her arm. "Let's go."

Domini shook him off. "Give me a minute."

She expected the vampire to drag her off, or at least protest, but Reynard stepped back and stood very still, his hands balled into fists at his sides, while she picked up the telephone handset. Domini felt a desperate need to catch up with the real world after several days of visiting the Twilight Zone. One way to reconnect seemed to be to call home to check her voice mail. Of the dozen messages in the inbox, only two were of any importance. One was from Holly.

"Andy said you saved my butt, then went off to have mad, passionate sex with Mr. Testicles. Actually, he said that you got hurt and Mr. T. was taking care of you. You aren't hurt bad, are you? You and Mr. T. are finally screwing like bunnies, right? You must be, or I would have heard from you. I *will* hear from you soon, Lancer. Thanks for taking care of me during the L.A. visit. The Venice show went off fine last night. I'm at the airport right now, off to Vancouver in a few minutes. Andy and a team are coming with to keep me safe on the road. Jo's meeting me there, so wish me luck and love. Wish you the same. Call."

"Wish you both," Domini said, and saved the message.

The other message was from her grandfather. He'd left it an hour earlier. "If you happen to decide to put in an appearance, I'll be at the office. Come in. We need to talk. Maxwell assures me that you're all right. I'm assuming you're catting around with Reynard. If so, consider your ass fired. Both your asses. Come talk to me anyway."

"Thanks, Grandpa." She saved that message, too. She put the phone back on the wall base.

"Let's go," Reynard said, taking her arm. "He wants to see us."

It occurred to her that he probably had extra good hearing, along with the other superpowers. "He didn't say he wanted to talk to you."

"But I want to talk to him." Reynard gave her a thin, tight smile, as though that was all he had the energy to offer. "Besides, maybe I want to be old-fashioned and ask for your hand."

"You can have the hand, if you promise to leave the old man alone."

Anger flashed over his already stern expression. "Come on." He tugged her back toward the front of the house. "Let's go."

Despite the growing heat of the morning, the dimness inside the office parking garage was blessedly cool against Alec's burning skin. It was much easier to see in here than out on the street. After he closed the car door, he leaned against it and took deep breaths, no longer feeling like he was drowning in light.

Even with the sunscreen, glasses, and dark polarized windows, riding in the car left him so sunsick, he was blind and wracked with pain when he finally stepped out into the parking garage. He knew it was a bad idea to leave Domini alone behind the wheel of the Jaguar, but he had to regain control before walking into the Lancer offices.

He was relieved that she made no effort to start the car and drive away. Oh, he could catch her if he had to, but the temper fit that would follow would not be good for their relationship. He hoped she sensed he was on the edge and was reacting with appropriate discretion.

Alec hooked his sunglasses onto the neck of his T-shirt and pressed his palms against his aching eyes. Even a week ago, sunlight had felt good against his skin; his vision had been sharp and clear both day and night. He could barely remember now how he'd noticed that his body was beginning to betray him. He'd been concerned but confident that Casmerek's renowned clinic would soon put everything to rights. He'd come in for a tune-up; he hadn't meant to go through hell. The treatment was complicated by the physical and psychic changes brought on by bonding. Maybe he should have mentioned it to Casmerek, but Prime pride and possessive paranoia got in the way.

He had the Purists to blame for this torture, as well. They threatened not only Domini but the clinic. The first serum hadn't worked, but the clinic was still his best hope. If he could get back there —

There was another way, of course. He could accept the night, give up sunlight and the discipline it took to live side by side with humans. It would only take blood and sex to ease the pain of the transition. Alec smiled, and felt the throb of fangs just beneath skin. He was so weary. It would be easy to give up, give in.

And betray everything the Clans stand for.

He wasn't a selfish Tribe boy, to do what he wanted when he wanted, or a pragmatic male of the Families, who did what was convenient in the name of survival. He was

Clan. He'd taken vows. Honor meant something, even though it was driving him mad.

Alec sighed. Soon he wasn't going to have a choice. Clan, Family, or Tribe, he was still a vampire. Nature would have its way eventually.

But not yet. For Domini's sake, he'd abide by the rules as long as he could.

He forced his eyes to focus, his senses to be alert. The sooner he talked with Ben Lancer, the sooner he could get on with hunting the Purist who'd attacked Domini.

Besides his red Jaguar, three dark Mercedeses, a black Hummer, and a dark blue Lincoln Navigator were parked in the Lancer office slots. There was a white Grand Cherokee parked near the building entrance, but no other cars occupied the spaces on this level.

Alec went around to the driver's-side door and opened it. "You have no idea how noble I'm being," he informed the woman he loved.

He took her hand and helped her out of the low-slung sports car. She didn't need the help, but his touch was a warning not to run. The feel of her soft skin on his was a comfort as well, and kept his mind off the pain.

"You all right?" she asked him.

He noted that Domini was annoyed with

herself for caring, but she did care.

"Maybe you should go home, lie down, and have a rest —"

"Come on." He twined his fingers firmly with hers and led her toward the building entrance.

He was taken by surprise when the door of the white Jeep opened as they neared it. Alec let out an angry snarl, thrust Domini behind him, and spun to face the Jeep. Instinct told him to make the leap with all claws and fangs extended, and he was barely able to hold instinct at bay. Instinct should also have let him know the other Prime was nearby before he actually saw him.

Anthony Crowe stepped cautiously to the concrete and held a hand out toward Alec. He held a white envelope in his other hand. "Peace, Brother Fox." He spoke quietly, and moved slowly to close the SUV door gently behind him.

Alec took the time the other Prime gave him to calm down. "Peace, Brother Crow," he answered when his vision had flashed back from red to something closer to normal.

From behind him, Domini said, "Hi, Tony."

Alec was aware that she was both relieved and annoyed at this evidence that she *really* hadn't imagined the encounter in the vampire bar. And that she was still *really* angry at him for having made her think it was her imagination. Okay, he'd been wrong to manipulate her like that. He wasn't going to apologize for it again.

You didn't apologize to begin with.

Alec heard her thought and ignored it. "What are you doing here?" he asked Crowe.

"Several reasons," Crowe answered. "I spent the last few hours waiting around to see if the Purists have any interest in Lancer Services. Haven't noticed anyone but me watching the place. Second, I wanted to let you know that Casmerek's team have packed up everything and headed out of town. Don't worry, he'll be in touch with you soon." Crowe took a cell phone from an inside jacket pocket and handed it to Alec. "You'll hear from the doc only on this number."

"Thanks." Alec put the phone in his pocket. Then he glanced at the small FedEx package. "What's that?"

"The main reason I'm here." Crowe passed the envelope to Alec. "I made those calls about your lady, and this came with instructions to deliver it to you."

Domini supposed this might be a good time to attempt an escape, but instead she peered curiously over Reynard's shoulder.

For one thing, she didn't figure she could outrun two vampires. And for another, she was completely flabbergasted at the idea of vampires getting FedEx packages. It didn't seem right, somehow, that supernatural creatures used cell phones and overnight delivery services. They should use mysterious white-haired messengers in swirling black capes who arrived at the stroke of midnight, holding out red velvet cases in their pale, long-fingered hands. She did notice that the address was written out in thick, dark ink, in rather ornate handwriting.

When Reynard hesitated to open the package, she grew impatient. "Who's it from?" she asked, practically bouncing on her toes with curiosity.

"His mother," Tony answered.

Domini stared at the other vampire. "What?"

"My Matri," Reynard said.

"Your who?"

"Which in this case happens to be his mother." Tony noticed her confusion and said, "Brother Fox, haven't you explained anything about your Clan to this girl? If you're getting married, she should know about her in-laws."

"We're not getting married," Domini announced.

"That's not what I heard," Tony answered.

Domini chose to ignore him and watched as Alec tore open the envelope with shaking fingers. What spilled into his palm was a small red velvet bag and a small folded square of heavy writing paper. Now, this had more of a vampire look to it.

The mysterious effect was spoiled somewhat by their standing in a concrete parking garage, and Tony Crowe's sharp whistle when he saw the bag.

"What is it?" Domini asked.

"Is that what I think it is?" Crowe asked.

They both peered closer.

Alec's stomach twisted with nerves. He very much did not want this to be what Crowe thought it was. The velvet pouch weighed heavily in his palm. It was almost warm, as though with the memory of the hand that had worn it, as though with the thoughts of the woman who had sent it only hours before.

He tugged open the braided silken strings that held the bag closed, and spilled the ring into his hand. The ruby-and-gold signet ring of the Matri of Clan Reynard. The same fox symbol he wore as a tattoo on his wrist was incised deeply into the rounded ruby bezel. It was a beautiful thing, ancient, symbolic.

The ring must be returned to the Matri.

Whatever command came with the ring must be obeyed instantly, without question. To fail to obey was a sentence of expulsion from the Clan, and of death as well. The clanless one would be hunted down and killed by all those he'd once called brother, sister, kinfolk, and parent. The ring of the Matri was far heavier than the pure gold and priceless gem that made up its physical form.

Crowe was solemn and silent, taking a step back. Domini's attention was sharply focused on Alec, curiosity mixed with sudden wariness. She sensed this was important, too important for any flippant questions or comments.

Alec unfolded the paper and recognized his Matri's handwriting.

Bring me Domini Lancer.

Fists of ice closed around Alec's heart and pounded into his gut. A small explosion of rebellion tried to evaporate his already shaky thinking processes. He didn't know what the Matri wanted, and for a second he didn't care. The world around him went blood red and boiling hot with his fury. He threw back his head and howled with rage.

Domini was *his*.

Lady Anjelica had no right to ask him to give up —

No right? Anjelica was Matri of the Clan.

His heart cracked open, but the fury subsided. The world went from red to dark. He was hollow, empty, an automaton.

He was Prime. He was Clan.

Duty. Honor. Obedience.

He sensed Domini's fear and confusion, even concern for him, but he could not bear to look at her. She belonged to the Matri now.

Alec tucked the ring back into the pouch, then turned to the cautiously watching Anthony Crowe. "We need to get to Idaho," he told the Prime of the allied Clan. "Can you help with the arrangements?"

CHAPTER TWENTY-FOUR

They were heading toward an isolated airport. The human captive was the designated driver.

Domini was following a map displayed on a small GPS screen in the center of the Jag's high-tech dashboard. Outside, the afternoon sun burned down on rolling desert hills spotted with the huge whirring fans of tall wind turbine towers. Traffic was light now that they'd left Route 10, and for someone used to driving in constant gridlock, this was weird.

She found the barren landscape eerie, but nowhere near as disconcerting as being on a road trip with Reynard. His head hurt. She knew, because her head hurt. She couldn't deny that they had a psychic connection; the more she was around him, the more attuned to him she was becoming. She suspected he was concealing a great deal of pain, and hiding something worse than physical pain. He was irritable, which set her nerves on edge. He was angry, but wouldn't say why. And there was the caged fiery beast prowling inside him, as well. The cage was weakening, and she didn't know what would happen if the monster escaped.

All she knew was that he and Tony Crowe had had a brief discussion involving routes, secrecy, and abandoned airfields. They'd sounded like a couple of drug smugglers coordinating an important shipment. Neither of them had asked her opinion about anything.

During their conversation she took the opportunity to make a break, running toward the building entrance, hoping to get to human help before the vampires noticed. Reynard proved to her that while he might not be feeling well, he could still move fast. He'd been waiting for her, leaning in front of the door before she got there, his arms casually crossed.

She'd let out a small squeak of rage, then swore vividly at him. He smiled. Actually, it was more of a snarl, and it showed her for the first time that he did have fangs: sharp, predatory, and thoroughly frightening. When she backed up in terror, she ran into Tony Crowe. He nudged her back toward Reynard, who grabbed her by the arm. She was then stuffed into the driver's seat of the Jaguar once more. Reynard called up directions to the Salton Sea Recreation Area on his GPS, and told her to drive.

Hours later Domini was still driving, and she was tired. There'd been one break for a gas and potty stop, but he'd given her no chance to escape.

The air-conditioning and dark windows didn't keep the heat at bay. Sweat sheened both their skins, but there was a lot more of her exposed than there was of Reynard in his dark shirt and jeans. Her micro-length skirt and midriff-baring top gave her no protection at all. She hesitated to ask for a hit of his super sunblock, because she was certain Reynard needed it more. She'd come to believe that the vampire definition of sunburn was spontaneous combustion. Maybe this was a good thing in the overall us-versus-the-monsters scheme of things, but she couldn't imagine it happening to Reynard.

Why she worried about him, she didn't know, but she did. More with every passing mile.

"You know, Mr. T., you make a terrible traveling companion."

Reynard lifted his head a bit and took a long gulp from a bottle of water. His throat still sounded parched when he asked, "Where are we?"

Domini checked the map on the screen. "We just passed Thermal. Heading toward Mecca. Nearly there," she added as the blue smudge of the inland sea grew larger on the map.

She'd never been to this part of California; she'd never been farther south than Palm Springs. She vaguely remembered from a geography class in junior high that the Salton Sea had been created by a Colorado River flood a long time ago. The Sea was actually a salty lake, only fed by polluted farm drainage. It had been quite a tourist spot once, but now it was mostly used by migrating birds.

"Pretty forlorn place you're taking me to," she said.

"That's the idea."

"Not my idea of a fun date."

Reynard put his head back against the soft leather headrest, seeming to have lost interest in the conversation. Then his hand reached across the gear shift to stroke the inside of her exposed thigh.

Heat rushed through Domini, and she let out a sharp gasp. The car veered across the sun-baked road.

"I could make it your idea of a date," he said.

Domini got the car under control. "I concede that." His fingers moved higher and continued to stroke. Domini's breath quickened.

She made herself concentrate on anything but what Reynard was doing. She saw a grove of date palms in the distance, and realized they were at the outskirts of a small town. A sign said to reduce speed to forty-five. She had to move Reynard's hand away so she could downshift.

"Mecca," Reynard said as the Jaguar moved through the outskirts of the small town. "Nine miles to go."

"Nine miles to what?"

"Nine miles to the Salt Shore Motel." He crossed his arms over his chest. "Wake me up then."

"I live to serve," she grumbled.

"Don't we all?" was his enigmatic answer.

She couldn't get a word out of him the rest of the way.

"What a lovely abandoned motel in the middle of nowhere you've brought me to, Reynard. I am *so* impressed."

"It's not abandoned," he answered after he closed the door. "The clerk told me that there are guests in two other rooms."

Domini had to admit that though the furnishings were seedy, the place was clean. An ancient air conditioner wheezed loudly away in the room's one window, drowning out any other noise and thinning down the late afternoon heat. The concrete walls were thick, but painted a cheery coral. The pale green indoor/outdoor carpet was thin but recently vacuumed. The spread on the queen-sized bed was beige chenille. The rest of the furnishings consisted of a chair and a table by the bed. There was a lamp on the table that boasted a bulb of such low wattage, it didn't even seem to bother Reynard's sensitive vision. There were also a chest of drawers and a television resting on an old coffee table. Hardly the Hotel Bel-Air, but at least there was a bathroom.

"Mind if I take a shower?"

Reynard was already pacing the room, like a restless prisoner measuring out the dimensions of his cell. He gestured jerkily toward the bathroom. "Fine."

Domini hesitated for a moment, studying him. She didn't like the look of him at all. He was more like a caged animal than a prisoner.

She curbed the impulse to go to him and take him in her arms. She was frightened of what would happen if she did. "You're getting worse, aren't you?"

He managed to curb his pacing long enough to give her a sardonic look. "You think?"

"Why?" she asked.

He went back to pacing. "Lots of reasons. I'm horny. Hungry. I'm hurting. I want to *bite* something."

"You left your medicine at your house."

"Yes." He gave her a sharp look. "I wish one of us had noticed that before now."

She could have pointed out that she wasn't the one who arranged this little road trip, but nagging an antsy vampire probably wasn't the safest course of action.

"You want to lie down?" she asked. "Can I get you a glass of water or anything?"

"Anything?" He took in a sharp breath. His muscles looked as tense as steel. "Domini, you have no idea —" Reynard rubbed his hands over his face. The lean lines were sharper than ever, pared down by pain. It gave him the beauty of a suffering saint, or the fierceness of a hungry predator. "It'll be dark soon. Maybe that will help."

He didn't sound at all confident. Reynard went back to pacing, and she went into the bathroom. There was no window in here. She stripped off the clothes she'd been wearing for far too long and stepped into the tiny shower cubicle. The shower head was positioned too low for comfort, and she couldn't get the overenthusiastic spray of water warmer or cooler than tepid. The pipes rattled like thunder, and the water roared enough to wake the dead. But at least there was a tiny square of soap and thin towels, so she managed to get clean and sort of dry.

Domini felt a bit more civilized when she was finished, but she hated having to put on her dirty clothes yet again. This was definitely not her idea of a glamorous resort getaway.

As kidnappings went, though, it could have been worse.

"There's a vampire out there," she said to her reflection in the bathroom mirror. "How do you define *worse?*"

A hungry vampire, she added, and a shiver of terror raced up her spine. Reality hit her hard, and she had to grab hold of the sink to keep from falling to her knees. She stayed where she was for a long time, shaking, her empty stomach twisting with nausea that left her panting with the effort not to throw up.

She was alone with a vampire.

Even worse, she wasn't alone with a vampire. There was the manager who'd rented them the room, and other people staying here.

Reynard had admitted to being hungry. To

wanting to bite something. Someone, he meant. She didn't think he *wanted* to — feed, or attack anyone. But she feared that soon he might not have any choice.

Domini opened the door and stepped into the bedroom. The chair and chest were smashed to kindling. The television had been shoved to the floor. Not only was Reynard still pacing, he'd left deep claw marks in the wall, baring pale lines of concrete beneath the cheerful coral paint. He whirled to face her. There was madness in the eyes that stared out of the tortured face, madness that struck her like a blow. His nails had grown sharp and pointed. She had to take a deep breath and remind herself that it wasn't blood under his nails, but dark pink paint. She tried to tell herself she imagined the feral gleam in his eyes. He was breathing hard, and pain radiated off of him like desert heat. He'd been keeping himself on a very tight leash, and now the leash was slipping badly.

Domini pushed the rising fear aside. "Are you going to hunt humans?" she asked him. "Do you need to drink blood?"

"I need blood."

He was on her in an instant, his hands tight on her shoulders, his body pressing hers hard against the wall. She was aware of his weight, his strength, his heat, his arousal.

There was no mistaking the fire in his eyes, a reflection of the burning inside him.

An answering fire stirred in her, quickening her breath, her body, her blood.

Reynard's face dipped close to hers; his lips brushed across hers without touching, yet she was aware of the slight bulge of needle fangs hidden beneath his lips. He breathed in her scent. She felt her heart begin to race in time with the frantic beat of his. His thoughts burned into her.

What do I want? What do I need?

The words mocked her, and himself.

"Me?" she asked.

"You!" The word was a snarl, of desire, of denial.

He spun away from her abruptly, before she could answer. Before either of them could move closer.

"I can't take what I want. You aren't mine to take."

Domini was left shaken, with only the battered wall to hold her up. Reynard was on the other side of the room, standing beneath the cold blast of the air conditioner, face turned upward and eyes closed. The wrecked room, the shredded walls, were evidence of his pent-up violence. Only the bed was left untouched, like an altar waiting for a sacrifice.

The monster wanted her. The monster needed her.

She glanced toward the door, only a few steps away. She took one step, her knees weak. She didn't think she had the strength to run, but she managed to walk out the door without Reynard noticing.

Domini had no idea what she intended to do when she stood outside. There were three cars in the small motel lot, each parked outside one of the occupied rooms. Domini fingered the Jaguar keys in the tiny pocket of her tiny skirt. She could leave if she wanted, run away from the whole mess. It wouldn't be hard to get in the car and drive away; she doubted Reynard could catch up to her. She doubted he'd even notice.

Then what?

Wash her hands of the whole affair? Write it off as a nightmare, or a hallucination brought on by her psychic gifts?

What would happen to Reynard? He was hurting. He needed help. She couldn't just leave him, and it wasn't like she could call the paramedics.

He did need help, and soon. She could feel the barriers shredding, the wildness building in him as though the emotions were her own.

She didn't believe that he wanted to hurt

anyone. He hadn't hurt her; he'd protected her. He'd protected Holly.

He'd made love to her. They'd made love. He'd made her feel like . . .

He tilted her head up and covered her mouth with his. She had not realized what deep, fiery pleasure the touching of lips, the delving of tongues, could bring. The kiss was a rich feast of sensation.

She felt sharp teeth press against her lips. Excitement overwhelmed fear. Perhaps fear enhanced her excitement. All she knew was that she moaned with loss when his mouth left hers.

"No — !"

"Peace," he whispered. He held her face in his hands, so that she must look into his eyes. They glowed faintly in the moonlight, as any night beast's would. "This night you are mine, to do with as I please."

The look in those eyes demanded an answer, an assent.

"I am yours."

"Do you want me? Do you want my body to cover yours? Do you want me inside you? I will have your consent."

She grabbed his thick black hair in her fists and pulled his mouth back to hers.

This kiss was as intense, but he did not let it last as long. "The night grows late," he whis-

pered against her mouth.

His hands skimmed over her then, and he kissed her throat and between her breasts and suckled at the tips, and moved on to her belly and thighs. Wherever he touched he left traces of fire behind. The heat pooled deep down in her belly, making her grind her hips and arch up against him, insistent, begging for more.

Every now and then there would be a slight sting as his sharp teeth penetrated her skin in ever more tender places. If he took a drop or two of her blood with each kiss, she welcomed the small sacrifice for the bright bursts of joy it brought. His fingers delved between her legs, caressed and teased until she thought she was about to die.

She opened to him and lifted her hips. She held her arms out, and looked up to meet his gaze.

Only she couldn't see his eyes, because he was wearing sunglasses. A glint of moonlight sparkled off his fangs.

"Reynard, what the hell are you doing in my dream?"

"Your dream? I thought it was mine."

Domini blinked, and found that she was standing in the motel parking lot, looking up at the sky. Stars were coming out as the last glow of sunset faded. For a moment she didn't realize what had happened.

Then she remembered that it *had* been a dream. A dream she'd shared with Reynard. Or was it a memory of a shared past, where he'd saved a city, and she'd been his reward?

He was the one who needed saving now.

Had they done this before? Been lovers through time? Soul mates?

Domini gave her head a hard shake. This was no time to go off on metaphysical theorizing. Not when a supernatural creature was tearing up the room behind her, and could be tearing up the rest of the building and the people in it any minute. He hadn't attacked anyone so far, but he was close to it.

She remembered the nightmare dream — vision — whatever it was.

The vampire's lust pounded through her, emotion as real and hard as the cock pounding ruthlessly inside her. There was no escape, only a storm overwhelming her. Driving total possession into her flesh, her blood, and being. She was spread out beneath him like a sacrifice. Her skin was smeared red with her blood, and his.

Which was real: the pleasure of the first dream, or the degradation of the second?

You don't live in dreams, she reminded herself harshly. Reality is what's back in that room.

Alexander Reynard needed her.

Domini turned on her heel and walked back to the door. Newfound determination didn't stop her from shaking like a leaf, but she went of her own free will. She knew what she had to do.

Domini opened the door and stepped inside. "You need me," she told the vampire who whirled to face her. She held out her arms. "You need me, and I'm here."

CHAPTER TWENTY-FIVE

"No!" He held his hands out before him, shaking his head with denial. "I can't!"

"The hell you can't," Domini answered. "I didn't just go through that whole crisis of conscience thing to come back in here and have you say no. If anybody's going to be self-sacrificing here, it's me."

She moved slowly closer to him. He backed up with each step she took, but she had the advantage; the wall was to his back. Eventually Reynard had nowhere else to go.

"Alexander," she said, putting her hands on him, cupping his face when he tried to turn away. His skin burned against her palms. "You've proved to be nothing but a good man. You're suffering. Let me help. I may not be the woman you deserve, but I'm here now, and you need me."

He took a deep breath and managed to say, "You don't belong to me."

"I belong to me." She smiled gently, stated very firmly, "I give myself to you. Whatever you vampires have going on about me doesn't mean shit. I don't care about magic rings. I don't care about secret societies. That's all bullshit, nothing to do with me. Nothing to do with us."

"It has — to do with — me."

"*You* have to do with me. Right here, right now. Nothing and no one else exists."

"Only us?"

It hurt to hear the way his voice rasped with pain. "Yes, Alexander."

"No. Too dangerous. You — go."

She shook her head, then stepped back and pulled off her clothes.

Alec could not help but look at Domini. He saw her with all his senses. It was the warmth of her flesh that called to him, the softness. The scent of her was sweet and sharp, all female. He meant to deny himself, but she smiled and held her arms wide, let all the barriers of her mind drop. She offered herself completely. Freely. Not unafraid, but with determination and her own rising hunger.

He could do nothing but reach out and touch.

He meant to be gentle, but intentions meant nothing. Claiming her meant everything. He drew her close, then lifted her into his arms. It was but a step to the bed.

Domini was aware of the unyielding firmness of the mattress, of the way the springs creaked beneath her weight, even of the faint bumps of the chenille bedspread. The moment Alexander touched her, she became supersensitized. Everything became *more.*

"Stay still," came his rough whisper. "Let it happen. Don't try to run. Don't fight. I don't want to hurt you."

His warning was not reassuring, but she stopped thinking a moment later when he kissed her. The kiss tasted of hot copper and electricity.

His hands moved over her, bringing pain, followed by pleasure. The combination was more than heady: at this moment, in this place, with him, it was perfect. Fear had no place here, only arousal.

He touched her everywhere, harsh, gentle, stimulating. His nails made the faintest of pinpricks, on her breasts, between them. Tiny spots of blood welled. His mouth found each mark, licked and suckled the beads of blood, took nourishment and gave back pleasure. Where fangs sank into flesh, she did not know.

Domini closed her eyes and let herself completely go. No barriers, nothing but sensation. Her orgasm sent flame through her blood and melted her bones. And that was only the beginning.

Fire filled her, consumed her, raised her up to explosive heights, brought her down into wells of swirling darkness where their twin heartbeats hammered together, then cycled her upward again. It took her higher and further each time, then dropped her deeper. She soared toward the sun, then dove into the depths of heavy darkness. She drowned, and each time she felt the spark go out of her, she was kindled back into fiery life.

She gradually became aware that their hearts were no longer in rhythm. His was stronger, so much stronger. His heart thundered, roared with life and power, while hers was drawing down to a faint echo, straining to keep time.

Straining to keep alive.

Domini understood what was happening. A trace of fear coiled through her, like smoke through flame. The fire would soon take her. Or the darkness. Either way, she would be consumed. She was dying.

She could not speak or move. Her spirit floated in a lava flow; slowly boiling away to nothing, but she'd lost all awareness of her body. She could barely find the will to call out a silent whisper. She hadn't enough strength to even call for help. All she could manage was his name.

Alexander.

An image of sparks turning to ash and falling around him like rain entered Alec's mind, interposing itself over the frenzied pleasure of feeding. The ash turned thick as snow, a blizzard blanketing the feverish greed, dulling it down to something manageable. He cried out angrily, not ready to lose the searing pleasure, the utter, satiating satisfaction. He had forgotten the power only the taste of blood could bring. Red lightning. There was nothing else like it in the universe.

Alexander.

The voice that called to him was faint, fading, unfamiliar in its weakness.

Alexander.

He barely recognized his own name. Didn't want to recognize it, because then he would have to *be* Alexander. Alexander was not the beast who fed and fed and wanted ever more.

Alexander was —

The man who loved Domini.

Domini?

The world came back in on him with a hard, heavy rush that brought him to orgasm

301

and left him sprawled on top of a soft, limp form. His vision shifted from seeing the world as degrees of heat, to something closer to human sight. He didn't remember when he'd entered her, taken her body as well as her blood, but they were twinned together, his seed inside her, her taste on his tongue.

And she was dying.

Alec let out a cry of pain. He'd taken too much, too quickly. He'd given nothing, shared nothing. She'd offered, but he should have refused. He'd lost control, lost himself. Now he was losing her before they'd even had time to —

Alexander.

Her voice was fainter than before.

His name sounded so beautiful in her mind. To hear it as her dying thought was soul-shattering.

"Selfish, stupid idiot!" Alec lifted his head, the fog clearing from his brain.

He sat on the edge of the bed, drew Domini into his lap, cradled her head against his shoulder, and brushed a wing of dark hair away from her face. He could detect no breath, and her normal paleness was changed to moonstone translucence.

He didn't have much time, and the only sharp objects available were his own claws and fangs. A quick, hard bite into the vein in his left wrist, then he opened her mouth and held his wrist to it.

Drink, he urged as blood began to flow into her. *Drink.* Alec sent the command into her fading thoughts. *Drink, and live. Please live.*

He waited, holding his breath, full of terror and guilt. And waited.

Domini!

Alexander?

She sounded miles away, fading fast.

I am with you, he sent his thoughts after her. *Do as I say!*

Bossy . . .

Alec laughed, though fear still rushed through him. *No time to argue. Suck, sweetheart. Swallow. Do it.*

No answer drifted back from the place where Domini sank into darkness. Alec could do no more — only wait, and pray, and bleed.

He caressed her throat, hoping that would make her swallow. He tried to find her pulse, but it was only the faintest flutter.

What the hell have I done —

Domini jerked, her mouth clamped around Alec's wrist, and she began to drink, fiercely reclaiming her life.

Alec let out a long gasp, and lost himself in

the intimate pleasure of giving the same fire he'd taken.

There was the light, and there was the voice. Both in the distance from where she hung in the dark. Both called to her. The flames had gone from the dark, hunger remained. She called out, and the voice answered. The light did not command, it did not call. The light offered peace, but the voice, the voice wanted her to live. The voice offered life. He wanted her.

She was Domini, he was her Alexander, her Alec, her Fox, and she wanted everything he was.

She was hungry for him. He offered, and she feasted.

Domini took from the fire, brought it inside her.

The tasting of sweet fire filled her senses for the longest time, but gradually, incrementally, Domini became aware of other things, things beyond the feeding. She had a body. She was aware of drying sweat and a cold breeze blowing over her. There was another body, hard and male, strong arms holding her, a heart beating like a drum. Underneath the drumbeat was another sound, an irritable, persistent ringing noise that hurt her ears. What was it?

A telephone?

A telephone. Yes.

After a while, it stopped.

Soon after that the darkness came back, but different now. She floated in it, mind and body and soul happy, exhausted, sated. She was herself again, too tired to move, almost awake, almost aware.

Aware enough to know Alexander was moving around the room when she wished he was beside her. She thought he might be getting dressed. That was too bad. She was not awake enough to protest that she wanted him to come to bed.

She heard the phone ring again. Then the knock came on the door. Then there were voices. Alexander barked out a question. There were answers. The air currents on her skin changed, and she knew he'd opened the door.

Alec had to open the door to the two men, but he blocked the doorway with his body. Dr. Casmerek, he recognized. The other must be the pilot.

Casmerek peered past Alec's shoulder. "What have you done?"

"She's mine," Alec answered.

"Let me in."

He was Prime. No one came near his mate. If Casmerek had been anything but a human physician, Alec's claws would have come out. As it was, he did show the faintest hint of fangs. The pilot had the sense to back off into the darkness.

Casmerek did not back off. He tried to take a step forward, but Alec put a hand on his shoulder. "Have you harmed her? Does she need a transfusion?"

Alec turned his wrist out so the doctor could see. "My blood. Only mine."

Casmerek's eyes widened. "Bonding? In your condition?" His features grew stern. "Step aside, Alec," he said calmly and with great authority. "For her sake. You know I won't harm her. She helped you; I can see that. Now let me help her."

Alec backed up, and the doctor followed. But he didn't let Casmerek near his woman. Instead, he wrapped the bedspread around Domini and lifted her in his arms.

"The plane's waiting?"

"Yes," Casmerek answered. "I brought the new serum. I was going to treat you during the flight."

"No need to change the plan." Alec marched out of the wrecked motel room. The darkness felt good. He hadn't felt so alive, so much himself, for a long time. He held Domini tight against his chest. He had her to thank for this night.

The doctor hurried into the parking lot

after them. "You're going to feel like hell to-morrow," he said, as though he'd read Alec's thoughts.

"Maybe."

Alec glanced at the pilot waiting in the shadows, leaning against a pickup truck with "Salt View Airport" painted on the door. Both the motel and the private airport were owned by the Clans. Both the humans were not only well paid, but had ties of family, friendship, and loyalty to the Clans.

Alec climbed into the back of the truck, cradling Domini in his lap. "Let's go," he ordered, a high-handed Prime who expected to be, and was, obeyed.

CHAPTER TWENTY-SIX

She knew her name was Domini; everything else was a blur.

The air smelled of pine; fresh and sweet, with just a hint of dampness to go along with the north woodsy tang. She remembered hearing raindrops on the windowpane sometime while she drifted in and out of sleep.

The bed was large, the mattress soft, the linens softer, and they smelled of lavender. This was not her bed.

She managed to open her eyes. It was a nice room, but totally unfamiliar. She made out botanical prints in dark wood frames hanging on a cream-colored wall. Sheer curtains fluttered in the breeze from a slightly open window. A pine-scented breeze was damp with recent rain. There was a pretty little pink glass lamp on the bedstand beside her. The lamp was turned on, but the bulb was about as dim as her thought processes at the moment. In the pinkish light she discovered she was wearing an old-fashioned long-sleeved cotton nightgown, elaborately embroidered white on white. How had she gotten into it?

When she tried to sit up, lights flared behind her eyes in fireworks that would have been pretty but for the pain. She fell back on the thick down pillows and lay very, very still. Maybe she wasn't ready to get up yet.

She let that thought percolate for a while, until it made her angry, and stubborn. She tried sitting up again, but this time she took it slowly. Her head still hurt when she moved, but she expected it, and she coped. There was a door on the other side of the room. She intended to go out that door.

Questions were beginning to form, and she wanted answers. She wasn't going to get them lying around in a soft bed in a pretty room somewhere very far from the smog, dust, and dry heat of Los Angeles.

She wanted to go home. And she wanted —

Loneliness stabbed at her, sharp and cutting, more painful than the ache in her head.

She wanted Alexander Reynard. Alec. Her Alexander.

"Where's Alexander?"

As if speaking the words activated a magic spell, the door opened — and a dark angel stepped in. The woman was beautiful; tall, lean, elegant, with supermodel cheekbones, green eyes, and long black satin hair; she was dressed all in black. She held her right hand out, and Domini recognized the ruby-and-gold ring the woman wore.

Domini wondered if she was supposed to curtsy, or kiss the ring.

"I am Lady Anjelica," the woman said, in a warm velvet voice. "Matri of Clan Reynard. Welcome to my Citadel."

"Uh-huh," Domini said, nodding slowly. She wondered if the woman was aware of how silly that all sounded. "And what century are we living in?"

The other woman only laughed.

"I'm living in the twenty-first. I suppose the title sounds a bit much to someone not used to our ways." She smiled, and her green eyes glinted with humor. "Would it help put you at ease if I told you that back in the sixties, I was known as the original Foxy Lady? Of course, that was long before you were born, though I swear you look exactly like your grandmother did then. We were quite the pair —"

"Whoa! Whoa! Whoa!" Domini waved her hands in front of her, which didn't help her headache, but the confusion was worse than the pain. "You didn't know my grandmother. You couldn't. You're a vampire; I can tell."

Lady Anjelica nodded. "Of course you can tell I'm a vampire. You and Alec have been busy." She shook a finger at Domini. "I wish you and my son hadn't begun the bond before I had a chance to talk to you both, but Dr. Casmerek tells me the feral incident couldn't be helped. I thank you for helping him. But what you don't yet understand is that his blood is beginning to change you."

Domini didn't understand a lot of what Lady Anjelica said. She couldn't remember — she couldn't remember past — "There was a ring. Your ring. Alexander —" His face flashed through her mind, pain-racked, tight with control, beautiful to her. She missed him desperately, needed to be with him. "Where's Alexander? Where's Reynard?"

A look of concern crossed Lady Anjelica's face. "He will be all right," she soothed Domini. "You can see him when he's better."

"I need to see him now."

"I understand."

Her expression was compassionate, but Lady Anjelica stood squarely between Domini and the door. Domini knew there was no getting past her. That didn't stop Domini from wanting to try; only the knowledge that she didn't know where to look stopped her.

Maybe if she concentrated on *wanting* to find Alexander, the wanting would lead her to him. But she didn't think the headache was going to let her concentrate enough for that. Besides the pain in her head, her whole body felt weak and drained, and not quite right. And there was panic growing in her, gnawing at her control.

"What happened?" she asked. "Why do I feel like this? Where am I? What happened?"

"All very good questions," Lady Anjelica answered. "Most of the answers, you'll be able to work out for yourself after you've had a bit more rest. And lots of nourishment. You were down a couple of quarts. You'll need lots of feeding to get your strength back."

"Down a couple of —"

What exactly did the vampire woman mean by "feeding"?

Domini found herself sitting on the edge of the bed. She was very confused, and even more dizzy. The pulse in her temples pounded, and she squinted to keep the other woman in focus. Nausea clenched her gut. "A couple quarts of what?"

"I think you need a bit more sleep," Lady Anjelica answered. Domini knew from the soft, insistent tone that the vampire was ordering rather than suggesting.

She waved a hand weakly toward Anjelica.

"Don't do that. I don't like it when you people do that." Her voice was a muffled slur.

"It's for your own good."

"You sound like Alexander."

"I am his mother."

"You look more like a sister."

"Thank you. I'll explain many things to you later. Sleep now," she ordered, and helped Domini lie back on the bed. Domini couldn't keep her eyes open any longer.

When she woke up again, Domini did feel better physically, but she wasn't happy about it. Not when she was haunted by dark dreams she couldn't recall, and woke with a lurking sense of dread. Something was coming, something she didn't want to face.

This time no one appeared in the room when she got up. She found clothes neatly folded on top of a chest at the foot of the bed. She found a bathroom as well, with vanilla-scented soap and thick, plush towels.

The clothes fit, from the underwear to the long black broomstick skirt, pine green silk sweater, and black slides she slipped on her feet. She felt much better with clothes on, armored to face the day, or the night, or the vampires that waited outside the door.

Well, she wasn't so sure about facing Alexander's mother. It wasn't just that the vampire queen, or whatever she was, was all magical and formidable, and far too glamorous for any other female's ego. It was that she was Alexander Reynard's *mother*, for God's sake!

She'd never been involved with a man long enough or seriously enough to meet his parents before. But she had a feeling that the only way she was going to get to Alexander was through his mom, so a meeting with Lady Anjelica was in the offing. Might as well get it over with.

Domini tried the door handle, and was surprised to find it wasn't locked. And *maybe* she was a touch disappointed that it wasn't. Being locked in would have been evidence of her being a prisoner. She had been brought here against her will, right? At Lady Anjelica's order. Domini's memory was still a little fuzzy, but she was pretty sure she hadn't volunteered to be a "guest" at the Citadel.

Domini walked out of the bedroom to find herself on a landing of polished hardwood that overlooked a huge room two stories below. Looking over the smooth wooden railing, she saw furniture, rugs, and a decor that was far more North Woods Lodge than Hollywood Vampire Castle. Of course, Reynard's house in Los Angeles had been perfectly normal, too. Maybe hearing the place called a citadel had given her notions. There wasn't a cobweb or coffin in sight in this airy house, and much of one wall of the great room that stretched up three stories was made of windows that looked out on a large lake.

"Pretty, isn't it?"

Domini jumped, and whirled to find Lady Anjelica standing beside her, leaning on the rail.

Anjelica was dressed in gray slacks and a gray-and-red patterned burn-out velvet tunic, her long hair framing her exquisite features. There was a wicked look on Anjelica's face.

"You enjoy giving people heart attacks, don't you?" Domini asked.

"Strokes," Anjelica answered. "Elevated blood pressure lends a certain carbonated effect to the victim's — I'm joking, I'm joking." She touched Domini's shoulder. "Don't look so horrified. Honestly, you young people have no macabre sense of humor these days."

"Not at the moment. Nice place," Domini added politely.

"Glad you like it."

"Can I leave now?"

"Come along," Anjelica said, ignoring Domini's request. "We need to talk." She walked down the landing and turned left at a long hallway. Domini followed. "My morning room," Anjelica said as she ushered Domini into a large windowless room at the end of the hall.

The decor here was more feminine, though strong colors dominated; the overhead lighting was subtle, and the furniture was leather, with a pair of chairs and a love seat grouped around a low table in the center of the room. There was a fire going in a white marble fireplace, and framed photographs on the wide mantel. A small desk was set against one wall, and a few other tables and straight-backed chairs were scattered around the room. The carpet was a deep plush, in a blue-and-white Chinese pattern.

"The great room downstairs is lovely in the morning, but I'm not much of a morning person," Anjelica told her.

Domini realized that Anjelica's conversation was meant to put her at ease, but what really drew her attention were the wonderful aromas coming from dishes on the table.

Domini's stomach rumbled as she walked past Anjelica and headed straight for the low table, where a small feast was set out on fancy china.

Domini pointed at a tall carafe. "Is that coffee?"

"I thought you might like some breakfast."

"Yes, please."

"Have a seat."

Domini had already settled into one of the leather wingback chairs. She poured two cups of coffee and passed one to Lady Anjelica before taking a long gulp. She sat back in the deep, butter-soft chair, savoring the coffee. "Wonderful."

"Try the orange juice," Anjelica directed. "It's good for you. There's eggs, bacon, and sausage. Never mind the cholesterol, you need protein right now. I'll talk while you eat, because there's a great deal you'll want to know, and much I can tell you before you need to ask any questions."

What Domini wanted was to know where Alexander was and if he was all right, but before she could ask, Lady Anjelica said, "I should tell you about Alec. About Primes in general, but Alec specifically, since he is your Prime. Eat your eggs while I explain."

Domini gave in to curiosity and hunger and let the woman talk.

"Primes are adult male vampires. They are proud, imperious, possessive, strong, territorial, intensely sexual, stubborn, haughty, protective, arrogant, handsome. Depending on the situation, they can be the most wonderful men in the world or complete pricks.

There tend to be more male vampires than females, so Primes frequently have sexual liaisons with human women. Sometimes those liaisons become long-term romantic relationships. And sometimes the same sort of lifemate soul-bond forms between a Prime and a female human as does between a vampire male and female. This bonding is on a psychic and physical level, and permanent. The Prime and his human soul mate share blood and psychic energy, which increases the human's life span and psychic gifts to match the life span of her mate. Due to a rare genetic abnormality in humans, occasionally, very rarely, a mortal woman bondmate can make the transition to vampire. This change doesn't grant immortality, because vampires are not immortal, though we do live significantly longer than our human cousins. Very close cousins, but I'll explain more about physiology, biology, and history in a bit."

"Okay," Domini agreed, around a mouthful of food. "Go on about Alexander and me."

She remembered now that she'd offered him her blood, and he must have shared blood with her. Anjelica's comment about her being down a couple of quarts made sense now. The experience had led to her feeling like hell, but Domini was willing to bet that her reaction came from the fact that Alexander had been so — feral — at the time.

"Absolutely correct. He took more of your blood than he should have, but he couldn't help it. He loves you," Anjelica said, "which is why he stopped before it was too late."

"I'm getting used to having my mind read, but I still don't like it."

Lady Anjelica didn't apologize for the intrusion, but said, "You'll develop barriers eventually."

"Fine. Go on."

"In the normal course of events, what appears to have happened between you and Alec is the meeting of two people meant to be bondmates. But the circumstances are not normal at all."

Dread clutched at Domini again. She was barely managing to accept the bondmate stuff. If you accepted that there were people like her who could see glimpses of the future, and that vampires really existed, then it was possible to believe that soul-deep love-for-all-time was possible. Now Lady Anjelica was throwing a wrench into the works.

"You're saying that your son and I *aren't* meant for each other? You don't approve?" Domini was not unaware of the irony here. A couple days ago, *she* wasn't sure she and Reynard belonged together.

"It is not for me to approve or disapprove," Lady Anjelica told her. "You are bonding. There is no stopping it. The problem might arise when the Matri of Clan Corvus finds out her granddaughter has bonded with a Reynard Prime, without any prior agreement or contract between clans." Anjelica waved an elegant hand while Domini gaped at her. "But that is a matter of paperwork and ceremony. I'm sure Cassandra Crowe and I will work something out; the Blackbird is a reasonable woman."

Domini stared at the vampire matriarch, dizzy with dread and the effort to make sense of what she'd heard. All that she knew was that her grandmother's name was Cassandra, and that her nickname was Blackbird. Everybody seemed to know that her nickname was Blackbird — at least all the vampires she met knew it. "What the hell are you talking about?"

Anjelica put down her coffee cup. "Let me explain about the Clans a bit, first. There are different sorts of vampires, different cultures, really. The Clans have always been the most closely associated with humans. We like humans — and not just as menu items. Though we do need to drink blood, we don't

have to kill to satisfy that hunger. We don't
even have to drink human blood, though we
prefer it. There's certainly a medical reason
for the craving, and we have researchers
working on the connection.

"The Clans do everything possible to
work for the welfare of our human cousins.
We always have and always will. There is an
ancient, sacred bond between us and our
human cousins. Once upon a time, we were
treated as gods by humans. We brought jus-
tice, protected them. Times changed, and
humans changed, and vampires became re-
viled and hunted. But the Clans stayed true
to our vows to protect humans.

"We went underground, and each of the
ancient Clans that had once been kings on
Earth took the name of a creature that humans needed, but hated. We became the
snakes, the wolves, the foxes, the crows, jackals, and so on. We took the names of creatures that humans called vermin, and wore
them with honor and irony. Never let it be
said that vampires don't have a sense of
humor.

"Corvus," she went on, "is the Crow Clan,
as Reynard is the Fox, Jackal is Shagal, and
so on. Your grandmother is from Clan
Corvus."

Domini wanted to protest, but arguing

with Anjelica wouldn't get the story out sooner.

"Since there are significantly fewer vampire women than men, traditionally, vampire women rarely had the same sorts of sexual liaisons as the Primes. For the last century, though, some of our young woman have ventured out into the world for a few decades before settling into their responsibilities as heads of the Clans. Once upon a time, Cassandra Crowe took herself a human lover."

"No."

Anjelica ignored Domini's faint protest. "They lived together for several decades. They had a son. Such offspring rarely exhibit any vampire traits. They might be a bit psychic, but for the most part they are completely human. Your father was human, Domini, but sometimes vampire traits skip a generation." She paused. "You are not completely human, Domini."

"That does it. I'm out of here."

Domini sprang to her feet and marched to the door. Nobody, no how, no way, was telling her that she was a vampire.

Domini! Come back here.

Anjelica's order snapped around her like a whip. Domini fought the urge to obey and kept on going.

I will not be disobeyed in my own house.

Don't bet on that, Domini thought back.

It took all her will, fueled by stubborn anger, but she made it to the door. Reaching for the knob and turning it was the hardest thing she'd ever done. It seemed to take a long time, but the door finally opened.

And when it did, Alexander came rushing in like a charging linebacker. He grabbed her, and his momentum carried them halfway across the room.

"What's the matter?" he demanded frantically, holding Domini in a tight embrace. Domini put her arms around him and held on tight to his hard muscle and flesh.

"Mother," he said, pulling her closer, "what the hell have you done to my woman?"

CHAPTER TWENTY-SEVEN

"I've been telling her the truth," Anjelica said, coming to her feet. "Truth I need to tell you, as well. I'm glad you feel up to joining us."

Alec was aware of his mother's anger. He had dared to enter the Matri's presence without asking permission; he'd also spoken rudely to her.

He didn't care. Even a Clan Matri had no right to cause pain to someone in the fragile beginning of a bond. He'd felt Domini's agitation and pain from the other side of the estate. Her need had been strong enough for him to throw off the effects of the sedatives Casmerek had given him, and come to his lover's aid.

He had not expected to find that his mother had caused Domini's distress.

"Domini is overreacting," his mother said, tightly controlling her impatience. "I was explaining her heritage to her, and she took it amiss."

Alec ran his hands soothingly up and down Domini's tense back and turned a puzzled look on his mother. "Her heritage?"

"Apparently her grandfather has been keeping secrets from her. I think that's what's disturbing her the most. Isn't it, Domini?"

Domini whirled out of Alec's embrace to face Anjelica. "I am not a vampire!" she declared.

The venom in her tone struck pain through him, but Alec reminded himself that Domini really didn't know anything about vampires yet. It certainly didn't help that he'd nearly killed her a few nights ago. "Of course you're not a vampire," he soothed. "Bonding to one, yes, but you cannot become —"

"She can and she will be changed," his mother interrupted. She turned a stern gaze on Alec. "Dr. Casmerek has done the blood tests to prove it. Why do you think the Purists pursue her?"

With everything else that had happened, Alec had all but forgotten that the fanatics had attacked the woman he loved. He put his hands on Domini's shoulders and gently turned her to face him. "Is there something you haven't been telling me?"

Her gaze met his in a fiery glare. "Of course not!"

"She had no idea about her family history," Anjelica said.

If Domini truly was of vampire lineage, their possibilities together might, just might, change drastically. Alec didn't dare to let himself hope yet. Having a bondmate, vampire or human, was more than many Primes ever achieved. Having Domini as his bondmate was more than enough. But . . .

Alec looked back at his mother. "Are you sure about this? How?"

"I knew her history before Dr. Casmerek ran his tests. Why do you think I sent for her?"

"I have no idea why. You commanded. I obeyed." He snapped the words out, hating that anyone, even his Clan Matri, dared to interfere with his private affairs.

"Sit down, both of you," Anjelica said. "And I will explain."

Domini was quivering with fury in his embrace. He knew that if he dared to let her go she would only try to march out again. The Matri would tell him to stop her, he would, and he and Domini would argue.

To avoid that argument, he forced his own anger at Anjelica to cool, and brought Domini to sit beside him on the love seat. He put his arm around her, keeping her close to comfort them both, and to keep her from bolting again.

"Anthony Crowe knew that his second cousin and I have always been friends," Anjelica explained after she resumed her own seat. "When no one at the Crowe Citadel knew where their Matri had gone on vacation, he called here to ask if I knew. I did, but if a Matri doesn't want to be disturbed, another Matri isn't going to disturb her for less than a Clan-threatening emergency." She gave Alec a faint smile. "When I asked what his business was, Anthony told me that you were involved with a young woman named Lancer who looked amazingly like his cousin Blackbird, and that Purists were active again in Los Angeles. Not only were they threatening vampires, but the Purists had an interest in the Lancer woman. He suspected a Crowe connection because of the strong resemblance between the women. He doesn't know about Blackbird's life among mortals, but I do. I knew who Domini had to be, so I sent for her."

Alec was still annoyed at Anjelica's interference, but he was also curious. "If she's Corvus, why not send her to the Corvus Clan?"

"Because I have a use for her."

He frowned at the Matri. "Other than being my mate, I take it."

"Yes."

"I'm sitting right here, you know," Domini chimed in. "What do you want with me?" she demanded of the Matri.

Anjelica looked directly at Domini. "I want you to talk to the hunters about the Purists."

After a pause, Domini said, "Of course you do." She turned to Alec. "This makes sense, how?"

"It does makes sense, when you know who the players are," Alec assured her.

"Explain to her, Alexander," Anjelica told him.

Domini's anxiety and anger weren't getting any better, and she was projecting all she felt very strongly. Her emotions were open to him; he wondered if Domini sensed his possessiveness for her, and his leashed anger at the Matri.

He did not want to talk. He was back in his right mind and certain of his physical responses. He wanted to celebrate this rebirth by taking his mate, over and over, until they were both blind, deaf, and dumb from sated lust. Then he wanted to start all over again.

Instead, he curbed desire and said, "It's a

staple of fiction, and a matter of fact. Where there are vampires, there are vampire hunters. Not all vampires are good. Not all hunters are as bad as the Purists. Over the millennia we've come to, if not exactly truces, at least unspoken understandings with the less fanatical of the hunters. They hunt the vampires that behave like monsters, and mostly leave the Clans alone. It's an uneasy understanding. Most hunters believe that the only good vampire is a 'staked through the heart, head cut off, mouth filled with garlic, burned to a cinder' dead vampire. Most vampires hate the hunters for all the persecutions of the past. Many resent the hunters taking out any vampire, no matter how evil, because there are so few left. There's bad blood on both sides, and no real trust. The situation is always tense, ready to spill over into bloodshed.

"The Purists are a supersecret fanatical cult that arose among the hunters a century ago. They hold to the original hunter doctrine that all vampires are the evil spawn of Satan and need to be destroyed."

"Hence the name Purist," Domini put in.

"Precisely, my love."

Are they right?

Alec caught Domini's thought, and told himself that no one could be damned for stray thoughts that crossed their minds. He exchanged a glance with his mother, and saw that she had also overheard Domini's flash of uncertainty.

"May I interject some facts and figures about what vampires really are?" Anjelica asked. Because she was the Clan Matri in her own citadel, the question was, of course, rhetorical. "We are not supernatural beings. We were not created by a pact with the devil, or any other such mythological nonsense. As long as there have been humans — no, as long as there have been hominids — there have been vampires. We are simply descended from a slightly different branch of the evolutionary tree."

This anthropological explanation drew Domini's complete attention. "Really? How so? How do you know?"

Anjelica was equally enthusiastic about explaining. "There is a legend about two sisters. Vampires have kept this legend alive for thousands of years. Our belief is that at the beginning of time, a pair of twin sisters were born deep in the heart of the world, in Africa. One sister walked by day, but feared the night. She was physically weaker than her twin, but very fertile. She gave birth to the race of men. The other sister was gifted with very long life, but she was not so prolific. The night was hers, as were many other gifts. She not only feared daylight, but it had the power to kill her. She was the mother of vampires. In the last few decades, proof has begun to emerge that there is a great deal of fact to our origin legend. You've heard of Eve?"

"You're not talking about Adam and Eve, are you?" Domini guessed. "You're referring to the study that traces all the mitochondrial DNA of everyone on earth back thousands of generations to the one hominid female that was the mother of us all. Some scientists, and the media, call her Eve."

"You watch the Discovery Channel a lot, don't you?" Alec murmured.

"Yes," Domini answered. "And I have a minor in anthropology."

Anjelica smiled with pleasure at Domini's interest. "That is indeed the Eve I referred to. Human scientists traced human origins back to this one primitive hominid woman. And vampire scientists have done work on finding Eve's sister. They have traced our DNA back to the same source — to the same family, rather."

"This is all very interesting," Alec said. *To someone, I suppose.* "But Domini and I would like to spend some time together — alone."

331

Anjelica lifted her head proudly. "Domini needed to understand that there is scientific proof that neither we, nor she, have any connection to demons or monsters."

"Fine. I'm glad that's settled."

He was aware that Domini was still uncomfortable, but only time and experience would fully settle her doubts. He wasn't all that comfortable with the scientific explanation of vampires, but if it helped Domini, he wasn't going to point out that he preferred a more romantic version of vampire origins.

"Now that I've explained about the Purists, will you tell us why you want Domini to talk to the hunters?"

"Because the hunters will be far more comfortable meeting face-to-face with a human to discuss our mutual problem with the Purists. We desperately need a liaison, and Domini's background will help her talk to both sides. There's tension building among all branches of vampires over recent increases in Purist attacks. Many of our kind are being swayed back to the old belief that the only good hunter is a dead one. I'm trying to keep a war from starting, and Domini can help stop that war. Fate has brought her to us at the moment we need her."

"I need her," Alec stated his claim. "She is mine."

"Domini's aid is needed by all the Clans," Anjelica went on. "I have called a Convocation." She glanced at the gold watch on her wrist. "I've been planning it for weeks, to begin tonight. Guests have been arriving from all over the country for several days."

"Convocation?" Domini asked Alec.

"Sort of a cross between a party, a religious ritual, and a board-of-directors meeting," he explained. "They're usually a lot of fun." Though he wasn't interested in socializing right now; he wanted to be alone with Domini. "Fun for those of us who don't have to work," he added with a respectful nod to his mother.

Anjelica actually took that as the hint he intended. "I have guests to greet," she said. "Staff to brief." She glanced toward her desk. "A speech to finish writing."

Alec rose to his feet, bringing Domini with him. "Then we'll leave you to your work." He had his lady out in the hallway and the door closed behind them before Anjelica could answer.

Anjelica sent telepathic laughter into his thoughts. *Show Domini the gazebo,* his mother thought at him. *You'll be private there.*

It was an excellent suggestion. Alec sent a thought of thanks, then said to Domini, "I'll show you the gardens and the lakeshore. You'll like the grounds."

Domini welcomed the chance to check out the area. She'd been trained to find all entrances and exits to wherever she was staying; you never knew when escape routes might come in handy.

"You're feeling better," she said as they stepped outside into the daylight.

It was overcast, a bit cool, but the pine-scented air was very refreshing. Alexander held her hand in his. It made her feel warm and secure, and the touch of his flesh sent little thrills of desire through her.

"How can you tell?" he asked, and raised her hand to his lips to kiss her knuckles one at a time.

It took Domini a moment to concentrate on anything but how those kisses made her feel. "You're not wearing sunglasses," she finally managed. "And you look . . ." The best she could manage was, "Good." Which was not nearly an adequate description.

His face was no longer gaunt or deathly pale. The sparkle in his eyes was wicked, but it wasn't feral. There was no sign of pain or weakness about him; just the opposite. He exuded confidence, strength, command, and bone-deep allure. He made her heart race and her knees weak, and sent desire careening through her. The man had it, knew he had it, and was perfectly comfortable living with an overdose of raw sexual appeal.

"Prime," Domini muttered.

"Uh-huh."

She'd spent time around movie stars, rock stars, and other high-powered men who oozed charisma and sexual confidence. She'd always been told that power was sexy. She'd certainly seen how women were attracted to that scent of power, but now she understood.

And Alexander Reynard stood there smiling at her in the middle of a vibrant garden, while she ignored the beautiful landscape and took in the wonder that was him. He accepted her awe as his due.

"You're — impressive," she said.

He drew her closer. "And you like it."

She draped her arms around his neck, pressed her body against the hard length of his, and let her fingers roam through his thick, dark hair. "And you like that I like it."

He put his hands on her, stroking her hips, her waist, and up and down her back, drawing small noises out of her and making her very aware of his own arousal.

He finally took a deep breath and held her

out at arm's length. "We can't stay here," he said.

"Why?" she wondered dreamily, trying to draw him back to her.

"Because we can be seen from every window in the back of the house." He turned her around.

Domini took in the huge three-story building. "That's a lot of windows," she agreed.

"Let's go down by the lake."

He put his arm around her shoulders and steered her to a red-brick path that took them in a zigzag pattern through the terraced grounds. Some of the property was beautifully landscaped, but much of it was wild woods. They crossed a meandering stream on log footbridges a couple of times.

Domini caught glimpses of other buildings through stands of trees and beyond low walls. "How big is this place?"

"We have a few acres, and a number of buildings. There's a small private school with dorms for the adolescents. Other things the Clan needs."

"How many people live here?"

"Most of us who call the Citadel home don't live here all the time. With the Convocation, there'll be a lot of guests."

"Where is this place?"

"On the shores of Lake Coeur d'Alene." He looked up at the mountains that rose in the distance. "Nice, isn't it?"

"Yes. How'd we get here?"

"We took a private plane from one private airport to another, then a helicopter to the helipad out by the garage. We have several copters, planes, and pilots always on standby. The Clans are fairly wealthy."

"Medieval treasure hordes?" she ventured.

"Investments in pharmaceutical firms, mostly. Biotech, genetic research, anything to do with medicine."

"How very — humanitarian of you."

"Partially."

They rounded a turn in the path and came upon a man sitting on a bench beneath a huge old pine tree. The man stood when he caught sight of them.

Alec winced, like a boy who'd been caught by the truant officer. "Dr. Casmerek," he said. "You've met the doctor," he told Domini, "but you don't remember him."

"Seems to be a lot of that going around," Domini muttered.

"I've been waiting for you, Alec. Nice to see you vertical, Ms. Lancer." The doctor came forward and held out his hand.

Domini was amused to realize after a moment that the doctor was more interested in taking her pulse than shaking her hand. Though she was aware that Alexander didn't approve of any male touching her but himself, she dutifully presented her wrist to the physician.

She wasn't amused a moment later when Casmerek's fingers settled on her skin; she found that *she* didn't like anyone's hands on her but Alexander's. But the doctor's exam was quick and impersonal.

He soon stepped back and said, "You're doing fine. You," he said, looking sternly at Alexander, "left the infirmary in the middle of your inoculations."

"Inoculations?" Domini gave Alec a quick, anxious look. "I thought you were all better."

"He is better," Casmerek said. "But he still needs — let's call them treatments for very serious allergies."

"Garlic, hawthorn wood, silver, that sort of thing," Alexander added.

Domini rubbed her wrists, remembering the bracelet that had irritated her skin a few days before. "I have trouble wearing silver sometimes," she said. "Wait a minute — I thought it was werewolves that were allergic to silver?"

"Not that I'm aware of," Alexander answered. "But silver's murder on vampires."

"And if you want to be one hundred percent in shape for tonight's gathering, Prime," Dr. Casmerek cut in, "you need to come with me right now."

Alec wanted to snarl with frustration. He was standing outside in the daylight and feeling just fine. He wanted to be with Domini. But Casmerek would never thwart a Prime without good reason. If he said Alec needed the rest of the shots, Alec needed them.

"All right, doc. Give me a second." He took Domini's hands and kissed them one by one before letting her go. "I'll see you tonight. Do me a favor, sweetheart." He kissed her palm one last time. "Wear anything but black to the party."

CHAPTER TWENTY-EIGHT

"Don't wear black, he said," Domini told Maja as they came down the stairs. She paused to take in the view of the room below, and Maja came to a halt beside her. "Do you see anyone wearing anything *but* black down there?"

"No." Maja was wearing a long-sleeved column of black velvet, very elegant, very Morticia Addams.

Maja had appeared at Domini's side when Alexander left her in the garden and hadn't let Domini out of her sight since. She wasn't particularly talkative, other than to tell Domini that she'd been sent to keep her company by Lady Anjelica and to answer "No" to any question Domini asked her. Her demeanor was completely neutral, and totally watchful. If Domini hadn't been so frustrated at having Maja dogging her every movement, she'd have complimented a fellow professional on her competence.

For all her polite inconspicuousness, Maja's presence reinforced Domini's belief that she was more a prisoner than a guest in Lady Anjelica's house. It infuriated her more than it frightened her. Being frightened all the time was far too wearing on the nerves. Besides, right now, all she wanted was to find Alexander; no one and nothing else in the Citadel mattered.

Except, possibly, what she was wearing.

She was wearing scarlet, and a lot of bare skin.

Domini had found the short, strapless red satin sheath among a closet full of clothes in her guest bedroom. The clothes and shoes stored in the closet ran in a wide range of sizes, leaving Domini to conclude that unexpected company was common. There'd been several dresses suitable for evening wear in Domini's size, two of them black. She'd decided to wear the red dress and a pair of stiletto heels partly to look sexy for Alexander, and partly because being inconspicuous was what she did at work, and tonight was a party. She hadn't planned on standing out quite so much in a crowd of strangers, though.

She continued down to the main floor and stepped into a sea of beautiful women in black — silk, satin, beading, lace, embroidery — all of it expensive, much of it stylish, some old-fashioned, some of it Goth. The men — and what men they were! — were dressed as darkly as the ladies. Many of them favored leather.

Heads turned her way instantly. Conversations stopped. She told herself it was the dress, but she could feel the psychic energy levels shift. She was being looked at, studied, assessed, and not with eyes alone. It reinforced that she was human, and that these people were not.

She needed Alexander. To see him, touch him, talk to him. She missed talking to him when he wasn't around. She'd wanted him all afternoon, her body humming with desire and anticipation. It was surprising how she'd gone from being wary of him to caring for him. But she also wanted to be near him because he was the one thing she was sure of in this place.

Maybe the one thing she was sure of in her life.

If her grandfather had lied to her about . . . If what Lady Anjelica said was true . . .

Domini pushed her doubts aside. She captured a glass of champagne from a roving server and moved farther into the huge room. At least, she hoped it was champagne

— for all she knew, vampires served carbonated plasma at their parties. She bravely took a sip, and discovered the flute did indeed hold champagne. Very good champagne.

Maja finally left Domini, walking past her, and was instantly surrounded by an admiring knot of vampire men.

Domini was glad to be rid of her watchdog, but it left her adrift in a room full of strangers. What was she supposed to do? Walk up to the nearest group and introduce herself? No one had filled her in on this culture's etiquette.

She supposed the best she could do was keep circulating until —

"Hello, beautiful."

Domini swung around to face the man who'd spoken. Even in heels, she had to look up quite a ways to meet his gaze. His eyes were dark, and his hair was blond. Broad shoulders filled out a high-necked, Russian-style tunic. His smile was confident to the point of being cocky. Even though she didn't have a clue about how vampires aged, her impression was that he was young.

"Hello, gorgeous," she answered without thinking, because he was.

He smirked. She'd figured he would.

"I'm Kiril."

Domini was very aware of all the eyes on

them, but Kiril didn't seem to notice, or at least care. He stood in front of her, and — preened for her pleasure, was the only phrase that came to mind for his attitude.

She took a sip of champagne. "You're trying to impress me, right?"

"I don't have to try." He held up a hand, his wrist turned outward so that she could see a small, stylized tattoo. "Wolf Clan," he announced proudly. "House Ariadne." He took a step closer to her. "I'm looking for a mate." He made a small gesture that somehow took in every other male in the room. "As are we all."

Domini's brows rose in shock. "Direct, aren't you?"

"I am Prime."

"You're a putz," someone behind Kiril said.

As the blond Prime whirled around, snarling, Domini thought she caught sight of a hint of fangs. He lunged toward another big blonde. Domini backed off hastily, while a laughing crowd formed around the fighting pair.

She remembered how Alexander and Tony had fought over her at the bar in Los Angeles. Apparently battles to claim mates were part of this alpha male culture. Looking around, she saw that there were far more men than women in the great room, and that each woman was surrounded by groups of men. No wonder Maja hadn't stuck with her when they joined the party. Why hang with a mortal female, when there were so many fine-looking studs to choose from?

Domini put more distance between herself and the altercation. She had no interest in being a party favor for the winner. Besides, if she couldn't find Alexander, she'd just find an unguarded exit. With everyone's attention focused on the brawl, maybe —

"Where are you going, pretty one?"

Oh, God, not another one!

When Domini turned around this time, the Prime who smiled at her was whipcord lean and sharp-featured, with thick, burgundy red hair that fell all the way down his back. He looked her over with a hot gaze that left her blushing, and far more intimidated than she'd been by Kiril's arrogance.

Domini fought the urge to take a step back. She faced the stranger and said, "You know I'm a human, right?"

"Yes." He came closer.

Domini did back up this time. "And involved with someone already?"

The vampire took a deep breath. "His blood's in you," he agreed with Domini. "But not so much that another couldn't claim you." Long fingers reached out and touched her cheek. "During Convocation, all is fair."

Domini took another step back. He followed, of course, and she finally noticed he was herding her toward a dark corner. Come to think of it, the room had a lot of dark nooks, crannies, and corners.

The red-haired vampire put his hand on her bare shoulder. "Warm, soft, and lovely," he murmured.

"Cold, hard bitch," she answered.

She threw her champagne into his face, glass and all, and spun away. He smiled and lunged forward over the wet floor and shards of broken crystal, and she used his momentum to toss him over her hip onto the hardwood floor.

He was on his feet before she could blink, and moving toward her again. "I like this game."

Domini stepped back and ran into a solid wall of muscle.

Strong hands came around Domini's shoulders. "I don't play games," Alexander said. "Go away, Colin, before I let my lady wipe the floor with you."

Domini didn't see Colin's exit, because Alexander turned her around, murmuring, "Kids," under his breath. Then he kissed her.

Pleasure swept through her, and the aching kindling of desire. His hands roved over her shoulders and back, and sifted through her hair. Her hands mirrored his movements while she drank in his scent and taste.

After a few minutes she came to herself enough to realize that he'd backed them into the dark corner she'd avoided earlier, and she was delighted at the privacy. Alec held her close as he nuzzled her throat, then kissed a line up her jaw and temple. His wide shoulders blocked her view of the room, but she heard music, laughter, the murmur of voices, and the occasional shout or snarl.

It pleased Alec that she wasn't wearing black. He reluctantly left off kissing her so that he could look at her. Her blue eyes were bright with desire, and her lush lips swollen from his kiss. She looked edible, but along with desire, he felt her curiosity, and a hint of annoyance.

"I'm sorry I'm late. Don't be offended by Colin or the other boys; they can't help but hit on anything in skirts."

She arched a brow. "Well, that's flattering."

He glanced briefly over his shoulder. "Flare's come back to the Citadel. That's one of the reasons for the Convocation;

every unattached Prime who could make it is here."

"Including you?"

He was pleased at the jealousy that shot through his lover. "I'm not unattached. And Flare's my sister."

"Flare?"

"Francesca. We call her Flare for her quick temper and tongue. My bet is that the Matri had to send Flare her ring, too, or she wouldn't have come home."

This was all interesting, but it was hard to think when he kept gently brushing her shoulders and chest and throat. The contact sent pulsing shivers through her. She touched his face in turn, tracing the long line of his jaw, his sensual lips, and the indentation in his chin. She wanted him, had never wanted anyone else, knew that she would never want anyone else. And she knew it was more than lust.

"I like you," she told him. "Even if you are wearing black." He wore a draping black jacket that set off his wide shoulders to perfection, with a black, tab-collared shirt beneath. She fought an impulse to rip off the shiny black buttons of his shirt to get to the skin beneath. "Then there's the lust thing."

Was it the bond they kept talking about that made her feel this way? Was it love? Were the two one and the same?

He put his hands around her waist and pulled her away from their cozy, dark corner. "Let's go somewhere."

"California?" she suggested, coming back to herself through the pleasurable burn of desire. "I need to go home. I need to talk to my grandfather."

He gave her a slightly annoyed look. "Did you ask to use a telephone?"

"Yes," she replied. "I was told the Matri didn't think I should make any calls. Polite or not, I'm a prisoner."

"Cherished guest," he corrected.

"Bullshit."

"I see," Alec said.

He swept Domini into one of the small alcoves off the great room and pulled the heavy drape across the doorway for privacy. The windowless little room had lounges piled high with thick pillows, low romantic lighting, and plush rugs; it was meant for nights like this.

"You see what?" Domini asked, after she'd taken in the romantic little boudoir.

Alec made sure that he was between Domini and the doorway when he answered. "I see that the Matri wishes you to stay here, incommunicado. Her word is law, Domini. There is nothing I can do about it."

Domini was outraged at such blind obedience. "What do you mean, there's nothing you can do about it?"

He ignored her anger. "Not blind," he answered her thoughts. "I stand by the choice I made to live as a son of the Clan on the day I came of age."

"But —"

He held up a hand to get her attention, then spoke very formally. "Lady Anjelica wants to keep you safe. And I would do anything to keep you safe. I *will* keep you safe. You saved my sanity," he added. "Even if I did not owe you that, I love you. And even if I did not love you, or owe you, you are a human in danger. A Prime's true and sacred duty is to protect humans from harm."

Domini glared at Alexander, her lips pressed tightly together. It wouldn't be right to make a man choose between what he saw as his duty and the woman he said he loved. Not and still respect herself. Not if she respected him.

But her grandfather needed her. He had to be frantic about her disappearance, and she desperately needed to talk to him. He was an old man, and she was all he had. If he had secrets, she needed to hear them from him.

"Then I suppose I'll have to escape on my own," she told Alexander.

He crossed his arms, looking dangerous and implacable. "I suppose you can try." He sighed and dropped his aggressive pose. "Or you could accept the Matri's hospitality and my protection. At least until she presents you to the Clan Council."

He came to her and took her in his arms. She stood stiffly in his embrace, fighting the temptation to be comforted, to give in. "I love you," he whispered. *I love you.*

And that did melt her heart, if not the stubborn shell that surrounded it.

She clung to him, accepting his comfort, even if she could not accept her imprisonment. She knew that he drew comfort from her as well, even though he thought she was a stubborn, prickly pain in the butt.

True, she acceded. *I don't know why you think you love me. Not that* you *aren't as stubborn and prickly.*

More puncturing than prickly, he corrected.

"Oh, yeah, fangs and claws."

"Standard equipment," he answered. "All the better to — Domini?"

You were down a couple of quarts. The memory of Anjelica's words ran with a tingling shock through Domini's mind, followed by Colin's, *His blood's in you, but not so much —*

"What the hell did they mean?"

351

Even as she asked, the memory came up out of the dark and hit her. The motel, the wrecked room, the suffering only she could aid. The choice. The fear and the burning ecstasy that mixed together into hunger. Deep, dying hunger. Sated by the sweetest taste in the world. Giving, taking, giving back and taking again.

They'd shared —

"More than blood," Alec told her. "More than sex. Both, but more." He held her face between his hands, looked into her eyes, and faced her shocked confusion. "That is how the bond begins. Our minds and souls recognize each other, our bodies crave no other touch, but it is the sharing of blood that makes a lover into a bondmate. I'm glad you remember, so I can thank you. But I wish it could have started now, when I could be gentle, careful." He stroked her cheek. "The way I will be in the future."

He glanced at the bed. Now would be a perfect time to strengthen what had started in that motel room. It would bind her closer to him, and help ease her doubts.

He moved his hands over her, soothing and arousing her. "You're strong, Domini, brave and giving. And you wonder why I love you? We were lucky. I might have driven you mad. But you gave yourself freely, and I think that saved us both. I might have killed you. I almost did. This time," he promised, leading her toward the bed, "it will be better."

As he talked, desire sang through Domini. She knew he played her like some fine instrument, and he was an expert musician, but she loved the tune. She covered his mouth with a hard, demanding kiss. She reached for his shirt buttons, to rip them off and —

The blue RAV-4 came to a halt beside a trio of palm trees. Sunset turned the water beyond the white crescent of beach molten bronze. The houses perched above the shore were dark silhouettes in the fading light of dusk. But the driver and three passengers weren't interested in the beauty of the place.

Another car pulled up behind them. Then a van rolled to a stop behind the second vehicle.

With the full team assembled, everyone got out of the vehicles. Everyone was carrying a weapon.

"Grandpa!"

Domini staggered away from Alexander. She couldn't see; her head was too fogged by passion, and the fading images of the vision. She stumbled to her hands and knees on the thick rug, and stayed there while her mind cleared.

"Domini?"

She was on her feet before Alexander could reach her. She waved him away when he would have taken her back into a comforting embrace.

"I have to get out of here," she said. "I have to." She turned, and ran in blind desperation out of the curtained alcove.

Chapter Twenty-nine

Alec moved faster than Domini. He caught her by the shoulders and drew her close as she stepped into the great room.

"Calm down," he whispered in her ear. He held her tight so that she couldn't move. She quivered beneath his hands. He projected calm at her while he looked around and stared down gazes that turned their way. "Don't *ever* run. Don't show fear. Don't panic. No one here wants to harm you, but there are kids here barely out of adolescence. Don't tempt them."

"I am not afraid of vampires," Domini whispered back angrily, her words precise and clipped. "I am afraid of vampire hunters. Your Purists are going to go after my grandfather, and I am going home to help him."

"What did you see?" Alec asked. "If you had a vision, I didn't share it."

"Why should you? It was my vision."

"We're bonding. We share —"

"Maybe your mind was occupied with thoughts of fucking," she snarled.

"So was yours," he countered.

"Until I saw my grandfather in trouble."

Alec tried to remain reasonable, calming. "You are worried about the Old Man. It's likely your subconscious —"

"Is minding its own business. When I see the future, Reynard, I see the future. I know a vision when I have one. And I saw —"

"There you are," Anjelica declared, emerging from the crowd and coming toward them. "Come along," she said, and everyone dutifully followed her into the central area of the great room. Domini and Alec were swept forward in the center of the crowd.

Domini was too intelligent to continue fighting with him in this situation, Alec knew. And far too intelligent to try to flee. So he twined his fingers with hers rather than hold her so tightly. *Relax,* he told her. *Enjoy the party.*

Domini visibly got hold of her temper. Anger remained hot in her eyes, but she put on a smile and squeezed his hand, as though to reassure him.

What was it Anjelica said about Primes?

Domini thought as she was led across the room. How they could be the most wonderful men in the world, or complete pricks? Lady Anjelica obviously knew what she was talking about, as her darling son was certainly on the prick side of Prime behavior at the moment. How dare he try to convince her that she hadn't seen what she'd seen, just because it didn't suit his or his beloved Clan's agendas?

Domini managed to train her attention on the present as they approached the free-standing fieldstone fireplace in the center of the room. A fire burned high in the hearth, and lit candles of all shapes and sizes were set out on the mantel and the deep stone bench that circled the fireplace. Five grave, dignified women stood before all this light. They were beautiful and ageless, and exuded confidence and power. Matris, Domini guessed; Clan leaders. No one had exactly explained the rules to her, but it wasn't hard to figure out that Clan society was matriarchal.

A group of men stood to one side of the Matris — strong, vital men, with hints of gray in their hair, lines of experience on their handsome faces. They were all past their youth, in the prime of life. Senior Primes? Silver foxes, definitely — and Wolves, Crows, and whatever the other Clans were called, she supposed.

Another group stood on the other side of the Matris; mostly younger Primes, but Maja was there. So was another young woman. She wore a burn-out velvet dress with nothing but pale skin beneath the semi-sheer black material. Her dark hair was cut buzz short and she was wearing far too much dark eye makeup, which didn't disguise the fact that she was probably the most beautiful woman in a room full of beautiful women. This had to be Flare, and she didn't look any happier to be there than Domini was.

Alec led Domini over to the younger group, and they took places in the front row. Domini found herself standing next to Flare, who threw her a hostile look before she turned a dagger stare on her mother.

Lady Anjelica took her place in the center of the Matris. Everyone at the party was gathered around the fireplace now.

Anjelica said a few words in a language Domini didn't know, and whatever she said got her a round of applause — except from Flare, who sneered. Something of a drama queen, Domini decided.

"Welcome," Anjelica said after she finished her speech in Vampirese. "Especially welcome home to my daughter Francesca."

More applause. More sneering from Flare, with a head-toss and a dirty look for everyone thrown in for good measure. Annoyed as she was with him, Domini couldn't keep from sharing an amused look with Alexander.

"And welcome to all the Primes who have come to Convocation for no other reason than to impress Francesca."

More laughter, and quite a few Primes exchanged challenging looks.

"It is time that Francesca founded her own House. I look forward to being a grandmother many times over in the next few decades."

There was another spattering of applause, especially from the Matris, who nodded their approval.

Domini found all this interplay interesting, until Lady Anjelica turned her attention on her and Alexander.

"My son Alexander brings the Clans good fortune, as well." Anjelica raked her gaze over the crowd before looking back at Domini. "All of us seek our bondmate," she said. "Some of us find this mate among vampire kind; many find their fulfillment with one of our human cousins. My son has found his mate."

More applause and enthusiastic cries of

congratulations filled the room. Alexander looked pleased and proud, and Domini couldn't help but feel a flutter of pleasure herself. When he put his arm around her shoulders, she leaned against him, happy to be with him, happy for him. She still planned on getting to her grandfather as soon as possible, though.

Anjelica held up a hand for silence. "Alec has brought us more than a bride. He has also brought back a daughter of the Clans. Welcome, Domini, bound to Prime Alexander, Reynard of House Reynard.

"Domini is human born, but bears a Founder's spark," Anjelica continued. "She is one of those rare women born of the day, but meant for the night."

Domini looked at Alexander. "This highfalutin stuff make sense to you?"

He was grinning. "Every word."

When she looked back at the crowd, Domini noticed that many of the women did not look particularly pleased at Anjelica's news. Vampire politics, she supposed.

"What am I being thrown into, here?" she whispered to Alec.

"Founders can start new clans," he whispered back. "Become Matris."

"Aren't all vampire women Matris?"

"Matris are heads of Clans. Most women

are heads of Houses within their Clans."

Anjelica finished her speech by throwing up her arms and declaring, "Tomorrow I will present Domini to the Matri, with whom we have much to discuss. Tonight, the Convocation of the Clans celebrates!"

The crowd cheered. Alec kept his arm around Domini and steered her into the party.

"That was very —"

"In a minute," Alec cut Domini off as Primes stepped up to them to offer their congratulations.

She kept quiet, but he felt her bursting with questions, and was aware of temper and impatience simmering under the polite veneer she put on. She really didn't pay attention to anything until Kiril stepped up to them.

"Congratulate me, cousin," the big blonde announced. He held up his arm, proudly showing off a wolf's-head tattoo. "I am going to be a fireman."

Alec gave the young Prime a pleased pat on the shoulder. "Congratulations. Welcome to the Force."

"Force?" Domini asked.

Kiril ducked his head in pleased embarrassment. When he looked back at Alec, his eyes were full of hero worship. "Will you be returning to the army?"

Alec shrugged. "Perhaps someday. For now, my lady and I will continue as bodyguards."

"We will?"

"Good," Kiril said. His attention was diverted as a woman walked by. "Excuse me," he said. "Maja!" he called, and headed after her.

"Isn't he cute?" Domini asked as the young Prime moved away.

"You've met?"

"He showed me his tattoo."

"Did it impress you?"

"Should it have?"

Alec disengaged himself from Domini to push up his left sleeve. He showed her the newly freshened fox on his own wrist. "Those of us who follow the old tradition of protecting humans wear our Clan mark like this. Not all of us choose to use the daylight drugs, but those who do, go into the military, police forces, that sort of thing. Becoming a fireman is a good beginning for a boy like Kiril."

"Boy? Idiot, you mean. You protectors are all idiots," said a female voice behind them.

Domini stood back as Alexander turned to face his sister. "How can you say that, Flare?"

"You know it's true." Flare gave a bitter laugh. "Humans don't need you, even if it does give you Primes a chance to play out in the real world."

"I thought you liked humans," Alec answered.

"I like them better than I do our kind. I like the real world, too."

"It's time you left their world."

"Because the Matri says so?"

Domini winced at the female vampire's toxic tone. She didn't like anyone speaking that way to Alexander, and she stepped between the siblings.

"Excuse me," she said to Flare. "I think —"

Flare's angry laugh cut Domini off. "What you think doesn't matter. What a woman wants doesn't matter. Are you going to defend your right to be a breeding sow because you're *bonded?* The bond's a prison. It makes you want whatever my brother wants. He's Prime. Primes want sons." Flare gestured at the room full of men. "All those Primes want is to get us pregnant and keep us that way. Whatever you were told, you were brought here as breeding stock, and nothing more. You're just a womb, and don't let anyone tell you differently."

With that angry pronouncement, Flare

turned on her high spiked heels and marched away. Several men followed her.

Domini turned back to Alexander.

He looked embarrassed and wary. "My sister's always been melodramatic."

Domini noticed that he didn't rush to deny what Flare had said. "Uh-huh."

His gaze followed his sister's haughty march through the room. "She's really not happy about being home, and she likes to give speeches even more than Mom. And her hormones are —"

"Was she telling the truth?"

He took instant umbrage, with a haughty, "Reynards do not lie."

"Uh-huh." She didn't know how much longer her frayed temper was going to hold.

"What do you mean, *uh-huh?*" he demanded.

"It means there are a hell of a lot of things you aren't telling me. You've got all these vampire rules and regs and expectations, which I'm supposed to obey without question. You expect me to trust you and to believe you, just because you're great in bed," she snapped. "But that's not how relationships work, and it's not how I work. And I didn't sign on to be anybody's baby factory! Do you understand me, Reynard?"

Alec grabbed Domini's shoulders and

pulled her to him until their faces were an inch apart. "Not anyone's children but mine. No one's babies but mine. Understand me, Lancer? You are *my* bondmate, and you will give *me* sons!"

Wait a minute — that wasn't what he'd meant to say!

The woman he loved looked at him with cold fury, and not a little fear. Emotionally, she was holding herself as distant from him as she had before they'd shared blood. It hurt him more now, because of what had happened between them.

Silence reigned around them, and everyone at the party stared. Never mind that struggles for dominance went on throughout every Convocation. This was no place for him and Domini to have a fight. From clear across the huge room, he saw his mother making her way toward them. Her interference was the last thing they needed.

"Damn!" Alec turned around and dragged Domini through the open doors, across the deck, and down into the dark garden. He didn't stop until they were assured of some privacy.

Then he let Domini go, held his hands out in front of him, and said, "That was the testosterone talking. Pure Prime possessiveness. I didn't mean it the way it sounded."

She wasn't ready to be placated. "How did you mean it?"

"I mean that I love you, and want us to have children together. If we can found a Clan —"

"I'm not a vampire."

"You are from Clan Corvus."

"So your *mother* says."

He felt his temper trying to get out of control again. "My mother doesn't lie."

Domini whirled back. "Don't you understand that I can't believe this vampire stuff coming from her?" She grabbed him by the shoulders and shook him. "It's my grandfather's story to confirm or deny. This is between him and me. Even if Anjelica is telling the truth, this is something I have to hear from *my* family. I have to talk to him. More importantly," she added, hands squeezing Alec's shoulders tightly, "I have to help him. I can't talk to him until I know he's safe."

Domini caught hold of her temper, and her desperation. A deep disappointment replaced her fury. She let Alec go, and stepped back. "Love is about trust."

Alec hated that he could not comfort this pain. "We're trying to keep you safe." It was all he had to offer.

"I know," she said, surprising him. "And I want to keep *him* safe."

366

"You don't know that you saw trouble." He held up a hand. "Remember that people with precognition rarely see any important visions of their own future." He hated to do it, but he added, "You told me that you did not foresee your parents' deaths."

She was exhausted, full of grief, but hope still burned deep inside her. "Maybe this time I got lucky. What I saw hasn't happened yet. You can change the future if you try. *I* need to try."

She sounded so sure, so desperate, that it tore Alec's heart. Love is about trust, she'd said. Trust your instincts. Trust the one you love.

At his back was the Citadel, full of light and friendship, his family, Clan, and all he believed in. Before him was his woman. Bondmate. Soul mate. She wasn't asking for her freedom, but she was asking him to believe in her. She told him what she must do.

"God damn it!" Alec snarled.

He turned his back on Domini and walked deeper into the shadows of the garden, where he took out his cell phone.

Domini watched his hunch-shouldered form anxiously, hearing only a faint murmur of what he was saying. When he turned around and approached her, she didn't know what to think. He held something in his hand, and tossed it to her when he was close enough.

She caught the car keys automatically.

"Spare set to the Jag," he said. He took her arm and led her across the lawn at a brisk pace.

"Where are we going?"

"The helipad's down by the garage. I told you we always keep flight crews on duty."

"Flight crews? Where are we going?"

"You're going home." He stopped to take her into a fierce hug. "Go talk to your grandfather. Do what you have to do." *Come back to me.*

Elation made her light as a balloon. "I love you!"

He kissed her fiercely. *You bet your ass you do, Lancer!*

She laughed, and the sound and sensation filled both their minds.

He hurried her down the path, and helped her into the small helicopter that would take her to the private airfield. She hugged him tight and kissed him again, but they'd said all that was needed. For now.

When she was in the air, Alec turned back to the house to face the wrath of his Matri. All he could tell her was the truth: that the needs of a bondmate overrode everything else in the world.

CHAPTER THIRTY

"It took you long enough to get here."

"The traffic on I-10 was pretty heavy," Domini answered from the doorway where she stood between the kitchen and living room.

She'd arrived only a few moments before, squealing the dusty Jaguar to a halt in the driveway. She'd run to the front door and knocked frantically until he opened the door, because she'd forgotten her key. He hadn't said a word when he saw her, but he had turned around, and she followed him.

Ben Lancer turned away from the kitchen sink, holding a carafe full of water. It was late afternoon, but he was in his bathrobe, and making coffee. Must be Sunday, he always slept in on Sundays. "You've been gone five days."

"I told you, the traffic was heavy."

He looked her over from head to foot. She

was still wearing the short, strapless red dress. She knew she looked like hell from lack of sleep and nerves.

"Been to a party?"

"Yes."

"With Reynard?"

"Yes. And possibly with some old friends of yours."

"Possibly?" The word came out as a deep, dark, suspicious rumble.

She'd anticipated this moment all the way back from Idaho. Now that it had come, she didn't know how to start. "Blackbird," she said at last. "Cassandra Crowe. Corvus Clan."

He carefully put the coffeepot down on the black marble counter. "So, Reynard's exactly who I thought he was."

"*Excuse* me?" She had not expected this response at all. She was annoyed to find her world spinning out of orbit again; you'd think by now, she'd be used to it. "You knew he's a vampire?"

"I thought so. It's getting harder to tell these days. The drugs the daylight ones take are getting better all the time. Knew you were destined to meet a vampire the minute you told me about your compulsion dream. That's how bonding starts with Primes and humans: fate kicking into high gear. Then

Reynard showed up. The way he looked at you — I thought, yeah, he's got the hunger the way only they can get it."

"Hunger?"

"Lust, honey. I can recognize it, even at my age."

Reeling, Domini said, "I need to sit down."

"Why don't you go get cleaned up?" he suggested instead. "You'll feel better when you're not dressed like a tart." He poured the water into the coffeemaker.

Domini didn't know which one of them was buying time with this diversion, but she went along with it. She took a few minutes to clean up and change into shorts and a shirt she kept in her old bedroom. It was odd how she kept bits of her belongings all over town, she reflected as she got dressed. Clothes here, at the office, at her dojo, at her place. Had she left any at Alexander's? Probably. Maybe it was because she didn't know where she belonged, or who she really was.

"Oh, please," she snorted at her reflection in the bathroom mirror as she brushed out her hair. "Well, at least I have a reflection. Quit stalling, Lancer."

She went back to face her grandfather, who'd also gotten dressed. He handed her a cup of steaming coffee, and they both took

371

seats at the kitchen counter. He handed her a bagel, and she ripped into it like she was starving. Come to think of it, she couldn't remember the last time she'd eaten. Breakfast with Lady Anjelica?

"Where've you been?" he asked after he put down his empty cup.

"Idaho," she said around the bagel. Then she swallowed, and added, "at a sort of party."

"Convocation? A Clan gathering?"

Domini nodded.

"What was it like?"

"Weird. Noisy. Sort of like I was part of the cast of *My Big Fat Vampire Wedding*. There was business going on, too. The Matris were gathered to talk . . . I don't know. Anjelica wants me to do something — diplomatic, I guess, but I have the impression the others have to approve. They — the vampires — were nice enough."

"Clans are all right, mostly. At least they make an effort to be civilized. Never can tell which way the Family ones will jump. And the Tribes are pure bloodsucking bastards. Glad you fell in with one of the Clan males, or I would have had to kill him. You look confused, girl. Didn't they tell you all about vampires?"

Domini shook her head. "I — Maybe

372

there wasn't time."

"Can see why they'd want to show you everything in a good light. The Clans are real snobs about how superior they are to other kinds of vampires."

"There was mention that not all vampires are good guys."

"Damn right, they're not." A considerable silence followed. Finally, the Old Man asked, "Was she there? At the Convocation?"

Domini knew that lost and lonely tone far too well. He always sounded like that when he talked about her grandmother. Especially around this time of year, around the anniversary of when —

"You always said you lost her." Domini swallowed a painful knot in her throat. "I thought you meant she was dead. She left you, didn't she? Abandoned you."

He turned a sharp, angry look on her. "Don't you ever think that! She did what she had to do. She did her duty." He looked down at the black counter. "It nearly killed me."

Domini knew how he felt, after only a few hours away from Alexander. There was a tugging ache in her being. She put her hand on her grandfather's shoulder. It was still hard muscled; there was no frailty about Benjamin Lancer. She thought she knew why now.

"You shared blood with her, didn't you? It makes you live longer, doesn't it? But if you were bonded, why would she leave — ?"

"We never bonded, exactly. The connection went deep between us, though. Once you love a vampire, you don't ever stop. The psychic and physical connection works differently with vampire females and mortal males than it does with human women and Primes. Species survival. Vampire women need a connection with their own kind if they're going to have vampire children."

"You had a child with her."

He gave her a slight smile. "Your dad wasn't a vampire, now, was he?"

Domini smiled back. "Not at all." Dad had been normal, prosaic; a kind, loving, practical man. "Not a bit of dangerous alpha male in him. Not like you still are."

"His mother and I were a tough pair. Reckless, too. We were glad when Junior turned out so sensible. Guess the wild streak skipped a generation to you. He didn't even know about her being a vampire. I raised him, and kept my secrets. Shouldn't have kept them from you. I knew I'd have to tell you one day, from that time you predicted the earthquake when you were still in diapers. I tried to prepare you."

"The bedtime stories you used to tell."

He ducked his head. "Got me in hot water with your mom."

"I remember."

Domini went to rummage in the refrigerator for more food. As she absorbed the conversation she realized that she hadn't really believed he'd refute any of it. It was only the confirmation that she needed. Loving Alexander made it real; made her real. Grandpa's saying it was so made it really real.

When she came back to him with a cold slice of pizza in her hand, she finally answered his earlier question. "Cassandra wasn't at the Convocation. She's a Matri, did you know that?"

He nodded. "That was why she had to leave me. She was heir to her Clan's leadership."

"Oh. You know a lot more about vampires than I do."

"Had a few decades to learn their real ways, and unlearn what I thought I knew."

Domini finished the pizza. "There's so much that doesn't make sense to me. Why would Lady Anjelica want me to be a liaison between the Clans and the hunters? Do you know about the humans that hunt vampires? About the Purists?"

He got up and went to the deck doorway.

He stared out at the rolling green Pacific, and the tenseness in his body language frightened her.

"Grandpa?"

"Let's go into the living room and get comfortable," he said.

She'd never known her grandfather to be interested in comfort. "Must be a long story," she said as he moved across the kitchen. A horrible certainty sent a chill through her, and she stood and touched his arm as he reached her. "You know about the Purists."

He said nothing, but took her hand and led her into the living room. It was darker in here, away from the sunlit kitchen. There was a view of the sea as well as the front lawn, with its hibiscus bushes and palm trees, but the curtains on both sides of the room were closed. He didn't turn on any lights before they sat down on the couch.

"Some stories need darkness, I guess," she said.

"Some do," he agreed.

Domini shivered with dread. But she'd never feared the truth. What kinds of ghosts was he about to conjure?

"This story is all about the dark," Ben told her. "You know about your grandmother." He let out a deep, aching sigh. "Now you need to know where I come from."

"Oh, shit." The words hissed out with a jolt of dread.

"Don't swear in my house." He rubbed the back of his neck, looked her in the eye, and went on. "Hunters and vampires have been at war since the Middle Ages. We killed them. They killed us."

"We?"

"Hush, and listen. Eventually folks on both sides got tired of the bloodshed. After a while the hunters started only going after the really bad ones, the ones even the other vampires disowned. But some among the hunters thought we were soft on the demons. That all vampires were demons, and demons need to burn. My grandparents and my parents, uncles, aunts, my brothers and sisters — and me — we were evangelists for returning to the old ways. That's why the Lancers founded the Purists."

Domini jumped to her feet. "What?"

He grabbed her hand and tugged her back down. "We had our reasons," he told her. "Good ones."

"But what could —"

"I told you, the Tribes were bastards. One of the things the Tribes like to do is keep humans, like cattle. They feed on their prisoners, use them as sex slaves. When I was about eleven, my mother was taken by a Prime of the Phoenix Tribe. He must have liked her, or maybe what he did to her was just to show his contempt for the hunters. He took her blood, used her body, and made her drink his blood."

"They bonded?"

"It was nothing like a bond. It was rape, repeated rape. Body, mind, and soul. It took us two years to track her down. My grandfather wanted to kill her, stake her through the heart, and burn her corpse — like any vampire. But my father wouldn't hear of it. He loved her, even if she was defiled and he never touched her again. My mother hated vampires. Hated them more than any other Purist. Eventually she became the leader of the movement."

Domini had a sudden memory of the old woman in the crowd outside the awards ceremony. Ancient but tough, and so very full of hate. Domini had a strong suspicion of who the ancient one was. It sent a cold shiver through her to think that her own great-grandmother had tried to have her killed. She needed to tell her grandfather this, but first she wanted to know more about her grandparents. So she kept it to herself as he went on with his story.

"I hunted vampires, hated vampires, until

I was sixteen. That's when I got caught by one myself. Blackbird caught me, but she had a fight on her hands to do it. I was hurt pretty bad, but instead of killing me, she took me to her Clan's citadel. I thought they were going to treat me like my mother had been treated. Instead, they civilized me. I was as wild as an adolescent vampire boy. Long and short of it is, I found out that not all vampires deserve killing; Blackbird and I fell in love; and we ran off together, away from her people and mine. We lived happily together for nearly thirty years. That's longer than most marriages last," he added regretfully. "Better than most marriages, too." He took Domini's hands and asked. "You love Reynard?"

"Yes," she answered, without hesitation.

She hadn't realized until this moment that she had no doubts, no questions, about what he was, what they had, and what they could build. Even if he wanted her to have lots of babies. There was nothing wrong with their having babies, when they were ready for them. Besides, Grandpa had been nagging her for great-grandchildren.

"Stick with him, or you'll regret it."

"I will." She slipped her hands from his and got up to cross the room and throw open the front curtains. She didn't want any more conversations in the dark. Even if daylight was starting to fade into evening shadow, the windows still let in a little light. "Then again, when he finds out my ancestry, he might not want me."

"He'd better want you."

"I don't know. Those people called me an abomination, and — Oh, my God! I completely forgot."

She turned to look outside. Were some of the shadows moving?

She crossed to the couch. "They know about me. About you. The Purists tracked us down somehow. They trapped me, setting up Holly's stalker as a smokescreen to attack me. Alexander saved me, and took me to his citadel. Last night, I saw them coming after you," she went on. "I've never had such a strong vision of the future. I ran home to help — then I forgot it when we started to talk about vampires."

He rose to his feet. "What did you see in this vision?"

"That they're going to attack the house."

He reached under a coaster on the coffee table and picked up the key to his gun case. "When?"

"Uh . . ." Domini glanced out the window again. "Now."

CHAPTER THIRTY-ONE

"Thanks for the call, Alec."

"No problem, Tony," Alec answered as he slid into the passenger seat of Crowe's white Grand Cherokee. Crowe was parked two blocks down from the Lancer house. It had been a long trip, one he would have made even if his Matri hadn't agreed that the plan was a good one.

"Your tip was what we needed to put these Purist assholes out of business."

"Not my tip. My lady's."

"Whatever. You called it in; gave us a target for the op."

Alec chafed at having been told to report to the Los Angeles Prime, instead of heading directly to Ben Lancer's house. He was used to commanding operations, and had no intention of being relegated to observer status. Not with Domini's life on the line.

"What's your team setup?"

Crowe gave him an aggravated look. "I've been a cop in this town for fifty years, D-Boy. I think I know what I'm doing. Besides," he added with a grin, "this is Shagal territory, and Old Barak's really running the show. He's a good strategist. The plan's to let all the Purists show up, then surround them and take them out when they attack the house."

Alec turned a furious glare on the other Prime. "You're putting human lives at stake."

Crowe held up a hand for silence, then cocked his head to one side to listen to the telepathic voice speaking in his head. Alec concentrated and picked up Barak's words as well.

We've got three vehicles parked under the palms. Fourteen humans have exited the vehicles. They've broken up into four teams and a couple stragglers. Each team is approaching the house from a different direction. Move up behind them. Take them before they reach the house. Alive.

"Alive?" Crowe sneered. "What fun is that?"

No blood on the beaches of Malibu, the elder thought back. *Take them prisoner now. We'll deal with them later.*

"No blood," Alec repeated. He opened the

car door and stepped out into the night air. He took a few deep sniffs, and found the scent he wanted. No one attacked his mate and got away with it. "No blood? I don't think so."

Crowe called out to him, but Alec quickly set off on the trail without looking back.

"I don't suppose you had the chance to get the alarm system repaired?" Domini asked her grandfather. He shook his head. "Want to call the police?"

"No." He gave her a stern look. "Some things need to be kept in the family."

Like vampires, and vampire wars. The Purists had gone out of their way to hide the attack on her behind a facade of threats to Holly. "Why are they attacking openly now?"

"Desperation," came the terse answer. "Local vampires are onto them by now. They're too fanatical to just leave town, so they'll try to take us out before they run. They'll make it look like a robbery-homicide."

"Charming." They were in the kitchen, and she was holding a 9mm Glock. "I don't think I want to let them make it as far as the house."

"Me, either."

Grandpa held a shotgun, and they both

had plenty of ammunition. Lancers didn't take kindly to being attacked.

"Wish I had the AK47 back from the shop," he complained. "And that this damn house didn't have so many windows."

It was full dark now. Domini took a quick glance out the window with a pair of nightscope glasses. "There's a lot of movement out there; at least two waves of attackers." She turned her head to look down at her grandfather, who was crouching by the center island. His attention was directed toward the glass deck door. "How many Purists are there?"

As she spoke, glass shattered. A bullet from a silenced weapon whizzed past, inches from her head.

Domini turned and fired before ducking to the floor. A scream of pain erupted from the yard.

"However many they started with, there's one less now," Ben said.

I said no blood! Barak's angry thought shot into Alec's head.

Tell the Lancers that! Crowe's thought shouted back.

Alec smiled, feeling Domini's surge of adrenaline through their bond. *That's my girl.* He went back to concentrating on his prey.

The man was crouched behind a dense hibiscus bush at the back of the house, near the deck staircase. Holding back from the main attack because of his broken wrist, Alec surmised.

Move in! Faster! Barak ordered. *Clean this up now!*

Vampires moved across the Lancer property toward their chosen targets. They moved silently, seeing in the dark, with superior hearing and scent, and able to sense thoughts and emotions. They were stronger and swifter than their human enemies as well, and the surrounded Purists didn't have a chance. Especially since the Purists were outnumbered, and the vampires had surprise on their side.

Alec sensed the Primes' elation as one by one they took out their targets. He kept his gaze on the Purist crouching in the bush, a gun clutched tight in the human's good hand. When the Purist thought it was safe to move, Alec followed him up the back stairway, a shadow one step behind his enemy. His hand, claws fully extended, was less than an inch from the man's shoulder.

Time for the punishment to begin.

A flicker at the edge of her vision and a faint whisper of warning in the back of her mind made Domini glance toward the deck. She saw a shadow silhouetted against the last dregs of sunset light. And a shadow behind the shadow, reaching out.

"Grandpa!"

"I see him."

The blast of the shotgun shattered the wall of glass. The Purist outside was hurled back and sideways onto the deck.

He hadn't been hit by the shotgun, Domini realized. Something else had pulled him down.

There was a struggle going on on the deck. Bodies rolled around, sliding and crunching on broken glass. Domini moved forward cautiously, trying to get a better view. She kept low, her Glock at the ready.

Inches away from the deck, she finally got a clear look at what was going on. Then she laughed, an unholy, triumphant sound. It made her bondmate turn around and grin at her. His fangs flashed in the faint light.

Sitting on the chest of one of the Purists, Alec stopped pummeling the other man's face and said, "Hi, hon. Be with you in a minute."

"Take your time." She'd never been so delighted to see anyone in her life. She had no sympathy for the man at all. "You came to rescue me, didn't you?"

Alec gave up punishing the Purist and hauled the man to his feet. He kept a firm hold on the cowering human as he spoke to Domini. "Yeah." He gave her a diffident look from under his eyelashes. "Do you mind?"

She shook her head and chuckled. Her emotions bubbled with pleasure. "Not a bit."

Benjamin Lancer came to stand behind his granddaughter. He leveled his shotgun at the Purist. "What have you got there?"

Barak came storming up onto the deck before Alec could answer. "Give me that," he demanded. He snatched the Purist from Alec's grip, knocked him out, and hauled him over his shoulder. "Sorry for the disturbance, Mr. Lancer," he said, and disappeared with his burden into the night.

Domini pointed after Barak. "What's he going to do with them?"

"Hypnotize them," Alec said. "The local vampires have rounded up all the Purists. They're going to make them forget all about vampires' existence. And the Lancers' existence," he added as he noticed the old man's frown. "The Clans don't kill if we don't have to," he pointed out.

"I know that," Lancer answered. He stepped back into the house through the shattered doorway, and pushed Domini forward onto the deck.

Alec scooped Domini into a tight embrace, and kissed her like he'd never kissed her before. *I couldn't let you face the Purists alone,* he whispered to her mind.

I know. I thought you'd come. I hoped . . .

You did?

Not until after they attacked, actually. But it did cross my mind that you might show up. She devoured him with the kiss, grinding her body against his. *I love you. Do you know how much I love you, Reynard? When you're with me, when you're not.*

I'll always be with you.

Forever?

Forever, Lancer.

Alec stopped kissing her and held her out at arm's length. She was grinning widely, the fire of battle as well as desire in her eyes. "You look like you enjoy a firefight way too much."

She pressed a finger into the cleft in his chin. "Hey, I'm bonded to a D-Boy, aren't I?"

They were so alike. Soul-deep alike. And just enough un-alike to add plenty of spice. He burned to take her to bed as soon as possible.

He pulled her close. "Woman, I think we're going to have an interesting life together."

"A long one." He nodded. She added, "With lots of kids. Eventually."

"Eventually," Alec agreed. He patted her on the bottom, then rested his hands over the tattoo riding low on her back. "And we'll call ourselves the Buzzard Clan."

"Condor," she corrected, and kissed him. *Someday we'll be the Founders of the Condor Clan.*

ABOUT THE AUTHOR

Susan Sizemore is the acclaimed author of the *Laws of the Blood* vampire fantasy series; she also writes historical romances. She lives in a house in the Midwest that contains a spoiled dog, a coffee maker, and many, many books. When she's not writing or reading or walking the dog, she's probably at the movies — most likely one with hobbits or young wizards. She loves vampires and basketball, collects art glass, and spends way too much time online. For more information, check out her almost-monthly newsletter at http://susansizemore.com.

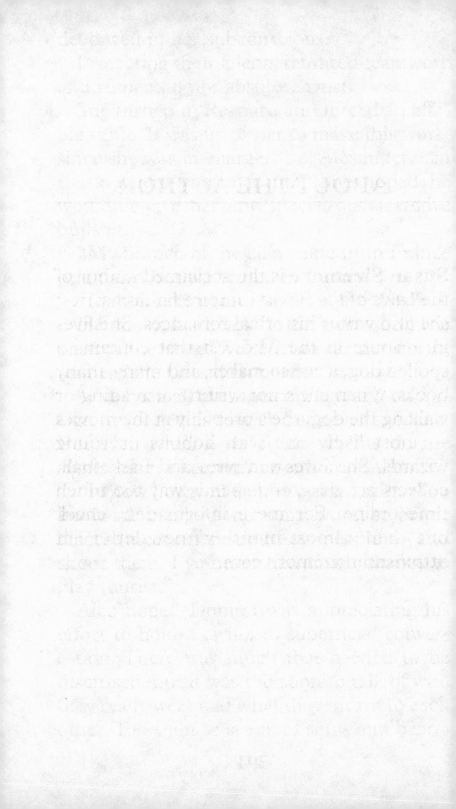